ENTRAPMENT

Copyright © Phil Oddy 2024

All rights reserved. No portion of this book may be reproduced, copied, distributed or adapted in any way, with the exception of certain activities permitted by applicable copyright laws, such as brief quotations in the context of a review or academic work. For permission to publish, distribute or otherwise reproduce this work, please contact the author at phil@philoddy.com.

This book is a work of fiction. Names, characters, places and incidents are either a product of the author's imagination or are used fictitiously. Any resemblance to actual people living or dead, events or locales is entirely coincidental.

Front cover designed by Getcovers

ENTRAPMENT

Entanglement Book II

Phil Oddy

Part One

CHAPTER 1

LEK

Once upon a time, Estrel Beck arrived in Trinity for the first time.

THREE WEEKS EARLIER

The sky is clear and the sun is high, but the peaks of the Proctean Mountains cast shadows that make it seem like dusk has hit the scar, this one specific rocky outcrop among the many. To the south, the sprawling city of Trinity basks in the hot sunshine, although how much of it is felt below the roofs and spires, down in the crevices where the people run and the city festers, is debatable.

There is a blinding flash, for a fraction of a second, and in its eclipse, a man appears. Maybe not "appears", maybe "falls". His momentum, whether from above or from another place, causes him to collapse to his knees, putting out his arms to catch his upper body on his hands rather than hit the ground with his face. He pauses there, eyes closed and panting for a moment, before he raises his head.

His hair is dark, his eyes clear, and he wears nondescript

fatigues that pinch around his shoulders and slip from his waist. They aren't his.

'Ho-ly...' he whispers, drawing out each syllable as if to test that he still has a voice after whatever he's just been through.

He becomes aware of his surroundings and his head snaps to each side, right before left before right. He looks down and then pushes his hands to his knees, watching his own limbs as he stiffly eases himself up, not entirely confident he is going to be able to complete the action.

'Yeah...' he breathes again, then, louder, 'Venn?'

His voice rasps. It's hoarse. He remembers screaming before.

'Venn?' he tries again, stronger, and then 'Lek?'

This time, the sound he makes is loud enough for the hint of an echo to reflect from the gully in front of him. But there is no actual reply.

I can, of course, hear him. I can, of course, see him. But he doesn't know that. He mustn't.

Also, he doesn't really mean me. Not this version of me.

The man closes his eyes. Other memories burst into his mind, like bubbles working their way through densely packed ferment to pop at the surface.

There's another one, he thinks.

"Grab the memories," she said. *"Grab them, grow them. It will bring you back."*

He tries to grab a memory.

How the hell do you catch a bursting bubble? No, that's just a metaphor. Focus...

He remembers the woman, her voice.

Mouse.

Not Mouse, older, greyer, more... what's the word for someone who knows stuff...?

Entrapment

Standing still on the top of the cliff, the man screws up his eyes and tries to bring back his own mind. He stands still for several hours, as he pieces his life back together, bubble by bubble, memory by memory.

When he has finished, he knows why he is there, and where he has come from, and what he has to do. And that starts with finding Venn, and a less omniscient version of me, and trying to explain to them who he is.

CHAPTER 2

LAGRANGE

'It goes right to the top,' they say, voice ever-so-slightly slurring from the drink.

I fight to stifle a yawn. I am so fucking tired, but I don't want to show it. I don't want to stop. I am drunk, but I am not drunk enough yet.

'Of course it does,' I say, too loud.

Mouse glances across the bar at me, checking I'm OK. I pull an "oops" face and check my volume. The three other people who turned around go back to their conversations.

'It always does,' I continue, keeping my voice low so Clar has to lean in to hear me over the bar chatter.

We've been here before, of course. Too much to drink, propping up the bar at Eamer's. Talking too loudly, spouting shit. It's a cycle.

I should know better. We both should. But particularly me. I'm an Authority agent. Although that, these days, means much less than it ought to.

I'm acutely aware of my mouth. I don't want to spit on

Clar, don't want to suffocate them in whisky breath. I choose my words.

'If it didn't,' I drawl, 'go right to the top, I mean, if it didn't, then they wouldn't be able to get away with it. Because these are not clever people. They are cruel people who do cruel things and get away with it because no one with enough power to stop them cares enough about the people they're doing them to.'

I drain my drink, tap the glass on the counter, nod to Mouse, who is there with the bottle. She refills me before the burn has hit my bowels.

I nod a "thank you". The drinks are free. I should feel more uncomfortable about that. My drinks are always free, which puts me in significant debt to Eamer. That's not the best idea given my job.

But the drinks are free.

'How many?' I ask.

Clar laughs through pursed lips, a splutter that erupts suddenly and attracts more attention. We need to be careful. We don't want to attract attention here. Here in the belly of the beast.

'How many here?' I ask, again, more specifically.

'Two,' they reply. 'Eamer's loyal to his girls, so he only wants to fill vacancies. It's worse on the docks.'

'And worse again in The Alleys,' I guess.

Clar is right, Eamer is loyal to his girls. It's coming to something, though. It's my job to stop people like Eamer. Instead, here we are praising his relative morality compared to how bad he theoretically could be.

Because there is no one worse than Eamer.

But like I said, the drinks are free.

I'm joking.

Not joking.

Clar nods, then knocks back their drink. I do the same and Mouse, bless her, refills us both. She taps her finger once on the side of my glass before she turns away. She thinks I've had enough. I disagree.

'What do you want me to do?' I ask. 'I don't think I can do anything.'

'I want you to know.' They drain their glass again and place it back, deliberately, carefully on the counter.

Mouse doesn't refill it. They're leaving.

'I know you can't do anything. I just want you to know. I want you to know that we can't give up. I owe… I owe them.'

I know they're talking about Hana. I know how much it hurts them that they let her down. The guilt still burns them inside. I can't do anything about that.

I can do something about this.

I drain my glass too, then I tap it again. I'm not leaving. I'm not done.

'Clar,' I say.

They stop and turn.

'Thank you,' I say. 'I'll do what I can.'

Clar nods, and then they go. Mouse pours me another drink. She hovers this time, instead of turning away. She has something to say.

'Go on.' I don't look up.

'You shouldn't indulge them,' she says. 'They won't let go if they think there's anything in it. You should have shut that down.'

Now I look up. Now I'm confused.

'"It goes all the way to the top",' she parrots.

I shrug. It does. Not in the way Clar means it, maybe, but it absolutely does.

'There's no fucking plan,' snarls Mouse.

She holds my gaze. She's wringing the towel, gripping it

between two fists and twisting.

'There's lots of fucking plans,' I grin, picking up my drink.

'That's the point,' she says, 'lots of little plans. No big overarching scheme. Lots of little plans allowed to run and fester and fuck everything up worse than it's already fucked. But no masterplan. No kingpin. No big bad.'

'Ha!'

I knock back the drink, tap the glass. Mouse pulls a face but fills it, anyway.

'Look at it from Clar's point of view,' I say. 'You know where they've come from. You know what they've seen, what they've been through.'

'They're a journalist. They should be objective.'

'Yes, but look at the stories they tell - you wouldn't blame them if they start to see the world from the perspective of the people they're standing up for. People who have been at the bottom of the pile for long enough that they can't see where the power that's stomping on them is coming from anymore.'

'That's my point,' Mouse is showing her frustration on her knotted brow. 'There is no power. There's a vacuum. A lack of power. They're a victim of circumstance, not a grand conspiracy.'

'I don't think it matters.'

I empty the glass again. It sticks in my throat, threatens to jump back up again. I swallow it down but I realise I've picked up the pace, without meaning to. I grind the base of the glass against the bar top.

'When you're bottom of the pile, it all feels the same. And a power vacuum doesn't exist in a… in a vacuum… in a…'

I lose my train of thought.

'You're drunk, Sim. Go home.'

I am drunk. But I'm not going home.

'I'm going to need their names,' I say.

Entrapment

Mouse shakes her head.

'You're drunk, Sim. Go home.'

She seems relieved when I stand up and wobble away from the bar.

I'm only going to piss.

Mouse sighs when she sees me come back. My face is wet from the water I splashed onto it. I feel refreshed, if not any more sober.

I can handle myself, though. You don't get to hold down a job like mine, whilst developing a dependence on alcohol like mine, without being able to handle yourself.

There's another drink waiting. Good. Mouse knows better than to argue with me. I down it, wait for the refill. Mouse's neck must be getting sore from all the shaking of her head.

Eventually, she gives in and gives me the names of the new girls. They're not Ashuanan names. They're likely not their real names.

I drain my latest drink, number three or four since I came back and I drop it back on the bar. Mouse doesn't refill it.

I lurch from my stool and launch myself across the saloon. I take a deep breath and imagine it's doing me some good, clearing my head. The air inside Eamer's is rotten. If anything, it should make my head spin worse.

I slip back down the corridor. It is dark and smells of stale piss. It's easy to think that's because of the toilets, but if anything, it's worse down the other end, near the Stairway to Heaven.

You have to be really horny to brave this, but plenty do.

The curtain is just past halfway down, but before you pull it aside, you have to gain Kurt's approval. Kurt is almost as wide as the stairway and growls when he breathes. He's also an exceedingly hairy man, and that's not the most bearlike thing about him.

Things Kurt doesn't like: drunkenness, over eagerness, people who think they can bribe him into turning a blind eye to either of the other two.

I am definitely too drunk for Kurt. He knows me though, and he knows why I'm here, so he moves aside into the specially created alcove, tipping his fedora. I say nothing.

I sigh and climb the stairs. Kurt growls. I like to think he recognises the sadness in the inevitability of where I'm headed.

Scandi is waiting at the top of the stairs. She knows me as well. This isn't my first visit to the girls at Eamer's and Scandi has been Madam for a long time.

'You look rough, Sim,' she says.

Her sympathy hits me weirdly hard. I feel myself tearing up.

'Long day.' I smile from one side of my mouth.

Scandi bobs her head. I don't think she believes me. But she's very good at keeping her counsel. It pays in a job like this.

'Who are you here to see?' she asks. 'It's Jak's night off.'

I know it's Jak's night off.

'It's a… uh… professional visit.'

That is a terrible line. It's also very untrue. I'm Authority and while I'm not in Vice my *professional* responsibilities would require me to shut down this entire operation.

But that includes the bar downstairs, which would be personally very painful to me, and would put a friend of mine out of work. So I'm not here in a professional capacity.

'I'm here to see the new girls,' I say.

Scandi raises her eyebrows. I shake my head.

'I see. I'm sure Laihla will appreciate that. Kari is with a client.'

That word makes me want to spit. It's too sanitised for what we're complicit in here.

Entrapment

Scandi turns to take me to Laihla's room. I sigh and take my Com from my jacket pocket. I go to tap it on the credit console, but Scandi turns and pushes my hand away with a scowl on her face.

'I'll take your credit when you come to take something from me.'

She knows why I'm here. She even opens the door for me.

The room is dark and smells of cherry. Laihla sits on the bed, her hands on her knees. She's trembling. I close my eyes and inhale. This doesn't get any easier.

She slinks her way up off the bed, doesn't say a word but her hand is on my shoulder, on my back, her arms wrap around my head, her body pushed close, her leg rubbing against me, her mouth on mine.

The cherry-scent fills my head. I reel. I push her away.

She falls to the floor. I didn't mean to push that hard.

'I'm sorry,' I say. 'Are you OK?'

She sniffs, wipes away a tear.

'Didn't you like it?' she whispers, barely making eye contact.

'I'm sorry,' I say again. 'I didn't mean to hurt you. I'm not here for what you think I am. I'm not here for the same thing as the other men.'

She shrugs.

'Some of the other men hurt me.'

My heart drops with the implication. She climbs back onto the bed, holding her shoulder. Her straps have slipped, the waistband of her underwear is askew. She looks so vulnerable.

Many men would want this. I don't give myself time to consider if I'm one of them. I fear the answer.

I step towards the bed. I can see the fear in her eyes, but she doesn't flinch, doesn't shrink back. She sits up tall, wets her lips with a seductive tongue. I reach out to her and hook her straps back onto her shoulders.

'That's not why I'm here,' I say, again.

The contact pad is next to the door, the same as in the other rooms, the same as in Jak's room. I pull out my Com again, hold it up, turn and walk to the door.

One hundred credits transfer. Laihla's eyes go wide. I want to say it again: "That's not why I'm here", but I put the Com back into my pocket and point at the contact pad.

'The credit is for you. Scandi knows. She'll transfer it quick. Eamer won't get his cut. When you need it, if you need anything, you ask Scandi.'

She nods. I reach into the pocket of my jacket and pull out a card. It's low tech.

'This is the address of my Com,' I say, handing it to her. 'My private Com. You need to keep that safe. No one can know you have it but if you ever need help...'

With a quivering hand, she reaches for the card. I take a step forward and let her take it.

'I work for Authority. You know what that means?'

She nods. I hope so. My protection is a double-edged sword.

She peers at the card. I think she understands what I'm saying.

'Simeon Lagrange,' she reads.

She looks up at me with big brown eyes. I don't give myself time to consider...

'You've given me cardboard,' she says, turning it over in her fingers. 'You're a smart man. Can't be hacked?'

'No, it can't,' I laugh. 'I mean it. If ever you need help. No one can know that you have it. No one except Kari.'

She nods and then reaches down and untucks the sheet. She slips the card underneath, next to the mattress, then tucks the sheet back in.

'It's safe,' she says. 'A secret.'

I'm relieved. She smiles as she smooths down the sheet, then looks back at me, pleased with herself.

'A secret. Thank you, Simeon Lagrange.'

'Good luck,' I say.

I leave Laihla's room. I'm doing what I can, I tell myself. I am not convinced it's true. It's left me feeling numb, but I've had enough to drink that I don't need to think any more. That's keeping me calm. Thinking isn't any good for me at a moment like this.

I am hungry, though. I should eat.

I can see Konoroz through the window. His expression is glazed, blank eyes staring out from behind the counter of his meat shop, as people stream past his window, half the city waking up, the other half going home to bed.

I must have missed the whistle because the PedWay is full of workers. The factories all change shift at the same time. It's always chaos.

I should know better than to hit the streets at this time, but I wasn't paying attention. I put my head down and plough on to my destination. I know it will be quiet inside.

A bell rings somewhere as I push the door open. It doesn't seem to rouse anything in the slight, balding man. He's usually very twitchy, but tonight he doesn't react.

I am hit with the warm aroma of gently frying meat, aromatic spices, sweat and sawdust. It's comfortable and I am glad I stepped in. I am also going to be very careful about what I touch while I am in here.

'Konoroz,' I say, sharply enough to get most people's attention.

Konoroz doesn't move. I suspect that his demeanour may be chemically induced and not a hypnotic state caused by watching the working masses stream past.

'Konoroz, have you been smoking up too hard?'

Konoroz's face creases and he pulls his gaze away from the window. He grins at me and pulls a small pill pot from his pocket, which rattles when he shakes it enthusiastically.

'Leetle haff-haff,' he croons. 'Takes the edge off.'

I sigh. This could be hard work. I lean my hand on the counter, immediately regretting it as a layer of grease imparts onto my skin. There isn't anywhere to wipe it, so I try to scrape off what I can on the edge of a menu.

'Not busy, Ko?' I ask, without looking up, although I already know the answer.

I am the only customer. I sometimes wonder if I am his only customer, full stop.

'They not buy from me.' Konoroz waves a dismissive hand at the window which, by now, shows an empty street. 'They not have the credits, but even if they did, their brains are washed. They couldn't handle the portion of truth I serve them up here.'

That takes me by surprise, and I splutter out an astonished laugh.

'Is that right?' I try to suppress the full extent of my mirth. 'Your meat is truth? Contains truth? Is pure truth?'

Konoroz nods.

'S'right,' he slurs. 'They feed the drugs in their water... they know no better.'

I sigh again. I should have known the direction in which this conversation was going to go.

'We've been through this, Ko,' I remind him. 'It's the same water that you drink and I drink. You live in the same tenement as half of them.'

Whilst I'm willing to accept that micro-dosing the population to keep them compliant sounds like exactly the sort of thing Chaguartay would do, the sheer complexity of managing such a thing without accidentally poisoning swathes of the workforce… Seductive an idea as it is, I think it unlikely.

'In the factories then,' insists Konoroz. 'Maybe they pump it though the air ducts, I don't know.'

He fixes me with an almost unbearably intense stare.

'They sombies, Sim. They have no thoughts, no life. They are walking machines for the factory. They are not people.'

'Zombies,' I correct him. 'And whilst that may be true, I don't think it's some big pharmaceutical conspiracy. They're just overworked and deficient in hope. Held back by their dependence.'

Konoroz shakes his head.

'Besides…' I nod at the pill pot he's still holding, clutched in a fist.

Konoroz looks down, apparently surprised that he's carrying drugs.

'Is not the same. These are herbal.'

They're not herbal. I know who cooks them, in the empty warehouse behind Eamer's. I would have arrested him before now, but he's a knowledgeable informant and he bakes good shit. Not that I partake. I'm not into chemicals.

I decide not to disabuse Konoroz, and just bob my head in apparent agreement.

'You need food?' asks Konoroz, appearing suddenly to remember what his shop is for. 'I have sausage…'

I have learned, through bitter experience, to be cautious when it comes to Konoroz's wares, however delicious they may smell.

'What's in the sausage?'

'Meat.' Konoroz's tone dares me to argue.

I am not convinced. I know that category covers a

multitude of sins, some of which I, personally, don't consider to be meat.

'If that's all the information you're willing to divulge,' I say, brow furrowed, 'then I think I'll pass and take the bread.'

This is a tactic. No one eats the bread.

'Is stale, idiot,' sulks Konoroz, taking a flatbread from the basket and banging it on the counter.

It clangs, if you can believe that.

'You cannot come to meat shop and eat stale bread.'

I scan the cabinet.

'Give me that tartare then.' I point at a shaped patty of raw, minced meat.

It is pink and has nothing obviously unpleasant or harmful to human health poking out of it.

'Is there plenty of spice in the mix?'

'The boy's special blend,' he cackles. 'I would say is just right...'

He scoops the patty into a greaseproof bag whilst delivering an ostentatious wink.

'...so you might want to take it with a glass of milk.'

I nod, secretly relieved. What I may have to endure in pain from the boy's patented spice blend would be nothing compared to the agony of digesting a sausage that has been reheated an undetermined number of times on a grill that hasn't been washed in a decade. The sausage smells so good, though.

'Where is he tonight?' I ask, referring to the aforementioned boy.

I've never been certain of the relationship. The way Konoroz refers to him I get the impression that he, at least, thinks he's his son. Seeing the two of them together, I've never been convinced that they weren't brothers.

Konoroz shrugs, handing the parcel across the counter.

'He not here. He drinks.'

I slide the meat up in its envelope and take a bite of my patty. It's ice cold and burns with raw garlic before the chilli even hits. My breath is going to be hell after this.

'Don't we all,' I say. 'We need to survive in this city, any way we can. How much do I owe you?'

'I do not know how much it is,' sighs Konoroz, looking lost.

I realise he's catching a second wave off the pills.

'It's OK, Ko,' I say, and pay him ten credits.

Konoroz seems OK with that which he should be as it would usually cost eight. I take another bite. Now it's warming up, it's developing a slightly slimy film which coats my tongue. It helps with the chilli.

I can feel the meat settling in my uncertain stomach, calming the waters. It is just what I need. That and tea, but I know how often Konoroz cleans his urn, and I'm not about to risk that now.

I pocket the rest of my burger and bid farewell to a now completely re-glazed Konoroz.

'Lay off the drugs,' I mutter, as the bell rings on my way out of the shop.

The street is quieter now. It's fast approaching three. It will be light before long.

The last of the night is the worst of the night, usually, but I don't see anyone around. A TransPod trundles past, a self-driving cab. I pull out my Com to hail it, but I don't hit the button. I could do with the walk.

I'm also not sure where I'm going. I don't think I'm going home. I need to walk. And it's time to think.

Something is nagging at me.

I feel helpless. I couldn't do anything for Laihla, nothing

real. I can't stop the trafficking. Mouse is right, there's no grand plan, nothing to dismantle, nothing to break apart. There's nothing I can do. There's nothing to do anything to.

But Clar is right too. It goes right to the top, whether it's control or neglect that's at the heart of it. There's only one way to stop this. You've got to cut the head off. Then the rest will wither and die.

But where is it? Chaguartay? One of his deputies? Borate in Authority? Toun in Administration? General Brooke in Military? Does the buck stop at Eamer?

In some ways, my life would be easier if it did. It would explain why I find it so hard to pin him down with any actual evidence of actual crimes.

A black cat slinks out of an alley as I pass, rubs itself on my ankle. I jump out of my skin. I thought it was a rat.

It's drizzling. I pause under the streetlight, the air sparkling in front of my eyes. I close them, stand still, swaying, letting the rain fleck my skin, cooling me, bringing me back to alertness.

Head, heart, gut. Those are the tools of my trade. Each one has its strengths, each one has its flaws. When they're in unanimous agreement, I know I'm onto something.

Head, heart, gut. I'd be lost without them. It's a shame that the side effects of my lifestyle are so focused on destroying them all.

Eamer feels wrong in my gut. If there's one thing that Authority, Administration and Military share, it's institutional inertia brought on by an excess of bureaucracy. My head tells me it's none of those.

Konoroz's contaminated water supply theory is implausible. There would have to be an entire department in the already-overstretched Administration dedicated to making that happen. But there is a ring of something, not exactly plausibility, but something close about it.

It feels like something Chaguartay would do, would want to do. Nothing happens in Trinity without him knowing, on some level. Nothing happens in Trinity without him being behind it, on some level. He's spent thirty years ripping the heart out of the place.

So, not drugs in the water, but the city is sick. And girls like Laihla, the victims of the system he allows to prevail, are the symptoms.

I check the time on my Com. It's past three. I'm closer to work than I am to home. I don't know that I've got any tea bags at home.

I feel the cat around my ankles again. I imagine the filth it lives in, the mites in its fur. I shudder, kick out.

The cat leaps away with a scrowl. I miss, spin around on the spot. For a reason that has more to do with instinct than rational thought, I pull my gun. The world tips and I'm crashing to the pavement. I feel my joints crunch, my teeth grind at the impact. I'm lucky I don't let off a shot.

Even if I wanted to go home, I have no confidence I'm going to make it.

I tuck my weapon away and check my pocket. My fingers close around my Authority identity token. I can access the building. I should go to work.

I pick myself up, creaking with the effort of it all. The cat sits on the low wall opposite, watching me. I want to fly at it, but I turn around and stagger to the junction. I take a left and head towards the safety of my office

CHAPTER 3

The sky is greying into morning. I sit alone in my office on the fourteenth floor of the Authority building. The world has just about stopped spinning. I wrenched my shoulder when I fell and my neck clicks every time I turn my head to the left.

Night shift rarely makes it up to this level, so I get to sit in peace. It's probably quieter than it is at home. I don't use my office for much, for precisely this reason. I prefer to work where there's noise and activity. The refectory is better, in the basement.

My office is a place for reprimanding Cadets and for thinking. There are no Cadets to be seen right now. Right now, I'm thinking.

I look out across the rooftops of Trinity, up to The Cliff, the giant scar that looms over the Eastern Quarter, then across to the Citadel with its precarious looking spires. Once, a long time ago, I would sit on the ledges of the south tower with the pigeons, looking the other way. It feels like a different world. I feel like a different person. I was a different person.

It's a different city.

It's too late now, though. I take none of it in. I'm thinking about something else.

My brain has rebooted and I'm already conjuring a whirl of competing thoughts and strategies. What Mouse said… What Clar said… What Konoroz said… It's too much. I need to thin it all down, get some focus. I'm no use to anyone like this.

"Leetle haff-haff?" Konoroz's voice echoes in my head. *"Takes the edge off…"*

If I really was looking for a handful of pills, it would be easy enough to swipe some from evidence. Winx, Crank, Flux… an entire shelf full of substances that don't even have names yet.

Every side effect you could want, along with a number that you wouldn't. None of which are herbal, whatever Konoroz might say. I'm not one for chemicals, though.

It's a principle thing. I don't care what I put into my body, what it does to me, but I don't want to line the pockets of the people I'm trying to bring down. The Black Knights traffic and deal all of those drugs.. Even the legal ones are gateways, and they're all produced by Chaguartay's factories. It's two sides of the same coin.

Alcohol, on the other hand, has been a cherished part of human culture for millennia. Also, I like the taste. And even though I drink in Eamer's bar, he's not making so much as a sub-credit from me. Remember, I don't pay for my drinks.

I need a drink now. The effects of last night's binge have subsided, and I have no problem with starting this early. Or on the job. Besides, my stomach is lined with Konoroz's best. I'm practically alcohol proof at the moment.

I slide open the lower drawer in my desk and pull out the bottle of clear, oily liquid. I pour a generous measure into the paper cup on my desk, where the liquid goes cloudy and brown as it mixes with the dregs from the spent tea bag I left in there.

Lagrange's Screwdriver.

I take a gulp and wince, then take another. I wince a bit less this time, and when I take a third, the edge has gone and my mind is calm. I settle back in my chair with my feet on the desk.

Head, heart, gut. I need to check in. Start again, at the beginning.

"It goes right to the top," Clar had said. And it's true that it always does, but it's equally true that it's a meaningless cliche if nobody knows where the top is.

Chaguartay, obviously, nothing happens in Trinity without the Mayor's blessing, even if it's implicit. He's untouchable, though, and too smart to take an active role in anything as sordid as people trafficking.

Also, he's there, in plain sight, so he's not what worries me. He's too visible. There's a very invisible hand moving this market.

I have a creeping anxiety that I may have overstepped the mark, stuck my head above the parapet, by reaching out to Laihla. It's probably my hangover talking, in which case, *Cheers!* I'm dealing with that.

What did I even do, anyway? I gave her credits that she won't get to keep and a Com address she will probably never get to use because she'll be dead before she finishes inputting the digits. That's if it's not discovered and taken from her first.

I was going to suggest she memorised it, but you can hack a brain with enough torture equipment. Not that it matters if someone gets it out of her, it's only a relay address. No one can trace it back to me.

I don't think it is that which is worrying me.

A light flickers on down the hallway. I see Jean walk past my window. The floor is waking up.

Any minute there will be a dozen offices filled with a dozen Oficiers, each with their own briefs and priorities. Each with their own pet projects.

My brief is the Black Knights and now, because of Clar, because of what happened with Hana, my pet project is Eamer's harem.

Jean's brief is Corruption. I just have to get her to tell me what her pet project is. And hope that it isn't me.

I've lost my thread, I realise, let my head wander off the path. I spend a lot of my time turning in circles. Or am I being thwarted at every turn?

There's a rot inside this building, a rot in Authority itself. I can't see it but I can smell it on the foetid breath of every floor, taste it on the sweat of the walls. But I can't see it, and that's what is causing me anxiety.

I don't know where it is; I don't know how high it goes. I can pretend that it doesn't matter to me, and I often do. I can protest that there's nothing I can do as much as I like. But firstly that's not true, I don't believe it's true, and secondly there are things I do, every day, that show that I don't believe it's true.

Someone has to do something, and if it isn't me, then who?

That is the question I can never satisfactorily answer. That's why I am like I am. That is why I do what I do.

I realise that my drink is finished. I didn't notice drinking it. That pretty much defeats the purpose of pouring it. I fix myself another and drink that instead. There is always another drink.

'Sir?'

There's a Cadet at my door, it's Parker. She's keen, it's early. But there's plenty of people you can impress by being here early. I'm not the only one who spends the night at my desk.

I like Parker. She's smart, makes excellent decisions. She looks like she needs to tell me something. She's twitchy and her eyes are flicking all over.

I put down the drink, the next drink, or the next but one, and wave her in. She remains hovering in the doorway.

'Sit down,' I tell her.

She doesn't.

'Sit down,' I tell her again.

She's almost hopping from one foot to the other and it's driving me crazy.

'Sit.' I stick my foot out the other side of the desk and kick the chair.

It skitters backwards. Parker steps forward to catch it before it falls over. And now she's in the room. She swings the chair around, throws herself into it, fidgeting nervously with the Com in her hand.

'Sorry to disturb you, sir,' she stammers.

It drives me mad that I make her this nervous. I am not *that* boss. Not all the time. She should be able to stand up to me.

'...but I thought you'd want to know this right away, so I didn't want to wait for this morning's Meeting and...'

The Meeting is in a little over an hour. This is either going to be really interesting or I'm about to feel a lot less positive about Parker's judgement.

'I was reviewing who was brought in overnight, you see and... Well, there's this Monk.'

'They don't call themselves Monks anymore,' I point out.

Surely Parker isn't old enough to remember when they did, but it's hard to change the words people use, especially when the thing they refer to hasn't.

'They're Clerics,' I remind her. 'The Citadel hasn't been a monastery since... Why is this something you felt the need to tell me? Our Division is Black Knights. You know that. We don't have a Devoted Division. They're not big lawbreakers...'

'That's just the thing, sir,' Parker cuts in.

I don't like it, but I let it slide. I don't let many people interrupt me.

'He did. Call himself a Monk and...'

'And he got brought in last night? For what?'

'He was drunk,' says Parker

Aren't we all?

'He was sleeping in the doorway.'

'The doorway?' I check. 'Of Authority?'

Not your average Cleric. They usually only get wasted within the relative safety and sanctuary of the Citadel walls. I assume he's pretty green.

'He said he was a Monk. He said he was with the Brotherhood.'

Parker raises her eyebrows, her eyes wide.

I guess it happens. Youthful exuberance, student politics - there must be a religious equivalent. Some new faction trying to recapture the glory days of a rose-tinted memory that bears little relation to the actual history, which they're too young to remember.

The Devoted are, despite the name, a pale imitation of the Brotherhood that preceded them, and a far more benign presence in that ancient building at the centre of Trinity. Geographical centre, at least.

The dissolution of the Brotherhood was one of Chaguartay's less controversial reforms. At least, it was at the time. If the people of Trinity have learned anything, it's that nothing he does can be separated from the man's lust for absolute power. You have to be suspicious of all his motives, even when you think you understand them. Even when you think you agree.

Entrapment

'The Brotherhood?' I repeated. 'Not the Devoted?'

It wasn't really a question. Parker didn't really answer it. Instead, she raised her eyebrows even further. I wouldn't have said that would be possible.

The Brotherhood would be a problem if I thought for a moment it was true. But this story, an inebriated, purported Monk claiming to be from the Brotherhood? It reads like a cosplay society member taking his art too seriously. I'm not worried. I also don't see what it's got to do with me.

'So, he's in the drunk tank?' I ask, seeking clarification. 'Street are aware? This feels like their jurisdiction. Fairly low level as well, if you don't mind me saying. I don't think this was worth your trek up to Fourteen. Even if Mortimer was in his office which…'

I check the time. It's still not quite eight.

'We both know he won't be.'

'The thing is,' says Parker, eyebrows snapping back into place, 'that he wouldn't give us his name. Not sure that he could, to be fair. But I got his ID.'

'Right,' I say.

I'm losing my patience now. Either she's wasting my time or she's leading me on. I don't care for either of those.

'So who is he?'

Parker places a shiny plastic token on the desk, face down, and slides it across to me. All very mysterious. I slide it off the edge of the desk and flip it over so I can read it. It's a Citizen's License. The picture that displays on the screen is, indeed, of a regular, contemporary Cleric. I read the name.

Bjorn Barlow.

Fuck.

'That's your guy, isn't it?' asks Parker. 'Your guy on the inside? Your Grey Knight? I had him transferred to our holding cell. I thought you'd want to talk to him.'

I nod, slowly. Bjorn Barlow is, indeed, my guy. But there's no way that Parker's Monk can be Bjorn Barlow.

'Thank you,' I say, slowly, standing.

The world has turned to treacle. Everything feels very slow and sticky compared to the speed the wheels in my brain are whirring.

'I think maybe I need to speak to Mr Barlow. You did the right thing bringing this to me.'

Parker looks pleased, stands up to go. I thank her again and she backs out of the room. I could swear she almost bows on the way out.

I breathe out. I hadn't realised that I was holding it in. I grab the bottle again, fill the cup and drink until it hurts. My heart is racing, my chest is tight, my head feels like it's shrinking in on itself.

I drop back into my chair and rub my face in my hands. None of this makes any sense.

Because Bjorn Barlow is, indeed, my guy. He's a double agent, a man on the inside who is supposed to be getting me closer to the activities of the Black Knights, who are, as I mentioned, my primary concern when I'm at work. And often when I'm not.

He's the Grey Knight.

There's no way that Parker's Monk can be Bjorn Barlow, and not for the reasons you may be thinking. Because Bjorn Barlow, despite the evidence of the apparently genuine Citizens License in my hand, does not exist. I don't actually have a man on the inside, although I really wanted everyone, Black Knights included, to think that I did.

We made him up.

Yet now he's in my holding cell.

I'm not ready to talk to Bjorn Barlow yet. Hell, I'm not ready to admit that he exists. Besides, we've got an hour to go before the Meeting and there's someone I need to give a bollocking too, first.

Heads turn as I stride into the Division's Operations Room. Of course they fucking do. I'm the hard-drinking bear with a sore head, just-woke-up-in-my-office bastard who runs this place. I'm the boss. And I will not be taken for a fool by an upstart Junior Oficier.

OK, I've just lapsed into being *that* boss. Maybe Parker isn't weak. Maybe I'm an arsehole.

James is in the conference room at the far end of Ops. It means that I have the entire length of the floor to stride, marching with purpose, scattering nervous Cadets as I pass.

My coat flaps and billows in my wake. The blinds are open, so James can see me coming. I catch his eye and I don't let go, leaving him in no doubt that I am on my way and that I am coming for him.

From twenty paces I can see him wind up the meeting, trying to pull his eyes away but unable to stop shooting nervous glances at me as I close in.

From ten paces I see the three Cadets push back their chairs and hurriedly stand, scooping up paper cups and plastic cartons and Com devices.

From five paces the door has already been opened and I'm within a stride it as the last of the Cadets scuttles out, leaving the way clear for me to enter.

I slam the door behind me with a flourish. I see James swallow nervously. Good. He stands up.

'Sir?'

'Who the fuck is Bjorn Barlow?' I demand.

'I... You... We...'

James seems to be having trouble with where to start. He falls back into his seat. He stares at me blankly. Apparently, he has no words. I will not help him.

'Bjorn Barlow. I take it you're familiar with that name?'

'I... Yes!' James splutters. 'But... I don't...'

'Who is he?'

James shakes his head, craning forward, furrowing his brow. I think he's trying to figure out if I'm making a joke. I make sure my expression is very clear that I am not.

'I thought you'd signed off on this, sir. I made him up. He doesn't exist. It was a test of the Knights' intelligence capabilities. We thought trying to find a mole that didn't exist might tie them in knots. It's an experiment.'

I'm nodding in violent agreement. James seems to relax. He thinks this is over. I haven't started yet.

'So you say. And yet there's a man in our holding cell who was carrying this. Maybe you can tell me what the hell it is?'

I slam the license onto the large, oval table, screen up. James peers over from his side. He takes a moment, but when he sees it, he turns white.

'I... I have never seen that before,' he stammers.

He holds his hands up, shrinks back in his chair. I think he's trying to get away from it. To his credit, he seems genuinely shocked. I'm inclined to believe him. I'm not letting him off, though.

'You didn't get a Citizen's License made up?' I suggested. 'Maybe to add some substance to the fiction?'

I raise my eyebrows, Parker-style.

'No. I... I thought about it, but I hadn't... I didn't get that far. All I did was put out the dispatch that you saw!'

I saw the dispatch. I also know it was intercepted by a Com known to be operated by the Knights. Did they see through this straight away? Create a "real" Barlow to let me know they knew? Did someone tip them off?

'Who else knew?'

'No one, sir, literally no one,'

James's hands are out. He's doing the eyebrows thing, too. He's gradually pulling out every piece of body language he can to protest his innocence.

'I brought the idea straight to you, told no one, executed it myself, told no one.'

'Then this is, what, a lucky guess?'

I stab my finger at the table, on the license token. James pulls the most demonstrative shrug that I have ever seen.

'I do not know,' he says, then, seeing the thunder in my face: 'No, I mean no. Not a lucky guess, obviously. Someone must know, somehow. But I have no idea how. Or who.'

I think I believe him. He looks pathetic, in this moment. The lack of dignity as he pleads and grovels for my forgiveness is definitely plausible. I don't rate James as a liar. I don't think he has it in him to do it this well.

'This is a shambles,' I announce, 'and a dangerous shambles at that.'

James is nodding vigorously. I'm pretty certain that I could get him to do anything I want right now. He's lucky that all I want is to understand what the hell is going on.

'You will find out what happened and how, and you will make it right.'

'Of course,' James begins, but I haven't finished.

I hold up a finger. He stops.

'But you will have to stay out of sight while you do so.'

If this was the Black Knights, then I don't want them to know that I know. If this wasn't the Black Knights, then I don't want them to find out.

'If this was the Knights, then it's a message that they know and you need to lie low. If this wasn't the Knights, then you've got other problems. Maybe even bigger problems. And just because it might not be the Knights doesn't mean that they don't now know, in which case your troubles just doubled. That's before you even get around to thinking about how I might react to this little clusterfuck...'

James is looking down now, shoulders slumped, head bowed. If this is bullshit, then it might turn out that he is, in fact, really, *really* good at it.

'Understood, sir,' he says, simply.

Damn it. I don't think I'm done yet. My mind is still whirring, trying to fit the pieces together. There's something else. If this wasn't the Black Knights, and it wasn't James, then maybe this would not be enough.

What if whoever it is, whoever is behind this, is here, in the building, part of Authority? Chances are they already know I know. I need them to think that I don't realise they could be involved. I need them to think that I think it's the Knights. Unless it is the Knights. In which case, I don't think it makes any difference.

'I can't have you here,' I sigh. 'Hand over your caseload. You're officially on desk duty. You're unofficially sorting this out. You need to get busy with other things, none of which I want to know about. You can start by sweeping my office for bugs. If that's how this got out, then I'm in all sorts of trouble.'

James fiddles with his Com, and I feel the beep of data received in my pocket. I take it out to double check, just as another transfer lands. There's a message. I don't have time for that right now.

'Borate on my back, I'll bring him up to speed,' I say, my voice barely hiding the groan.

I definitely won't bring him up to speed. Not on this. There are more than enough other things for him to be on my back about. I'll deal with Borate at the Meeting.

I glance up. James is standing, but he's not moving very fast.

'Fix this,' I bark.

James scuttles off.

Everyone just calls it the Meeting. It's gone under several names over the years. It was the Strategy Meeting for a while. It was called ROAM after that. It stood for Operational Authority Meeting. I do not remember what the R stood for. That's if I ever knew.

It has a name now, which I also don't remember and which is never used. If you called it anything other than the Meeting I don't think anyone would know what you were talking about.

The membership is Chief Gerstley Borate, who heads up Authority, and us, his faithful band of Oficiers, senior officers of the Trinity police. Emerald Jean is already in the room when I arrive.

I have fresh tea, which I've spiked for the occasion. You need help to get through the next half hour.

Everyone else floats in soon after, eyes fixed on their Com or their tablet, shuffling bacon sandwiches or muffins and, in Oda's case, fermented fruit. Baran, Rey and Bonheur all take their seats before Borate appears, his hulking frame filling the doorway and blocking the light until we all look up from our screens and acknowledge his presence.

No Mortimer, of course. Mortimer isn't here yet.

'Where's the prick?' asks Borate.

Everyone makes noncommittal grunting noises and fixates back on their screens. Borate takes his seat.

No one sees the point of the Meeting. As Oficiers, we spend a significant proportion of our working day trying to avoid sharing information about the cases we have ongoing, the status of our investigations, or our feeling about the weather at this time of year.

Authority is not a collaborative environment. It does not encourage creativity, or problem solving, and thinking outside the box is positively discouraged. We need to be busy. More importantly, we need to be seen to be busy. And nothing keeps us busy like trying to hide everything we're doing from our colleagues lest it turns out that they can help.

A problem shared is a problem halved, they say. We do not want that.

I think that's why Borate insists on the Meeting every morning. It's proof, for him, that we're all here, therefore that we're all keeping busy, in the most pointless and futile ways. Except Mortimer, of course.

The updates are, as usual, banal and uninformative in anything but the most basic way. Oda is still conducting investigations to ascertain whether Resistance is running a recruitment campaign in the refugee camps across the Northern Exposure. The investigation has been ongoing for at least eighteen months. Everyone around the table knows that, yes, Resistance has been recruiting from the refugee camps for years. Many of us know Agent Jones personally.

Baran gives a financial update. We have money. We always have money. It is the major benefit of being part of Trinity's saturated bureaucracy. It serves the political leadership of the city to tie a significant proportion of its crime fighting resource up in excessive red tape. Red tape costs. Nothing encourages ingenuity like budgetary restraint, whereas the one thing that can freeze an investigation in its tracks is the wait that comes with the prospect of a funding application coming through. The trick is to keep it on the cusp of coming through, but never to actually deliver the money.

Rey's personnel update is even less enlightening. We have a new intake arriving this month, following last month's wave of compulsory retirement, timed to ensure zero opportunity for handover. Continuity, institutional knowledge, these would also be a significant threat to the way things work around here.

Bonheur is a project manager. They have nothing to offer.

I do not, it turns out, mention Barlow. I didn't tell them about the plan before; I do not feel the need to update them on progress. They don't know there is any progress. Without Mortimer here, there are no awkward questions about who might or might not have been transferred from Street's cells to ours overnight. I'm in the clear.

I'm in the clear on Barlow, anyway. It seems that this is not what Borate was so keen to talk to me about.

'And the Manukan situation?' asks Borate.

Fuck, what is this? I cough and flick at my tablet, as if trying to call up a briefing paper.

'The Manukan situation?' I ask, feigning ignorance.

Ralph Manukan was an aide to Mayor Chaguartay. He was found a few weeks ago with a knife in his back, or maybe a bullet wound. I suddenly can't even remember how he was murdered. That's not a good look.

He can't genuinely want an update, can he?

Everyone said that it was Black Knights. I categorically said that it wasn't. I thought that was the end of things.

'I'm sure you understand how sensitive this is.' Borate's smile is without warmth.

The penny drops. Ralph Manukan was on Chaguartay's staff. Borate is under pressure to deliver. There is a minor problem. I haven't been actively pursuing any leads.

'Absolutely.'

I furrow my brow. I get a sharp pain behind my eyes. My skin feels tight. It can't be possible that I'm sobering up. This is not a good time. I slurp my tea. It needs to act fast.

'And I'm sure we all…' I sweep a hand around the

conference table. '...we all want to see a swift resolution to this case. And whoever is responsible held to account.'

'You make it sound like a mild dose of fraud,' snarls Borate. 'A man is dead. A significant member of the government is dead.'

Was he? Was he, though? He was a junior political strategist. Working for a man who has one strategy for all things: put pressure on everyone until he gets what he wants.

'The very fabric of our society, the values that hold Trinity together, all of that is under threat. Our department is under the microscope. I want results.'

This isn't my fault. I thought we agreed this.

'I'm uncertain that we've established that the Black Knights are responsible, sir,' I say.

To be fair, it makes no sense. The Black Knights are entirely, although not directly, under the command of Trinity's mayor. Why would they bump off someone who Chaguartay, apparently, holds in such esteem?

'I think you should ask my colleagues here...' another sweep around the table. '...why so little progress has been made? I'm doing my best but...'

Borate is staring at me. I stare back. He holds my stare, keeps on holding it until my eyes water. I feel like shit. This isn't worth it.

'I'll check with my team and get back to you, sir,' I whisper.

'See that you do.'

Borate rises and leaves the room.

I want to throw up.

CHAPTER 4

Borate can wait, Manukan can wait. I'm not ready to talk to Bjorn Barlow yet, but I'm going to do it, anyway.

I take the lift down to lower ground, flash my way through security and head to the back, where our cells are. My cells.

The door slides closed behind me and there is silence. I check the screen on the wall, only one is occupied. I can see Barlow on the monitor, sat perched on the side of his cot. He looks like any other Cleric, shaved head, azure robe…

Well, pale grey robe on the monochrome monitor, but I assume it's blue. Definitely not saffron, which is what the Brotherhood wore. Shiny, smooth head, no hint of a tonsure. I push a button next to the screen.

'Bjorn Barlow,' I bellow.

He jumps. I push another button, hold it down.

'Hello. The door is front of you is about to open. I'd like you to move into the room next door and take a seat. We need to have a conversation.'

Barlow nods, as if to himself, and stands, before moving slowly, elegantly, across the floor of his cell and through into the interview room. I let go of the button and the door swishes back out of the wall and closes behind him.

I watch him sit at the far end of the table, sliding himself into the chair which is bolted to the floor. I check behind me to make sure the door is secured, that there's no chance of him escaping, then open the door from the anteroom and enter the interview room myself.

I take an uncomfortable seat opposite him. I'm a little rounder than I really need to be to slide easily between the chair and the table. This side should have cushions. The Cleric is wearing a loose linen habit. If anything, he's got to be even more uncomfortable.

You wouldn't know it from his expression. He looks serene. I instantly dislike him.

'Hello again,' says the Cleric.

He must have confused me with someone else. Not Parker. James? Seems unlikely. He's a lot younger than me. And he's Ashuanan. James, that is, not Barlow.

'We haven't spoken before,' I say. 'My name is Oficier Lagrange. I head up this Division, here at Authority. My remit is Black Knight activity. Criminal activity. We'll come on to why I've come to talk to you but... You're with the Devoted, I understand.'

Barlow smiles. I want to punch him. This surging rage is not a good sign.

I can feel the frustration boiling in the pit of my stomach, the anxiety spreading through my veins. I think I'm going to have a full on panic attack. I shouldn't be here. I'm going to explode, implode, fuck this whole thing up, because I think I'm indestructible and I don't know when to stop.

I stretch my eyes wide, try to get some air to my brain. I don't know. I don't know what I'm doing here.

'That is correct, sir.' He is softly spoken.

'You told my Junior that you were from the Brotherhood?'

'I did.' Barlow holds his hands up, in a gesture that protests innocence. 'I apologise. I have been a little discombobulated of late.'

'You were drunk?'

'I was not.'

He doesn't seem drunk now, although my capacity to judge may be tempered by the fact that I am. He doesn't seem troubled by a hangover either, and he's not a young man so he really should be if he consumed enough to forget the last thirty years.

'You were "discombobulated" for other reasons?' I ask.

He smiles again. It's unnerving.

'My mind wanders,' he says. 'I'm still adjusting.'

I pause. I may not be dealing with a well man. I feel a bit out of my depth. I don't think he's done anything wrong. I don't believe he was drunk.

'You don't need to keep calling me "sir",' I say. 'The people I interview are usually disinclined to be polite to me. Your name is Bjorn Barlow?'

It's not really a question. There has to be a simple explanation for this, and the only one that holds water is it being a massive coincidence.

'Is that the question you really want to ask?'

'There are many questions that I want to ask,' I snap. 'I didn't realise that I had a quota, though. To be honest, that wasn't one of them.'

'Ask the right one and I may answer them all.'

He certainly talks like a Cleric. My mood has turned. I want to squeeze his smug face between my fists.

He's being evasive. *Head, heart, gut.* What's the non-simple explanation here? Let's interrogate that.

Confused old man forgets who he is, hears a name, assumes it's his. Could this apologetic - apparently coherent - man in front of me have forgotten who he was? Maybe. For long enough to get a new Citizen's License configured? Maybe not. Also, there are biometric records. You can't just get any old name bonded to a license token.

Head, heart, gut. It doesn't check out. Where would he have heard the name, apart from anything else? That question alone takes us down a new labyrinth of rabbit holes.

I rub my chin. It sandpapers my hand. The simple explanation. It sounds right, but I don't feel it yet.

I wave the Citizen's License at him.

'This is yours?'

'No.' He smiles again. 'That's not it.'

I bristle. This isn't falling into place. I keep running up the same blind alley, backtracking, then running up it again because it's the only sensible way to go.

I'm more drunk than I should be. I shouldn't be drunk at all. That won't be helping.

I clench my hands into fists and relax them again. I look up at the ceiling, trying to find the next question. What can I say to get him to talk? Everyone wants to talk, deep down. I'm very good at helping them to do so. To get them to talk to me. But today I have nothing. I look back at the Cleric in front of me.

I shouldn't be talking to Bjorn Barlow.

I'm not ready to talk to Bjorn Barlow.

I can't talk to Bjorn Barlow.

Bjorn Barlow does not exist.

'I could ask you a question, if you like,' says not-Barlow.

I stare at him.

'That's not how this works,' I grunt. 'But go ahead.'

'Who wanted Ralph Manukan dead, and how are you going to stop them?'

I stare at him some more.

'What do you know about Ralph Manukan?'

This is too much of a coincidence, too lucky. Barlow/not-Barlow wants me to think he knows something. I don't believe him. Someone is trying to get to me. Confuse me, trip me up, set me up in a trap.

I'm angry. I can feel the rage rising.

'That question doesn't even make sense. Ralph Manukan is already dead. They succeeded. I can't stop them. But I can catch them. I will catch them.'

It's time for me to go. I shouldn't be here right now.

'I'm not finished,' I say as I stand up to leave. 'I will be back.'

He nods. He fucking nods. Doesn't say a word. Just like he knows something. Anything. Everything. And in that moment, I really think that he does.

I stagger out of Authority and hail a TransPod. There's a regular stream of vehicles circulating outside the building. Everyone wants to get away from here, fast.

Now that I've admitted defeat, now that I've accepted that my bloody minded spiralling has left me unable to cope, now that I've decided to go home, the exhaustion hits me like a fist.

When I get in the Pod, the interface asks me what conversational mode I would prefer for my journey.

'Just drive,' I snarl.

I don't hear another word from the interface. The robot knows where it's going - that information was transferred from my Com when I hailed it. It takes me straight there.

Phil Oddy

My Accommodation block is dark. I could take an Authority apartment in a gleaming complex. They have facilities. Both the kind to use for leisure, and the kind that would provide the support I need to sort my life out.

But I grew up here and I'm not ready to leave. I'm not ready to stop being me, being the person I've become. I tell myself that it keeps me real, keeps me grounded, keeps me closer to the people I'm supposed to protect.

When I lie still, quiet, in bed in the middle of the night, I don't think that's true. I think I'm scared to stop being me, because I worry that there's nobody else in here. I think that I have to be this person or I won't be anybody.

I slide down an alley. The shadows cast deep here, voids that suck the life from the air. The doors of every apartment are locked tight. Nothing gets out: no light, no sound, no life, no death. No evil.

I don't need to go there. I would only have to do something about it and, right now, I don't have the energy. I close my eyes, breathe in the night air. It stinks, but it's my city, our stink. It's comforting. It's home.

I don't know how long it's been since I was home. I don't really sleep, you'll have noticed. As I strain every sinew climbing the steps, the aromas of a dozen lives hit me on a tide of warmth leaking from the neighbouring flats.

The smell. The smell can escape. The stench of life and death, that's the one thing you can't hide. Spice and fat and candles and incense and sweat and vomit and shit, the reek of human existence pushed out on a wave of perfume.

The light outside my apartment flickers as I unlock my door. I cross the threshold and deep bass rumbles from the floor above. In here, I'm connected to other lives. One above, one below, three on each side. We're a cell, a network, a hub. I don't know their names, but I know their habits and the familiarity of their intrusions tells me I am home.

I tap the Com unit on the wall. The flat is dark, so the meter has probably run down because the light in the kitchen doesn't turn off, usually. I bring up the meter on the Com screen and top it up.

I would get around to putting that on automatic, but I'm so rarely here it doesn't seem worth the admin. My foot slips slightly as I shuffle in and I glance down. There's an envelope on the mat. It's got a footprint on it from when I stepped in just now.

That's very old school. Like the card I gave to Laihla earlier, its physical nature, its analogue lack-of-tech, promises secrets. I deal in secrets every day, it's my job, but even I don't get many letters. You can't buy envelopes in many stores. No one ever has a pen.

I pick it up, turning it over in my hands. The envelope isn't new, it's been reused many times. Words are scribbled out and rubbed off, the corners tatty and several generations of tape are peeling from around the flap.

I peel up the latest one and look inside. There's a single sheet of paper, which I draw out. The writing is oversized, looping, like someone trying to zero in on the shapes required to form actual letters.

It's a foreign hand, not a standard script, and a long way away from what I usually read, fed through a translation software to smooth out all the rough edges. It's real, personal, not blunted by the algorithm.

I find it easier to read Clar's messages at arm's length, where I can get a sense of the shape of the sentence. You get lost trying to read the words themselves. I hold it out in front of me, turn the light on.

I take a moment, but I get there. It says: "Laihla says thank you. One good turn deserves another..."

I run a glass under a tap and down the water. I want a different drink, but when even I think that's a bad idea, then it's probably time to stop.

I think I'm hungry. I'm tired. And hungry. And tired. I can feel my brain grinding to a halt.

I stagger to the kitchen and check the cupboard, where all I find is a half box of off-brand fish sticks. I don't even bother to check the fridge for milk. If I left any in there, it will be solid by now. I shake the box, and suddenly I'm not as hungry as I thought I was.

I realise that Clar's message didn't seem to finish. I flip the paper. Taped to it, with the words "Sweet dreams" scrawled next to it, is a small plastic bag containing a few, precious, golden strands.

Rosaan's finest. These most definitely are herbal.

I'm almost too tired to roll them into a smokable packet, but I manage it. My fingers can retrieve memories that my brain cannot.

I stumble back to the living room, pause by the couch, then make a smarter decision and head for the bedroom. I don't so much throw myself onto the bed as trip and fall. But I'm where I need to be now.

One last drag, save the rest for tomorrow. I've got this far without burning myself to death in my bed, and I've got what I need. It's the trick to continuing to function with habits like mine. Know when to push it, know when to coast. I feel my whole body sink, consciousness running from me fast.

I don't chase it. I don't react to the solvent tang seeping through the floorboards. I guess the Tweak palace in the flat below is still in operation.

Someone should close that down. But not me. Not now. Do I really want Vice poking around this close to home?

Head…

Bjorn Barlow wanted me to ask him questions. I wanted to ask Bjorn Barlow questions. But they weren't the same questions. Except…

…Heart…

Did I ask the questions I wanted the answers to? He knows something. I remember thinking that. Anything. Everything. Isn't that what I want…?

…Gut.

I'm not going to figure out what the right question is. That's not how it works. That's not how I work. It's out there, though. I'll know it when I see it.

I'll know it when I hear it.

I'll know it when I feel it…

The alley already stinks of death. Also, urine and rotting vegetation. Each one assaults my sense of smell, like repeated blows to the olfactory nerve. I know this, but I don't feel it. I can't feel it. I'm not really here. I float an arm's length from my body. I'm not living this scene for the first time. I remember all of this. I know what's going to happen.

The body on the floor may stink of these things also, some or none. I'm not getting close enough to find out. The Cadet, the new one – not Parker – drops the blanket as I turn away, pulling my pipe from the pocket inside my jacket as I turn. It's empty, the pipe, has been for years. I keep it in the pocket because it's easier than trying to break the reflex. I place it in my mouth and bite down, hard.

'Sir?' repeats not-Parker. 'Is it him?'

'Dunno,' I growl through gritted teeth. 'He's a mess.'

He is a mess. Even if I wasn't almost profoundly face-blind, I doubt I would have recognised the victim. I don't fancy his wife's chances when we need an ID. I do, of course, know who it is. It's my number one priority at the moment. Bjorn Barlow.

No, not Bjorn Barlow. Borate's voice echoes in my head. "A man is dead. A significant member of the government is dead." It's that one. I'll remember his name in a minute.

'Did you find her?' *I demand of Parker. Now it's Parker. I don't know what I was thinking before.* 'Manukan's wife?'

There it is. Manukan. I'm catching up.

Parker shakes her head. It feels better, now that it's Parker. I think it was Parker all along, both in this scenario and in the original one. I wonder who she was before.

'Spoke to the sister, sir,' *she replies matter-of-factly.*

She taps her Com, brings up her notes.

'She said that she'd gone out for the evening. She was looking after their daughter. It was… a tough conversation. I didn't go into details, so she doesn't know why we want to talk to her. I thought it was best, but that means that she has no reason to hurry home. We could be waiting a while.'

Parker pauses. Stair rods crash into the deepening puddles on the less-sheltered side of the alleyway. She seems momentarily hypnotised by the rain.

'Hell of a night for a stroll,' *I say.*

I'm trying to pull her back in. I don't know what's going on. She's never normally like this. She wasn't like this the first time around.

Parker shakes her head. I raise an eyebrow. Parker is a good Cadet, will be a great Oficier one day. She can read people. There is something she isn't saying.

'You can say it.'

Having given my permission, I am slightly perturbed to see Parker turn her head and glance up and down the alley before she speaks. It's fine that she's apprehensive about speaking out of turn, but it's doesn't seem to be me she's afraid of. Finally, she says something.

'There's something she wasn't saying.' *She is staring at the floor.* 'I don't know what, but I've heard a member of that particular family swear up was down when it suited them, often enough to know what it feels like.'

I spit out my pipe out with the force of the laugh that explodes, unbidden, from within. It clatters onto the cobbles and smashes into three pieces. I stare at the broken relic of old habits, while I bring myself back under control.

I wipe a small tear from my eye and look up to Parker, only just managing to drop my grin before I make eye contact with the younger woman.

'Nicely put, Cadet. So we're open to the idea that she's gone AWOL. I would get someone on that…'

I trail off. Suddenly we're not talking about Manukan's wife anymore. "A member of that particular family…" *is a phrase only used about one particular family.*

'Already done, sir.'

I don't ask who she's having followed. A female "member of that particular family" *could only be Evie White. I mean, it could be her sister, but what is anyone going to learn following Sara Chaguartay from salon to salon?*

I look at the body on the ground. It's still Manukan, best as I can tell. I'll piece this together later. It will make sense when my head is straighter.

I'm tired, I remember, and hungover. I can wait for it to make sense. I just need to soak it all up right now. I nod.

'Who?'

'Solzinger,' *she says.*

I had wondered where Solzinger was. I think. At some stage.

'Anything else I should know?' I ask.

I need to get inside. Parker looks at me again, withholding.

'Good grief, Cadet. Anyone would think I was some Alley drunk who had wandered into your crime scene and was trying to piss all over your corpse.'

Parker winces at the inelegance of the analogy. She sighs.

'I don't know yet, sir,' she admits. 'But something doesn't make sense.'

She isn't wrong, but I didn't think she was experiencing this scene the same way I was.

'This is meant to be the Black Knights, right?' she continues, 'but apart from where we are, there's nothing that points at them. I'm waiting on the ballistics analysis, but I don't think any firearms that we've ever seen them use caused that wound. If anything, I'd said the gun was Military. They didn't call it in, not with any recognised code words. Anyway, I've got Phonics combing the downloads to triple check but there was nothing reported...'

'Wait.' I hold up a hand, brow furrowed, mouth bent into a frown. 'This wasn't called in?'

Parker is right. That makes little sense. The Black Knights have the city by the balls, and they like to make sure we don't forget it. They like to give them a little twist from time to time.

For them to murder a man in the street and not take credit. That's unusual, to say the least.

'No, sir, not by the usual channels...' Parker falls silent.

I see her catch sight of my expression. She knows better than to interrupt this face.

'So..?'

Parker remains silent. She knows better than to second guess this face, as well. I'm not having it though. That's not what I've trained her for.

'What am I thinking, Cadet?'

Entrapment

'How did we find him?' she guesses, despite herself.

I nod, lower my hand and wave it in a circular motion to suggest that she should continue.

'Civilian,' explains Parker. *'Stumbled across it, or tripped over it, I think. They reported it. Text over Com. Anonymous.'*

I suck air in through my teeth. Not the Black Knights, not my problem, but now that I'm involved, I have a nasty suspicion that I'm going to find it hard to extricate myself. I'm feeling a little stitched up. I need to talk to Borate.

'I'm going to assume you don't think this is Street?' I ask. *'If it's not Knights?'*

Parker shakes her head.

'It's not Knights, but it's still professional,' she confirms.

She says nothing more. She doesn't need to.

'He worked for Chaguartay,' I complain.

Maybe that was the problem.

'Maybe it's not linked.' Parker raises a hopeful eyebrow.

I fix my steely gaze on the young Cadet for whom I had harboured so much hope. So much potential... I sigh, shake my head, turn away and step into the rain.

'Not you, too, Parker. There's no hope for us, is there?'

She fixes me with a steely stare. I feel my testicles shrink. She turns and points to something that's painted on the wall. I hadn't taken any notice of it before. It's just graffiti.

'Sir, what's the elephant for?' she asks.

CHAPTER 5

It takes a while for the alarm from my Com to cut through, but eventually I am awake.

I was asleep. That was a dream. It's an immense relief because the Manukan case is baffling enough without me having to figure out what the hell all of that nonsense meant.

It takes a moment to shake it all off; oddly, I'm most bothered by the idea that I might be face blind. I'm not face blind.

I roll over and sit up. I'm still wearing my clothes. They stick to my skin. I feel disgusting. My head feels surprisingly clear, however. I should worry about how good I'm getting at tolerating the amount I abuse myself. I'm not going to.

I realise that it's not the alarm, that's not what woke me up. Someone is calling my Com. I grab it from the bed next to me and blink the screen into focus.

My heart sinks at the name on the screen. That's not someone I'm mentally prepared to talk to.

I don't know that I'm ever going to be ready for this conversation, however, and there's only so long I can dodge this. I've rejected several calls already, over the last couple of days.

I think I have to do this. I answer it.

I don't need to worry about holo mode. Where this call is coming from, that's not an option.

There's a long pause, but I say nothing. I'm waiting, waiting for a familiar recorded message telling me that this call originates from Detention. Then a beep. Then a voice, an angry voice.

'Sim, what the fuck? I thought you'd call.'

I groan.

'Kamla. I don't... You can't...'

I can't form coherent thoughts. It's not altogether down to the hangover, which I now realise that I do have. It's the fact of who I'm talking to. It's what she wants from me, how unprepared I am to discuss it. It's why she's in this situation in the first place, and how much of it is my fault.

I sit up, swing my legs off the bed, and stand. I shuffle to the window and pull the blinds open. Murky grey light soaks in. It's early. Early tomorrow?

'Why are you calling so early?' I ask.

'I thought you would call me. I waited all day. What do you mean early?'

So it's not early, it's still today. Man, I hurt. There's an ache in my shoulders and scuffs all up one shin. As I stretch and flex my arms to restore some flow of blood to my hands, I notice that one of my biceps is strained as well.

Battered. I feel battered, like a man repeatedly pummelled with a baseball bat... or a man tossed in flour and flung into greasy hot fat. Come to think of it, my skin is burning, with a low level background radiation that prickles, pretty much all over. Brilliant.

'Were you asleep? Are you drunk?'

I can't decide if she's pissed off or concerned. She has every right to be pissed off, and I don't deserve concern, so I probably shouldn't worry about this, but... we had something, once.

'I'm working a case,' I say.

That, she knows, is no indicator of whether I'm drunk. But I want her to know that I'm busy, with real stuff, with proper work. Nothing, if I'm honest, that is going to help her, but I don't need to admit to that.

I also don't think I can count dreaming about a case as "working it", either. Especially when the fundamentals are so wrong. Manukan wasn't married, there was no baby, no sister. And that really wasn't Parker.

'Bullshit. I need the money, Sim.'

Ah, right, she doesn't believe me. That's fair enough, and good to know. Also, very perceptive of her, although she has met me, so it wasn't the wildest stab in the dark.

'I'll get you the money,' I groan, rubbing my head. I need a glass of water.

The money will get her out of Detention. She hasn't done much wrong. Her arrest - which was somewhat my fault - was because of what and who she knew, rather than what she'd done. She was only initially detained because she couldn't pay the fine.

'You'd better. It's your fault that I'm stuck here.'

It is my fault. Not just because of my part in her arrest, but also because I told her she had nothing to worry about, that the fine would be small, that she'd be able to pay. I got that wrong.

That she's still in there is also my fault. I have the money she needs, but I have to figure out a few things before I'm ready to admit that. Just a few more amongst the many things I have to figure out. It's a weight on my mind.

'I know it's my fault,' I say. 'Hang in there.'

She ends the call. Or somebody ends it for her. I do feel

bad. I worry about her in there. But the *real* reason she's in there, the reason that I had to put her in the situation that led to her arrest, that was *not* my fault and I can't get her out until I know whose fault it is.

Regardless, very little of it is *her* fault.

I turn away from the window and check my Com for messages. There are thirty-seven notifications. Many from James, many more from Borate. He seems to know what's been going on, vis-à-vis Bjorn Barlow, and he doesn't seem happy that he didn't hear it from me.

That's not surprising, and there was definitely a point yesterday - this morning - when I was going to tell him. I got sidetracked. Because I was drunk and didn't think that I could handle it.

I know how weak an excuse that is.

There's a message from Lomax, though. Noise from Borate is one thing, but I need to go back in if it's got to the stage where Lomax is messaging me. *Damn it!*

I was working a case. Working my case. That's an excuse. I should stop making excuses and actually do it.

I find some different clothes on the floor, change into them, grab my Com and make a dash for the door.

'Sim!' Lomax nods at me from behind his desk.

'Lomax.'

This is several orders of magnitude more respect and courtesy than I would usually show anyone in the building, Borate included. Lomax Churchill is a special case, though. Lomax Churchill is worth his weight in gold.

Lomax looks at me over the top of his screen. He doesn't look impressed.

'You disappeared on me, Sim,' he scolds. 'The boss has been throwing things around all afternoon. He's really, really pissed off with you. It's taking all my special skills to calm him down. You'd better not have just been sleeping off another bender.'

I bite my tongue.

'I was busy,' I mumble.

'Too busy to check your Com?' Lomax raises an eyebrow into a perfect arch.

'I came running when you called,' I plead.

'Too bloody right you did!' Lomax seems incredulous that I would have reacted otherwise. It's a good job that Kamla called when she did. In retrospect, of course.

'I'm here now…'

'You are here now,' he concedes. 'So all's well that ends well? He'll see you in a minute.'

There's a bang on the other side of the wall. It's made of glass but the tinting can be turned up and down and currently it's opaque. Maybe Lomax wasn't being metaphorical when he mentioned Borate throwing things.

'Who's in there?' I'm not worried. If anything, it would be good for the boss to get all the throwing out of his system before I'm called in.

'Ha!' Lomax looks up again from his screen. 'Mortimer.'

Who else?

'Has he been in there long?'

Lomax shrugs.

'A while,' he says. 'I don't think that's important, though. That bang suggests to me that the boss hasn't quite worked out all of his frustration yet. My guess is that our Morty won't get out of there until he has. He's a bit of a punching bag, I'd say.'

Poor guy. I'd feel sorry for him if he wasn't so useless. We go back a long way and he's always been useless. It was a ridiculous decision to put him in charge of something as tough and all-consuming as Street. Nobody knew what Borate was thinking. Nobody is surprised at how it's turned out. Except for Borate.

There are raised voices. I agree with Lomax. I'll be waiting for a while.

'So how's married life?' I ask.

This is what I do. This is how important Lomax Churchill is to the quality of my life. This is how much I care about what Lomax Churchill thinks about me. This is how much I want Lomax Churchill to like me…

I'm doing small talk.

I know Lomax got married recently. Maybe as recently as last month? That's a detail too far, as is the actual name of his actual wife. I've done well, though. Lomax appreciates the effort and grins at the question.

'It's heaven!' He holds up a small, wooden box painted jade green with some kind of golden trim. 'Look at what she gives me!'

'Her grandmother's jewellery box?'

It's not a serious guess, and fortunately, Lomax is not seriously offended.

'No, silly.' He opens the box up. It's lined with greasy paper, and he extracts what I can only describe as a nugget of meat. 'It's a lunch box.'

'Is she trying to give you a heart attack?'

'No, no, no! She'd be horrified if she saw what I replace her nuts and seeds and berries with. Poor darling wants me to live forever but I can't be doing with that… I put the bird food in a bowl in the break room. The sparrows swoop in and it's gone in an instant. Poor, hungry things…'

The sparrows are not, in fact, sparrows, but what Lomax calls the Cadets, on account of them all looking "like tiny, undernourished birds". He says it's a sign of them being too underpaid to afford to eat properly. I think it's more likely that a young metabolism and having to spend twelve hours a day on their feet, putting in the legwork that us, more senior Oficiers, can't be arsed to, means that they're always hungry. They will eat anything, though. I'm not sure that sparrows are the best analogy.

'And then you pop into Café Konoroz and...'

'...get some proper food, exactly.' Lomax finishes my sentence for me.

He will have a heart attack one of these days. He doesn't move more than ten paces from that chair in the course of a working day, and I know he uses Borate's personal pilot to get chauffeured door-to-door. He manages the central transport calendar, so he can block out some time whenever he needs to go anywhere.

I know for a fact that he's not above sending Borate in a pool Pod when they need to leave at the same time. He's shameless.

'So what have you been doing?' asks Lomax. Again, with the arched eyebrows.

'Working the case.' I'm lying to myself as much as anything. Apparently, vague dreams do now count.

'The Manukan case?'

Lomax knows everything. Before I got painfully put on the spot in The Meeting earlier, there's no way Oda, or Baran, or Rey knew anything about the Manukan case, or that I hadn't already handed it over to Mortimer. It would make sense to hand it over to Mortimer.

Maybe that's what Borate is doing now? Maybe I'm off the hook. *Is that too hopeful?*

'Yes. Only I'm not sure it should be my case. It doesn't feel like the Knights...'

'Borate is pretty certain that it's yours.'

That extinguishes that vague hope then, I guess. If anyone

would know what was on Borate's mind, I'm talking to him. I'm going to need some actual leads, though. We have the weapon type, but that led us nowhere useful. Beyond that, nothing. No idea of Manukan the man. As far as I can tell, he led a simple life of work, eat, sleep, repeat. And as all of his work was confidential…

Images from the dream keep seeping into my train of thought, though. Not-Parker, the confusion between Manukan's home life and that of the Chaguartay family, something about an elephant… None of this is fact, none of this is even close to being evidence. But I don't have a lot to go on apart from gut feel and experience tells me that my gut sometimes has strange ways of getting through to me.

'I can't shake the feeling that there's something bigger going on around this, you know,' I wonder aloud.

'How so?' Lomax's attention seems to be on something else, on whatever just flashed up on his screen. But that's OK. I'm really only thinking aloud.

'I don't understand why everyone is insisting it's my case,' I start. 'Apart from where the body was found, there is no sign that this was Black Knight activity. Wrong firearm, no call-in, their alignment with…'

Lomax's head snaps up and I remember where I am. We do not acknowledge the connection between Chaguartay and the Knights.

'It just doesn't fit,' I say, and leave it at that. 'But somewhere there is pressure. Pressure on Borate, meaning pressure on me. Pressure from where, though? Not Manukan's family. He doesn't have one. Not from Administration, they wouldn't sully themselves to get political. There has been no debate in The Dome, so not Opposition. It has to be from Chaguartay, which makes sense, but…'

I run into the same difficulty but, again, I can't say

anything. This is the trouble with all of this, with everything we do. We tie ourselves in knots, run around in circles and keep ending up looking at the big man.

It makes no sense that Chaguartay's team would point fingers at the Black Knights. So what if it was more personal? I think about the conversation with not-Parker in the dream. The whole thing was invented by my subconscious. What was I trying to tell myself?

If it was the Black Knights, and I was still very much on the fence about whether it was, then they wouldn't have risked this action on their own. Taking out a close aide of the very man whose patronage ensured their ongoing protection and survival would be apocalyptic if it wasn't sanctioned.

So Chaguartay ordered it. For personal reasons. To protect someone. Someone in his family.

Pieces fall into place. Sara. Something happened between Manukan and Sara and Chaguartay ordered him killed. It all makes perfect sense.

Except it doesn't. If he ordered the kill, why does he want it investigated so badly?

Head, heart, gut. It feels almost right, though. My gut likes this theory, even if my heart doesn't love it. I just need to find the holes and work out how to fill them in. And experience tells me that when I can't see the complete picture like this, it's usually because someone is hiding the pieces from me.

Not-Parker. Someone is working against me. Someone I trust, like Parker. Someone who has another agenda, though. Could that be Parker? I don't know yet…

Borate's door swings open, and Mortimer skulks out. He looks harassed and harangued but physically unscathed.

Lomax waits for the door to click shut again before he exclaims,

'You're alive!'

Mortimer glances at him. It's a nervous look. I'd be scowling right now, but Mortimer doesn't look like he's got it in him. He nervously glances in Lomax's direction, mumbles something in his shaky little voice, completely blanks me, and then scuttles off into the main corridor.

His scuttle is pretty fast. I'd describe him as running away if he could lift his feet more than a few inches off the floor.

Lomax sighs.

'Looks like he's had the sense of humour beaten out of him.' He stands up and stretches, putting his fists into the small of his back as his spine audibly cracks. 'Or he would have if he'd had one in the first place.'

I go to stand up too. It's my turn. Lomax waves a hand to indicate that I should stay where I am.

'I'll check on the weather,' he explains. 'You don't want to walk into a hurricane-force Borate.'

'That would be something I'd rather avoid,' I say gratefully.

Lomax's a nice guy, don't get me wrong, but I don't know what I've done for him to be looking after me like this. I don't like it; it makes me uncomfortable. But so does the prospect of copping the wrong end of Gerstley Borate's wrath, so I let it happen.

Lomax grins and taps a few keys before turning to Borate's door.

'Just a jiff,' he says, and slips through into Borate's office.

I recognise the sing-song tone he uses as he says this. It usually means that he's incredibly pleased with himself. The most common reason for Lomax Churchill to be incredibly pleased with himself is that he's just realised that you're going to owe him. Big time.

'I'll be brief.'

Borate leans farther back in his seat. His brow is slick, his usually robustly glowing skin pasty, his dark hair slicked to his scalp. He doesn't look well.

'I seem to be a busy man,' he chuckles, without humour.

I nod. I don't want to catch whatever he's contracted. Keeping it brief is fine with me, and I don't need to extend the encounter with unnecessary words. Borate lifts a file, an actual cardboard folder, and tosses it across the desk towards me. Interesting. More analogue input.

'That record is off the record,' he chuckles again, until it develops into a wheezing cough.

He puts his hand over his mouth and waves at me to pick it up. It's full of pictures. All of them of me. Me letting myself into my building; me coming out of my building; me getting coffee; me talking to Clar; me drinking at Eamer's; me standing over the dead body of Ralph Manukan, with actual Parker standing in the background.

'You've had me watched?'

'No,' Borate shakes his head. 'But someone has. I was passed this by persons who shall remain nameless, but it worries me you did not know.'

Shit, I really didn't.

'I see you have a body.' He doesn't wait for me to reply. 'Who are your suspects?'

'We don't have any at the moment,' I confess. There is only so far it's advisable to flannel the Chief. 'I'm becoming increasingly sceptical that the Black Knights are involved at all. It doesn't have their hallmarks, and it seems odd that they'd go against Chaguartay given...'

Borate coughs, motioning me to hush and cupping his ears. He thinks his office is bugged. If his office is bugged, then I'm even more convinced that mine is. Maybe I was a little harsh on James.

I will not proffer the Manukan-banging-Chaguartay's-daughter theory. I didn't think I was going to anyway, and I'm definitely not going to now. Not if the big man is listening in. Either I'm wrong, in which case that's going to go badly for me, or I'm right, which could also go badly for me.

I need to formulate a new theory, fast. My brain makes a leap. I conjure a new hypothesis out of thin air, with very little awareness of what triggered it.

'What I mean is that it seems more likely that someone linked to a group openly opposed to the mayor...' I say this slowly.

I think I know where I'm going, where I'll end up. I'm not sure I believe that I'm about to say this. Heart all the way. There is no input from either my rational brain, or indeed my raw instinct, going on right now.

'Resistance?'

'Not Resistance.'

I take a deep breath. I am going to say it. I can't believe that I'm going to do this now, in front of Chief Borate, when I have next to no evidence other than... not even a hunch. A half-remembered dream. It's strange. It's like I want this to be true.

'Opposition.' I say.

Yep, that's what I'm giving him. Jack and Evie White arranged for the murder of her father's aide. Possibly because he was involved with her sister. Although I don't know why she'd care.

Is this career suicide?

Is this actual suicide?

I've said it now. The cards are going to have to fall where they fall; I guess. I feel strangely light, lifted, freed. I'm a bit giddy. Is this who I am when I'm sober? Am I sober?

'Opposition?' Borate leans back. 'That seems like a stretch. We've seen many things in Trinity, but so far our politicians have steered clear of kidnap. And murder.'

He turns in his seat and moves to stand up. I don't think that what he's just said is even remotely true, but this is the cue that the conversation is over. I stand up as well. Borate shakes his head, subtly but definitively.

'Street,' he says.

This is encouraging. I've put him off. Downside is he now thinks I'm a terrible detective. Upside is he's going to give the case to Mortimer. Who will get nowhere.

'You have contacts.' My heart sinks. 'Go use them.'

He shakes my hand, and I leave his office.

He won't let me off the hook.

Street. He wants me to investigate small-time crooks and petty thieves. It's a blind alley. Which is where I'm likely to find a lot of them, but I want to know why he's so keen to send me up there.

I don't believe for a moment that he doesn't think that this is part of the power struggle that passes for business and politics in Trinity. I didn't expect him to go for the Opposition hunch. In the cold light of the corridor I don't know why I mentioned it, but I know that no knife wielding street gambler murdered Ralph Manukan.

That said, he's right. I have Street contacts.

Despite her Black Knight connections - working for Eamer being the most obvious expression of these - Mouse lives and breathes the streets of Trinity. There is no one more Street. There is no one else I would turn to.

I find her sat on a barrel by the back door of Eamer's. She's smoking something and drinking from a mug, lost in her own world. In unguarded moments like these, when she doesn't know that anyone is watching, she reminds me so much of her mother it hurts.

I squash that thought down quickly. I was there, at the end, when she held Mouse for the first and last time. I've watched Mouse grow up, watched her scrap and scramble into the woman she's become today. I'm proud of her. There are plenty who wouldn't have made it.

As I approach, she looks up. Nodding a greeting, she stands and tosses the remains of her coffee against the wall.

'You'd think the sign would be enough to keep The Alleys' dog population from using our back garden as a urinal,' she shrugs, 'but the dredge from the bottom of the coffee pot is the only thing that seems to keep them away.'

I look at the sign. It used to say No Parking, but someone has changed the P to a B.

'Ha ha,' I say. I don't actually laugh.

I look at the yard. "Back garden" is really pushing it. There are things that are green here, but none of them are alive, at least not in a good way.

'What do you need?' asks Mouse, leaning on the wall next to the loading ramp. Mouse knows I don't do social calls.

'Manukan,' I say.

Mouse sucks air in through her teeth.

'I read that was your case.'

This is Mouse being funny. She knows that it's my case. We discussed it last week.

'Ha ha,' I say, again.

'You know I can't talk about that. Walls have ears.'

I gesture around us.

'We're outside.'

'Just because you can't see the wall doesn't mean it's not holding us back.' She sucks in smoke.

I'm very tempted to ask her to pass it to me. I am feeling quite agitated, and more than a little ill. I know this feeling, and it's not one that I like. It's one that I probably need right now, though.

I make decisions when I'm agitated. Better decisions. I make connections, figure things out. I need to make some progress.

Progress hurts.

'Very enigmatic. You're really not going to tell me anything?'

'I really am not,' Mouse exhales.

She stares at me. It's defiant, a challenge. A challenge to my authority, to my seniority.

I accept the challenge.

'But you know something?'

'I…' Mouse hesitates, sucks in another lungful.

She knows something. Mouse always knows something, of course, but I think she knows something specific. I push it.

'Mouse. Who are you scared of?'

She splutters in response to that, streaming smoke from her mouth and nostrils like an enraged dragon.

'Not scared.' She shakes her head.

I look at her. I think that if I say nothing right now, she'll crack. Seven seconds of silence is all it's going to take.

'Not scared,' she repeats, within four.

She's good, but I'm better.

'So..?' I ask.

I have to admit that I'm confused. Mouse is smart, she moves in unsavoury circles; she has a knack for getting things done. That all comes from knowing things, but from knowing them in a way that means she will not incriminate herself. She is scared of something. It's something big, as well.

'I can't, Sim. I have to protect myself.'

I get that, but it's never got in the way of her helping me out before. I remain silent. Seven more seconds.

'Look, they didn't come through me,' she says, cracking.

She screws her glowing stub into the wall and flicks the butt away. She didn't offer me any. She puts her hands up.

'I had nothing to do with it. Any of it. No one approached me. I arranged nothing. And anyway, I know you don't think it was the Knights. Why are you still chasing this one, Sim?'

'I seem to be stuck with it,' I growl. 'Borate won't let it go. Won't let me let it go. I don't know if he knows something, or if he just doesn't think that Mortimer is up to the job.'

Mouse isn't telling me something, so I'm not going to give her any of my batshit theories. I suspect that's not quite the tit-for-tat I'm presenting it as.

'Look, I know nothing,' she says, wearily, 'like genuinely know nothing. But, based on the things I don't know, you could do worse than starting at Bridge.'

'Bridge?' I ask. 'As in Bridge Terminus?'

'Ask for Bennett. Come back…'

I cut her off.

'I'm not having this. I'm an Authority Oficier. I'm not running around the city on some scavenger hunt looking for…'

'Ask for Bennett,' insists Mouse, cutting across me this time. 'Bennett's who they go to when I say no.'

At last, a glimmer of information. I jump on it.

'Mouse, who did you say no to?'

Mouse shakes her head, gives me a half smile.

'That's just the thing. They were smart enough not to ask in the first place.'

I strongly suspect that Mouse is giving me the runaround, but I don't think I can do anything about that. Saying nothing else, I leave her and find my way home via The Alleys.

CHAPTER 6

Here I am, though. It's the next morning and I'm at Bridge. Bennett Holman is nominally the Station Master, but his heart doesn't seem to be in his work. He seems to be delighted to have someone to talk to.

'Given how easy this job is,' he says, 'I really ought to try harder to be better at it.'

Bridge Terminus is the entry point into Trinity for rail passengers, but there aren't a lot of passenger trains. As Holman has been explaining, most of the locomotives carry freight, which is unloaded by robots onto self-driving Pods for onward transport. He doesn't have to do much.

'That's the 11.45.' He points at the ceiling that is rumbling as a train passes overhead. The clock says 11.47. He flicks a switch and turns a dial and it loses two minutes. 'Listen…'

I hear the station concourse echo with a click-click-click as the update is received by the rest of the clocks in the building.

'Like thousands of tiny ants, tap-dancing,' says Holman. 'I change the clock a lot. I don't even know what the right time is most of the day. That's why I reset it when a train comes through. Mr Toun keeps the system running like clockwork.

That's good enough for me.'

'It's important.'

It is not important. It is irrelevant. I don't know what I'm doing here. This man is an idiot.

'The problem is that I just don't care enough,' he says, 'but nor does anyone else. There's no one watching, no one checking. The notice on the wall is a lie.'

The notice on the wall starts with the words "YOUR JOB IS IMPORTANT". You see it all over, Trinity. It usually is a lie.

The hall now fills with the clank and hiss of hydraulics wheezing into action, loading the carriages from the newly arrived train onto the Pods. Holman pulls the service window closed to muffle the cacophony.

'My work is trivial,' he says, before sliding a greasy package from under the counter. 'I haven't had breakfast…'

It looks like it came from Konoroz's. As he unwraps the paper, I see rice congealed into a fatty lump underneath what it's best to assume is lamb.

It's odd, I think, how I never see anyone in Café Konoroz, and yet everyone I'm meeting at the moment seems to get their tiffin from his palace of grease. That also feels irrelevant, but I tuck it away. I've learned not to ignore the strange places my mind wanders, especially when I'm in this mood.

I still haven't had a drink. Dear Creator, I need a drink. I am sorely tempted to reward myself later, and by later, I mean as soon as humanly possible.

'Not a single mistake I make, and I make plenty, believe me, has consequence. It's a lie. Do you have a fork? I need to mash this up…' Holman is still talking.

This guy does not refer people to hitmen. It's frustrating. I don't know why I'm here. I don't know what I'm supposed to ask. I don't know what I'm meant to get from this man.

I trust Mouse. It's the only thing keeping me here. But is it possible she's mistaken?

Could there be more than one Bennett Holman? Does someone else work here when he's not on duty? Are they my man?

'It's not as if we usually even get any...' Holman stops talking as a loud grating sound, possibly signifying a misaligned ramp and some superficial damage to the 11:45's paintwork ends abruptly, and I notice a repetitive thudding from right in front of me.

Holman raises the window shutter to reveal a flustered looking man dressed in a suit and tie. Holman seems surprised, which shows in both the look on his face and the clumsy way he bundles his breakfast into a ball and shoves it back under the counter.

Licking his greasy thumb on one hand, he fumbles to clip the shutter into place so that it doesn't slide back down.

'Excuse me?' says the man, before the window is fully open.

'Yes,' Holman regains his composure. Turns out he is trying to be better at his job after all. 'ah - Welcome to Trinity! Can I help you?'

'I'm looking for the left luggage.' The visitor looks pained and impatient. He either needs to go to the toilet or he's late for something.

'We don't have a left luggage office,' Holman explains, 'but if...'

The man cuts him off.

'Lockers..?'

'If you'll allow me to explain,' Holman cuts in. 'What I can do for you is arrange for your baggage to be taken to Tunnel terminus...'

'To where?' he asks.

'Tunnel. It's our sister station, if you like. For departures.'

'Departures? You mean I don't..?'

'You've obviously not been to Trinity before, sir. That's correct. Bridge Terminus is for arrivals only. To continue your onward journey...'

'So I can leave my bag with you?' the man asks.

'Yes you can,' Holman affirms. 'And when you arrive at Tunnel to continue on your way, it will be there, ready and waiting. Just pop it in the bin to your right and I'll sort you out a ticket.'

Holman pulls a small lever on the desk and, on the other side of the wall, a metal hatch tilts open. The man hefts a wheeled suitcase up from the floor and, with a little effort, wedges it in. Holman pushes the lever, and the hatch tilts back, pulling the bag into the booth.

The man taps his Com to the contact pad next to the window.

'And you're done,' says Holman. 'Your receipt will be uploaded to your device. Present that at Tunnel before you depart and your bag will be returned.'

The man stares at Holman for a moment.

'Don't you need my name, or something, in case there's... a mix-up... or something?'

'Not really,' Holman shrugs. 'we don't really get mix-ups.'

I can see why it must be hard to get one bag mixed up with no other bags. Holman looks a bit lost. He doesn't seem to know what to do. He doesn't seem to have anticipated someone deviating from the script. He probably doesn't get to use it often.

'But if you like...' He slides a piece of paper out from a pile and gets ready to write on it. 'What's your name?'

'Deleon,' says the man. 'That's D-E-L-...'

I assume that Mr Deleon spots the look on Holman's face, because he stops. We've all met a few Deleons in our time.

'Deleon,' he repeats, sheepishly. 'Lukas Deleon.'

Holman writes it down, slides out a drawer and puts the piece of paper in it. There is a screen right in front of him. He makes no attempt to input the information.

'Thank you.' He smiles. 'Have a great day.'

Lukas Deleon backs away a few paces, then bends to pick up a second, heavier-looking case that I hadn't seen on the floor. He turns and walks across the ticket hall towards the stairs at the far end.

Holman scratches at the back of his head.

'Mr Lukas Deleon has annoyed me a bit at the end there,' he mutters. 'I might not care about the job, but I'm not an idiot.'

I can't decide what Bennett Holman is, but I agree that Deleon was acting strangely. Not, granted, as strangely as the Oficier who turns up at the railway station to shadow the Station Master whose job description must read more like that of a Ticket Clerk. Whatever, this man is not the man that people go to when Mouse says "no".

'I'm going to go,' I say. 'Thank you for your time.'

At which point Deleon's case suddenly bulges and rocks on its chassis, as if it contains something alive.

'Hey, Mr Deleon,' Holman calls out. 'What have you got in the case? We can't take live animals. There are terms and conditions!'

But Lukas Deleon has gone. I look at Bennett Holman, who is so obviously not the guy I'm looking for, but…

Fuck this, I think. I needed a lead and Mouse gave me a lead. Time to follow said lead, even if it, excuse the pun, leads nowhere. Most leads do.

'Bennett Holman, you're under arrest,' I say.

I am expecting Parker, because I called her. She turns up with a squad in the usual span of time, which is to say not particularly quickly. It's long enough for me to second guess my decision to arrest Holman. I should have followed Deleon. Now, enough time has passed that his trail will have gone cold.

Maybe I'm past my creative peak. It only lasts for so long. *Head, heart, gut,* in need of lubrication. That's why I always end up drinking again.

Ha! Yes, that's why...

So Parker I'm expecting but Sergey James is also in tow, and him I am not.

'You cleared your caseload,' I remind him. 'I cleared your caseload.'

'I'm working my one remaining case,' he says.

'Barlow? Here?' I know that's what he's talking about, but how does that work?

James sighs. It seems to be an effort to have to explain himself to me.

'Bjorn Barlow didn't exist until two days ago,' he says. 'That's not possible, so I'm working on the assumption that he did exist, just not in the Trinity archives. He must have come from somewhere else. This seems to be a likely entry point. I've come to talk to your man, Holman. Quietly. I didn't know you were about to flood the place with Authority uniforms.'

'Blow your cover, did I? Parker's talking to him,' I say.

His reasoning is fair, but he's overlooking a logical flaw.

'You can take over when she's finished. I suggest that the first question you ask him is how he got a Citizen's License so fast?'

James looks put out. I'm not surprised. He's incredibly concerned about seniority.

'But Parker's...'

'Parker is working for me,' I point out. 'Parker has Bennett Holman for now. You can wait.'

I sit down on Holman's swivel chair, pick up the suitcase

that Deleon left behind. I've confiscated it now. I should probably admit it into evidence. I should at least let the folks at Tunnel know that it's been delayed en route to its destination. I'm not going to do any of that.

'What do you make of this, though? While you're waiting.' I hold it up for James to get a good look at. It's no longer twitching, no longer seems as bulky, or as heavy, as it did half an hour ago.

James is irritating me, has been for weeks, but I'm not convinced he's dodgy. I think he's a good Junior and he might have a perspective that I'm lacking. An irritating little shit's perspective. Nevertheless, it might be useful.

I unzip the case. James leans across to peer inside. Then leans back again. I can see from the look on his face that he's confused.

'There's nothing in there,' he says. 'It's empty.'

'I'm glad you think so, because I can't see anything in there either. Which is odd because if you'd seen it rock like I did, if you'd heard it squeal... then you'd be expecting to see rather more in that bag than there actually appears to be,'

'Squeal?' James asks.

I nod.

'Like air escaping from a small hole in a balloon. Or a tiny elephant about to stampede.'

James laughs. The tension leaves his face, and he seems relaxed for a moment. It's quite heartwarming to see. Maybe I need to take him for a drink sometime? It doesn't have to be a slippery slope.

'How tiny?' asks James. 'Have you checked the lining?'

I suppress the urge to gawp in amazement. I think that was a joke.

'Ha ha,' I say, zipping the bag back up.

I hate this case. Not the suitcase, the... *see, I can make jokes too.* Too many questions, not enough answers. This question doesn't even make sense. I don't even know what this question is.

Who is Lukas Deleon? What's his business in Trinity? Was there something in this bag that has now disappeared? If there was, is that an indication of anything criminal, or at least untoward? What about his other case?

Why did I arrest Bennett Holman when Lukas Deleon is easily more interesting? James was going to come along and nab Holman, anyway. Shit.

You may be interesting, Mr Deleon, but I really hope you're not up to anything or I've made a big mistake.

'I hate this case,' I say.

'I know what you mean,' says James, and I feel sorry for him in the moment.

He's not talking about the same case, but we're in the same boat. *What kind of job is this?*

Parker appears in the doorway. James stands up.

'That was quick,' I say.

Parker is shaking her head. Parker, I'm on the fence about. *No, wait, that was a dream… what am I thinking?* Parker is keen. She impresses me. By being early. I shouldn't be looking at Parker like that.

'I'm not done, sir. This is going to take a while, I think. He likes to talk, this one. Not necessarily about anything particularly relevant, but every time I decide I'm going to cut him off, he drops in another nugget and I have to let him go on.'

'So..?' I'm confused. It seems to be a constant today.

'Just a hunch, sir, but I'm getting a distinct impression that he knows more than he's letting on. Lukas Deleon, for example.'

'He knows him?'

'I think so.'

Bennett Holman is a much better actor than I would have given him credit for. But Deleon is important. Frustratingly, I knew it and I missed my opportunity. I blame Mouse for putting me on the wrong track. Although, if she hadn't, I wouldn't be here and I wouldn't know who Lukas Deleon is.

Although, of course, I don't actually know who Lukas Deleon is. I should have kept him here. I should have followed him. One of those.

'You think we need to speak to him?' I bang my fist on the table.

'I do, sir. That's what I came to say.'

'Damn it! I let him leave. He was right here and I…'

'Tunnel,' says James. 'Eventually he'll go to Tunnel. To pick up his empty bag. You could add a tracker…'

'Damn it!'

The last thing I need right now is James solving my problems, but that's actually a great idea. I didn't even let Tunnel know that I'd taken the bag. As far as they're aware, it's on its way.

I don't say anything, I just get up, growl, swipe the bag and march out.

It doesn't do to let them think you're grateful.

There's a direct miniTram from Bridge to Tunnel, so I'm going to take the miniTram. I couldn't get a Pod here quickly enough anyway and the traffic at this time of day would be impossible to get through, even with the sirens. The regular Pods can't get out of the way if there's nowhere to go.

That's unfortunate, because I hate getting the trams. I usually try to avoid them as the motion from side to side makes me nauseous if I don't close my eyes. I already have closed my eyes and I'm already feeling like I want to throw up.

It's perhaps as well that I haven't eaten anything. It's definitely a good thing that I've not been drinking.

We lurch to a halt. I don't know the route so I don't know what the stop is, but if I were to take a guess, it would be Apt Nodding. I hear the doors open to let a load of passengers on. I sit up straighter and open my eyes.

They file onboard and into the vacant seats. The tram is filling rapidly but, for now, no one sits next to me. I congratulate myself on seeming appropriately intimidating. I work hard on that, so it's gratifying.

I don't want to engage, don't want to make eye contact, so I do what anyone would do in this situation and take out my Com. I need to concentrate on something that isn't the creeping miasma from the surrounding plebs.

I have a cluster of notifications building up, but there isn't anything from anyone I care about, so I'm going to ignore them until there is.

I try to play a bit of Bomb but I can't really concentrate and the motion of the miniTram keeps causing me to tap the wrong pod with my thumb and blow myself up. I sigh, blank the screen and close my eyes again. I can hear the dull buzz of the Com stream below, the murmurs of conversation. The driver isn't supposed to have that on.

I wonder about James, about Barlow. He's right, if the Monk was from out of town, then that would explain his lack of records, but it doesn't fit with so many other things. He's got a Citizen's License. He says he's from the Citadel. He looks like he's from the Citadel.

Not a Cleric, though. *Brotherhood*. That's a blast from the past. Not an unwelcome one, but one that I very much thought was buried. He didn't confirm that he was Barlow, either. He very pointedly avoided that question.

Head, heart, gut. I don't believe that it is him. But the picture was him. Every thought, every turn, I face a new contradiction...

My eyes spring open. What if he's not from out of town? What if he's from another time?

That's insane.

But it would fit with his suggestion that he comes from a religious order that hasn't existed for nearly thirty years. My breath is shallow, my heart is racing.

It fits. Does it fit?

It can fit all it likes, but it isn't possible.

I think about the day James brought the idea of Bjorn Barlow to me. *No, not the idea of Bjorn Barlow.* He didn't have a name at that point. The idea of a fictitious man on the inside. I came up with the name.

I don't know where it came from. It just seemed to fit. And now I'm wondering...

Was there a real Bjorn Barlow? Did I ever know a Bjorn Barlow? In another place, in another life, long, long ago...

The tram jerks to another halt, and I open my eyes.

I thought my eyes were already open.

I was asleep. Reality quickly flows in and flushes out the wonky thinking and mazy logic of the space between waking and sleep. The place where time travelling Monks are a reasonable explanation for the chaos that passes for everyday life in Trinity.

The radio cuts across my thoughts before they have a chance to get any wilder.

'...Authority Chief Gerstley Borate has reiterated his commitment to restricting the activities of the Black Knights, despite a lukewarm reception from Mayor Chaguartay...'

I take a deep breath and wince. I appreciate my work earning coverage on the news, but it's both very kind of them and a terrible indictment of their journalistic standards that they fail to point out that the restriction of Black Knight activities is currently limited to one arrest, one measly imprisonment.

My personal sneaking suspicion, unavoidable in the face of the spectacular lack of progress by my department, is that Black Knight infiltration of Authority is rife to the point of suffocation.

I let out the deep breath. The woman in the seat in front of me turns around, looking annoyed. I raise my hand in apology.

The news has moved on. Even they don't care what I'm up to that much.

'...Begrade score three times in Docklands' latest victory over local rivals Academy, but the game ended in controversy as he was stretchered off after a vicious tackle by Academy defender Lesinge...'

They aren't kidding. It was vicious. I saw the game in Eamer's. It was packed. Almost entirely Docklands fans, so I'd had to keep my mouth shut and my head down. I'd pretended to celebrate each of Begrade's goals, but even my reaction to Lesinge's tackle had been real and unfiltered. You could see the hatred in his eyes as he jabbed the pike through his opponent's ankle.

I shudder at the thought. He is looking at a hefty ban now, which will not be good news for the rest of Academy's season.

'...and the schedule for this evening is rain, so make the most of this afternoon's late autumn sunshine - this might be the last we see of it until next year...'

The brakes hiss us to a halt. It's Ogre Awarded, so the next stop is mine. "Barley Omen, for Tunnel Terminus" scrolls across the LED display and I get to my feet, Deleon's mysterious, empty bag in my hand.

Except it's not so empty anymore. It's got an Authority tracker tucked into the lining.

CHAPTER 7

They're effectively sister stations, but Tunnel and Bridge are very different buildings. Bridge is all marble and shine and those weird-as-shit gates. Whereas Tunnel is rough concrete and more rough concrete. It's as if we're trying to con people as they arrive into thinking that Trinity is a nice place. We seem to care much less on the way out.

Tunnel is much better run than Bridge, as well. No busier though - people leaving Trinity are no more common than those arriving, at least by this mode of transport.

I walk up to the office door and knock.

'Come in!'

The door unlocks as I push at it and I step into the warmth of Nolan's office. The furnishings are soft, the air fragrant and warm, the lighting just the right side of subtle. It feels less like a place of work and more like a meditation space. No fuss, no complications, just comfort and calm.

'Sim!' says Nolan, sounding genuinely pleased to see me.

Few people ever sound pleased to see me. That two of them shared a womb is not lost on me. Nolan Churchill is

Lomax's twin. He is every bit the man that his brother is.

I lift Deleon's empty suitcase onto the desk beside him and drop into the very comfortable chair that Nolan keeps for visitors. It doesn't look anything special. To all intents and purposes it's a normal swivel chair, but it is the most comfortable place I have ever sat. Bar none, without exaggeration.

'Morning Nolan,' I say, leaning back.

'What have you brought me?' Nolan nods at the suitcase.

'Left luggage,' I say.

I need to explain what the deal is, I know, but I'll do that in a minute. Suddenly I'm so comfortable that I realise just how tired I really am. It's not even lunchtime but, right now, I could go to sleep for a very long time.

'Are you OK, Sim?' asks Nolan.

I sigh.

'I'm just tired, Nolan,' I say. 'I'm just very, very tired. Of all of it.

'Is that all?' Nolan laughs. 'How long has it been?'

'How long has it been since..?'

I know what he's getting at. I'm pretending that I don't because even I recognise that this is no way to live a life. No way to live my life.

Except, who am I kidding? This is the only way to live my life. It's the only way I live my life.

'Come on, Sim. You've sobered up, haven't you? It's not good for you, you know it's not. Thinking like this. You're not used to it. You're a victim of your own brilliance, you know you are. You can't burn like this for very long. No one human being can take it.'

I stare at him. His straight face doesn't last for very long.

'Those are very profound words,' I say, watching him corpse in front of me. 'I take it they're mine.'

'The number of times I've had to listen to you spout this nonsense about your brilliance, and how it is that very brilliance that prompts, nay, *necessitates* your borderline suicidal drinking habit... well, I think I'm due a small amount of affectionate ribbing.'

I continue to stare at him.

'That was quite a speech,' I say. 'Have you finished? And did you really say "nay"?'

'I did,' Nolan nods. 'I absolutely did. You were asking for it.'

'Right,' I say, closing my eyes. 'That's lovely. I'm just going to rest here until you've got it out of your system, then I can tell you why I'm actually here.'

I hear Nolan chuckle, and then I hear the scraping of a tin on a desktop, the popping of a lid, and an aroma of butter and spice surrounds me.

'Conciliatory pastry?' Nolan says.

My eyes snap open. *Now we're talking.* "Never let them think you're grateful" might be a principle I live by, but "Never pass on anything baked by Nolan Churchill" is one that I'd die for. I take a small, light brown package from the proffered tin.

I sink my teeth into it and a rich, aromatic softness consumes my senses. I couldn't begin to tell you what was in it, but I'm certain that if I could eat nothing else for the rest of my life, then it wouldn't be a hardship. I don't even think there is meat in it.

'Good?' asks Nolan.

He can see my expression. I know he's not in any doubt.

'So good,' I mumble through a mouthful of crumbs.

'Thanks,' he says, 'that means a lot. Ahj tried some, obviously, but he says that everything I do is divine, so his feedback is meaningless. You, on the other hand, couldn't bullshit me if you wanted to. Which I know you don't.'

Ahji is Nolan's husband. Ahji is a lucky man.

'What's in it?' I ask.

'Mushroom,' Nolan shrugs. 'Amongst other things. There's a… erm… shall we say *premium* version where I use a different variety of mushroom, the kind that gets harvested by naked eunuchs on the moonlit slopes of the Northern Exposure…'

I shake my head. That's not a thing that happens. All the mushrooms on the streets of Trinity are lab grown and smuggled out by unscrupulous Researchers. That's the official line, anyway. Makes you wonder why they grow hallucinogenic mushrooms in Research. Makes you wonder how the Researchers got so tight with the Black Knights.

I have enough trouble keeping tabs on them above ground, however. What they're up to under our feet is more than I have the capacity to deal with.

'…but those kind are not for working hours,' he finishes.

I think I'd like to try those. But I have business to attend to. This has already become far too much of a friendly chat. I have a persona to maintain, and people to shout at.

'That's not why I'm here,' I say.

Nolan adopts a serious face. It is hard to take it seriously. He looks like a small child.

'You've brought me a suitcase,' he observes.

'I have,' I agree. 'It was left at Bridge a couple of hours ago. It needs to go into your left luggage store.'

'Sim,' says Nolan, faux concern creeping into his tone. 'You know that we have automation for that sort of thing? You don't need to be carrying people's bags for them. It's a little below your pay grade.'

I ignore him. I'm very fond of the Churchill twins, but that fondness has a limit. Nolan just found it.

'I intercepted it. I added a tracking device. And while I don't expect the owner to return to collect it for some time, it is very important to my investigation that it is here when they do so and that I can track them from that point onwards.'

'Right,' says Nolan.

His voice has dropped. He's wondering what this means. He may be contemplating whether he's in any danger. He doesn't ask, though, which is as well, because I wouldn't be able to reassure him that he isn't.

'What's in the case?'

'Right now?' I ask. 'Nothing.'

'Nothing?'

'No. It's not completely clear if there was ever anything in the case. The evidence is… inconclusive. But…'

'Hang on, you mean there *was* something in the case?'

'There may have been.'

'But now there isn't?'

'No.'

'But how does that work? Did you take it out?'

'No. To stop this getting out of control, nor did I destroy it, nor was anything stolen from it by person or persons known or unknown. You don't need to understand what happened to the contents of the case. If, indeed, there were any contents of the case…'

'I've got to be honest, Sim, you're not making sense right now.'

'Regardless, you don't need to concern yourself with any of those questions. You just need to put this suitcase into storage. I suggest you do it now.'

We are interrupted by a banging on the service window.

'Hello? Hello?' says a voice, which I recognise instantly.

I push myself back with my feet and my chair wheels out of view of the window. Pulling a confused face, Nolan turns to speak to the customer on the other side.

'Good morning... afternoon,' Nolan checks the clock and corrects himself. 'Good afternoon. Welcome to Tunnel Terminus. How can I help you?'

'Hello,' says Lukas Deleon. 'I have a left luggage query. In that I wanted to check on my left luggage.'

'You want to check in some left luggage?' asks Nolan, reaching for the lever for the luggage drawer.

This seems like a wilful misunderstanding on Nolan's part, and I wonder why he's being difficult, but of course he doesn't know who this is. He doesn't know that this man has already checked in his luggage and that said luggage is currently sitting within reaching distance of Nolan's left hand.

'No, no, no,' says Deleon.

He seems worried. There is a waver in his voice that I am very interested in.

'Oh, right,' says Nolan, confused. 'What can I do for you?'

'I checked some luggage in earlier today, at the other station,' says Deleon.

'Ah, and you'd like to collect it,' Nolan cuts in. 'Well, if you could...'

'No, no, no,' says Deleon, again.

'No?' Nolan remains confused.

'No, I just want to check on it. Make sure it got here OK. It is very important that it is here when I'm ready for it and, well, your system...'

Deleon trails off. He seems not to want to cause offence by criticising the, frankly, bizarre and over engineered solution that Administration have come up with for a problem that, if we're all being honest, they created.

Welcome to Trinity.

This hesitancy amuses Nolan.

'If the system isn't clear to you, I could explain,' he offers.

He pulls a piece of paper from a drawer next to his desk and pushes it towards the service window. He quickly draws several Xs on it. I'm uncertain what they represent. I suspect they represent nothing more than Nolan's offbeat sense of humour.

'No, no, no,' says Deleon a third time.

Nolan seems to deflate, his fun spoiled before he even got started.

'Your system is fine...'

It isn't.

'...but for my peace of mind, could you check? My name is...'

'Just register your Com on the contact pad and I'll check for you,' says Nolan, robotically.

I recognise this as his sad voice.

Deleon taps his Com on the pad and I see a "Not Found" message pop up on Nolan's screen. I lean forward as much as I dare, as much as I can without revealing my presence to Deleon, and nudge the case across the table toward Nolan.

He doesn't notice.

'I'm very sorry, but I don't seem to have...' he begins.

I throw caution to the wind and push the case harder. It skids across the table and hits Noland on the elbow. He registers the contact and glances in my direction. I nod towards the case, a furious, stabbing motion with my entire head and neck. I'm not sure how he gets the message, but he does.

Nolan picks up the suitcase and holds it so that Deleon can see it. It seems, if anything, even less weighty than before, so he lifts it with ease, one handed, no evident strain.

'Is this your bag?' he asks hopefully.

'Yes, yes, it is,' says an audibly relieved Deleon.

'Just came in,' grins Nolan, lying.

That's not how anything works around here.

'Wasn't processed yet. You sure you don't want it now?'

'No, no, no,' says Deleon. 'No need. Just keep it safe for me. I'll be back in a few hours.'

He's turning and walking away before Nolan has a real chance to react.

'Rude,' he says, as he turns to me.

I'm already standing up and making for the door. Nolan sighs.

'I expect little more from you, though. See you later, Sim. Make sure you come back and tell me what the hell all of that was about.'

I grunt and slip through the door, back onto the station concourse. Lukas Deleon is standing by the exit, staring at me. He doesn't have his second case with him.

I wonder where he left that.

We lock eyes. He turns and pushes his way through the crowd, disappearing from view as I break into a run.

By the time I make it to the gates, he's halfway up the street. I can just see his head bobbing beyond a crowd of pedestrians. I could get out my Authority ID token or, even more effectively, my gun, but I don't want to draw attention to myself or to spook Deleon.

I'm not sure if I could spook him. I felt like he was looking out for me, like he knows who I am and knows I'm trying to track him down. That feels unlikely, feels paranoid, but that doesn't mean it isn't what is happening.

If anything, that it seems unlikely and yet also probable makes me suspect that it's exactly what's happening. I'm just missing a piece of the puzzle. The piece that makes it obvious.

Head, heart, gut. Doesn't matter which, at this point.

He can't have seen me in the office at Tunnel. I don't think he saw me at Bridge. He could have seen me on my way into

Nolan's office.

Shit, I was carrying his bag. He would have recognised that. That would have made me stand out, made him take notice. *Sloppy, Simeon.* That was sloppy.

I put my head down and push through the crowd, letting out a kind of low-level growl as I speed up from a standing start into a trot and then, when I realise that, against all odds, this bizarre behaviour is having the desired effect and the crowd is parting, a full run.

I guess it's human nature to recoil from the strange and confusing. It's self-preservation, to get away from a situation that doesn't seem safe. I am rarely concerned with whether people think I'm safe.

I burst out the other side of the small knot of people and can see Deleon round a corner up ahead. This gives me some cover. With him out of sight, the way is now clear for me to make up some ground.

I run to the corner and then stop abruptly, peering around to check the way. Deleon has slowed now. He either doesn't know that I'm following, or doesn't care anymore.

He is barely fifty yards ahead. He is looking up and down at the wall to his left, as if searching for something.

Head, heart, gut. The way he looked at me, as if he'd been waiting, before he took off. That doesn't sit right. Nor does the fact that he's not running. He's not trying to get away from me.

I don't think I'm following him. I think he's leading me.

What do you want to show me? I wonder. *And why?*

The wall in question is part of the perimeter of the Citadel. The windows cut into it are irregular and varied in size, shape and condition, giving away little of the rooms and courtyards they belong to on the other side. There are no doors to be seen, but I am certain that a door is what Deleon is looking for.

What can he be doing? Who is he, really? Parker seemed

pretty certain that Bennett Holman knew him and, if Mouse is to be believed - and she usually is, despite my reservations when I talked to Holman - that makes Deleon what? A hitman?

He doesn't seem to be armed, not in any serious way. There's always the possibility that he's carrying something hidden, a knife or a small gun, but knife wielding assassins are ten-a-penny in The Alleys so why would someone go outside Trinity to hire services they could easily find inside, at more desperate prices?

Maybe he's a go-between? *Going between whom?* Holman and... Is it too much to hope it's whoever hired someone to kill Manukan? There are several unknown people in that theory, so I recognise this is speculative, but if he was..?

Why so interested in the Citadel? There's nothing to connect Manukan's murder with the Devoted. Is this a new lead?

Reductio ad absurdam, I think I'm ruling out Deleon having anything to do with Manukan.

Head, heart, gut. It doesn't feel like it has anything to do with Manukan, but...

I can't get Bjorn Barlow out of my head. Barlow mentioned Manukan. James was looking into Barlow. Mouse sent me to Holman to ask about Manukan. James was coming to talk to Holman. It feels like there's something there.

I just wish I could figure out how to join the dots. It would help if the dots stopped moving.

I hear a grinding of gears and the roar of an overworked TransPod. My attention is grabbed by a vehicle speeding down the street, the cloud of rubber and overloaded circuits making me cough and bringing tears to my eyes.

Joyriders. It's become a problem ever since the city fleet specs were leaked onto an anonymous Com channel. I know Administration has people working on it, trying to get a patch out there before they lose too many vehicles. I know they aren't having a lot of luck.

For now, they're easy pickings. Most of the Pods are driverless, so it will feel like a victimless crime. Also, it looks like fun. The Pod twists off the ground and corkscrews around the corner. I used to drive like that, once.

When I can breathe again, I can't see Deleon anymore. Cursing my bad luck, which I'm uncertain actually was bad luck, I stumble up the street, my head flicking back and forth, up and down, looking for a clue, anything to follow.

There isn't a sign of the man. I run a few more paces, still nothing. I spin on the spot, arms flailing, searching frantically. I was disabled by the wake of the speeding TransPod, but he can't have disappeared so quickly, so completely. There hasn't been enough time. He has to be…

Ahead, I spy a gap in the wall. I take the last few paces towards it. A narrow alley retreats into the stone, just wide enough for me to walk down. Or for Deleon to walk down.

There's a door at the far end, small and wooden and painted black. I try it. It's locked.

I bang on it, but it doesn't even echo. I kick at the door in frustration. It's as robust as it appears, and I have to thank the steel at the end of my boots for saving me from a broken toe.

If this is where Deleon went, then I won't be following him. Cursing, I back out of the alley.

Now what?

I don't even know why I'm here. I don't even know why I care. Borate doesn't like my theories about how Manukan's murder is nothing to do with the Black Knights - and therefore nothing to do with my Division - so he sends me off to talk to Mouse who sends me to Holman who leads me to Deleon.

James is interested in Holman, not me. And Deleon is only

of interest because Parker thinks Holman knows him. Which should only interest James, aside from me not knowing if I fully trust Parker.

No, but... wasn't that a dream?

Bottom line: Deleon couldn't be responsible for Manukan's death. Deleon has only just arrived in town.

I'm wasting my time.

This entire job is a waste of my time. Seven years I've been tasked with investigating Black Knight activity and taking them down. So far, I have one mid-ranking Knight imprisoned.

One. Plus an unfortunate undercover Cadet who I was not entirely careful with the welfare and aftercare for.

That was why I invented my second undercover operative and let a rumour infiltrate the Knights rather than an actual person who could get hurt. And now he has manifested and wound up in my interview room.

And he claims to know about Manukan, which brings things right back round full circle and points to Manukan's murder being Knight activity after all.

Except that I don't believe him. I don't believe he knows anything about Manukan and I don't believe he's anything to do with the Black Knights, and *I don't believe he's Bjorn fucking Barlow.*

Bjorn fucking Barlow does not exist.

I scrunch up my fists and push them into my eyes until I see stars. It doesn't help, the pounding pressure building in my head is still there. I have an overwhelming urge to give up, to curl up right there in the alleyway and sleep.

This is it. I've run out of road. I'm shutting down. I've had too much time without a filter on. I can't deal with the noise or the smell, the dirt and the chaos. I can't deal with my own thoughts. I need to do something about this.

I shuffle back to the pavement and look either way up and

down the road. There is a bar there. That is no good. I don't have time to sit down. If I sit down, I won't get back up again.

There's a store the other way, and that's more what I'm looking for. Checking for further runaway TransPods, I cross the empty street and push my way inside with my shoulder. That's a door handle I know better than to touch with an uncovered hand.

The interior of the store is dark and smells of refrigerator coolant. There's a chest in the corner filled with cured meats. The light keeps flickering on and off. I can almost taste the food poisoning in the air. It's like Konoroz without the promise of a good time before you lose your bowel.

The shopkeeper is short and looks suspicious of me. The drinks are out of sight. What isn't out of sight is the rifle they're holding. Nice part of town, this.

'What can I get you?' The shopkeeper's voice is a purr, rolling consonants I didn't know could be rolled. I can't place the accent. That also means I don't know what they're likely to be selling.

'What have you got?' I ask. 'It needs to be as efficiently alcoholic as possible.'

The shopkeeper nods and, without taking either their eyes or the gun off me, bends at the knee and lifts a bottle filled with a green liquid.

'It is green,' they say unnecessarily.

'I can see,' I say.

'No, I mean it is *Green.*' This time I can hear the proper noun. I'm not fussy. It's probably cheap.

I flash my Com over the payment pad without registering the price, and take the bottle.

'Thanks,' I throw, over my shoulder, when I'm already halfway out of the store.

I really hope this stuff does the trick. I'm out of leads,

completely at a loss.

Not a whisper of a signal from my head, heart, or gut. They've all gone quiet.

There's only one place for me to try now.

Because I know someone who might know something about Manukan. Someone who will definitely know if the Knights were involved.

I've not been mentioning it, because it's a fucked up situation which is all my fault. This you already know, but I deliberately kept that story separate, deliberately didn't link it when I was telling you about it. I don't want to face this, but I don't think I have a choice at this point.

I need to get to the bottom of who killed Manukan.

I'm going to have to go see Kamla.

CHAPTER 8

I have a very large pocket in the lining of my coat. The bottle of Green nestles in it, close to my heart. I can feel its firm weight pressing on my ribcage, supporting my chest, both inside and out. I am breathing more freely; the pressure is easing.

Thanks to its appley goodness, I am becoming myself again.

I hail a TransPod to Detention and, as I climb in, my Com notifies me that Governor Herrera is on their way to Authority. This is good news, that I can turn to my advantage.

This happens to me regularly, too often to be mere good luck. It's a scheduled meeting. It happens every month, but I don't think I was conscious of it when I decided to visit Kamla.

I wonder on what level I know these things, and how I can access them more readily. I've learned that my instincts - *head, heart, gut* - are good enough for me to trust them, but I never know why. I think I'd feel a lot calmer if I could see more of the picture.

Drinking, taking drugs, not drinking, not taking drugs...

I've existed on many plains of consciousness, but I've never quite found that one. Maybe I should be meditating. Maybe I should stop overthinking and go with the flow.

It intrigues me, though. I can't rest until I've put all the pieces together. I suspect that, if I ever solve the mystery of what goes on in my subconscious mind, it will be the last thing I ever do.

Borate is asking, via Lomax, for updates pertinent to his meeting with Herrera. I send some, but he will struggle to make sense of them. For once, this isn't his failing. They're all three months out of date and copied-and-pasted from other cases. Some of them aren't even mine.

I'm running interference. I don't need Herrera to come back too early. I don't really want them to know about my visit and, whilst it will obviously be logged, there will be no reason for them to look.

Also, I'm pissed off with Borate. More than usual. I didn't like that thing with the pictures in the folder. That felt like a threat. I won't put up with him telling me how to work a case. I don't like him and barely trust him.

On the other hand, I'm nobody's best friend, am as reliable as a broken clock and am about to lie my way into a high security prison. I'm a model employee.

It's completely different.

My rank means that I can turn up at Detention unannounced, which I do. Unfortunately, the lackey on the gate doesn't seem to be aware of this. I've flashed my token three times now, and all he does is check my name against his database and peer down at me from his seat, high in the booth, with an apologetic look of bafflement on his oily face.

'I'm sorry.' He pushes his hair out of his eyes for the third time. 'I can't find you on the list. Is there a chance your name got misspelled?'

If it wasn't for the large swig of Green I took after I jumped out of the Pod, a stiffener to put me on before I stashed the bottle behind a grit bin around the corner, then the pressure in my head would be at exploding-brain proportions by now.

As it is, I am calm. I am peace. I raise my eyebrows and let the frustration float on.

'My name doesn't need to be on the list.'

I say it firmly, but quietly.

The youth cracks his fingers. It looks like a nervous tick. I think it's good that he's nervous. I think he should be more nervous than this. Maybe even downright scared.

'I'm an Oficier. I'm allowed to come in and talk to the Detained, if it will help my investigations.'

'And will it?' asks the child in front of me.

I don't know where they find them. This one is taking the piss. It's not just that I'm an Oficier. I'd understand Mortimer having these difficulties, wet, limp lettuce leaf that he is, but I have bearing, I have gravitas. I also have a fucking reputation that he should be fucking aware of.

Oh look, I'm getting angry.

Drink or no drink, I'm about to grab the grotty little scrote by the neck and shake him until his head wobbles off. This has escalated quickly or, should I say, I have escalated quickly.

'I need to talk to the Governor,' I say.

'The Governor's not here,' says the gateman.

I know the Governor isn't there. I wait for the kid to offer me an alternative plan. I was hoping this visit would be under the radar. I don't think that's going to be possible now.

I realise that I'm going to have to offer the kid an alternative plan because he is apparently incapable of coming up with one himself.

'So I need to talk to the Governor's second-in-command?'

I suggest.

The gateman doesn't react initially. He seems to take time to process the words, like he's weighing up the pros and cons of breaking protocol. Only, as he's already ably demonstrated, he hasn't got a fucking clue what the fucking protocol is, so I don't know what's taking all the time.

Finally, he hits a button on the desk. After a moment, a familiar voice answers.

'Burns.'

The clipped voice makes the tinny speaker buzz. If he hadn't said his name, I might have doubted it was him. Westley Burns is Governor Herrera's deputy. We know each other well. We went through training together, before we took different paths into the vast bureaucratic nightmare that is Trinity's civil services.

Despite knowing me well, I think that Westley actually likes me. I might even describe him as a friend.

'Sir, I've got a...' begins the gateman, a quaver in his voice helping to illustrate just how out of his depth he has now realised he is.

'Wes, it's Sim,' I shout, hoping the microphone is good enough to pick me up.

There is a pause.

'Tramayne?' Burns's voice becomes even more stern.

I could feel sorry for young Tramayne at this point, but he's been a massive pain in my arse, so I don't.

'Why are you keeping Simeon Lagrange hanging around at the gates?'

Gateman Tramayne goes a purply shade of red as he realises that his superior officer doesn't think that he's been doing a good job, in all his efforts to prevent me accessing the building.

'I... I...' he stammers. 'I didn't...'

'Didn't know?' asks the disembodied voice of Westley Burns. 'Didn't think? Didn't care?'

I can see the cogs whirring as Tramayne weighs up whether any of these options are things he should own up to.

Burns doesn't wait for him to come to a conclusion.

'Let him in, gateman. And report to me at the end of your shift, please. I have some reading material for you to revise overnight…'

Tramayne's finger stabs as another button, desperate for it to engage and free him from the situation he's got himself into.

The gates buzz and swing open. I walk on through. It shouldn't have to be this hard. I hope the bottle of Green is still where I left it when I get back out. I think I'm going to need that.

So, it's useful to have friends in high places. But that also makes it harder to get away with things it would be helpful that they didn't know. Like who I'm really here to see.

I cross the yard and am buzzed through several sets of gates. I know I'm being scanned at every one. It's a surprisingly efficient system, certainly for Trinity. I barely have to break stride.

The last gate, a metal panel that runs from floor to ceiling, slides away into the wall and I step through into the familiar long corridor. My fillings ache and throb as I do so, but no alarms go off. No one comes running with a spray or a baton or a gun.

I've passed security. I'm just visiting.

The corridor gives access to twenty or more visiting rooms, but every door is closed, every window one-way. I march along the length, only guessing at the eyes that may be on the other side. Who is watching me?

I keep my eyes straight ahead, my head back and high. My

strides are long, determined, purposeful. I'm not putting on a show, but I'm not risking giving the wrong impression about who I am and why I'm here.

It's entirely possible that nobody sees.

Burns's door is open when I reach the end of the corridor. He greets me with a bear hug as I step into his office. I don't respond, but he's used to that. I'm not a fan of hugs in a professional context. I don't have a lot of use for them in a personal one.

'He's gone on hunger strike again, you know.' That's the first thing he says.

Burns takes a seat in front of his desk. I take the other. There isn't enough room for us both. I take a minute to realise who he's talking about.

I nod. He's assumed I'm here to see Vocat. As well he should. My privileges to come and go as I please only extend to Detainees of the Division for which I'm Senior Oficier. We didn't arrest Kamla. In fact, I tried very hard to avoid it. Very hard and very successfully.

'Shit,' I say. 'I was hoping to pump him for information. I have some leads on a murder and I need to narrow them down.'

This, at least, is plausible. If I did actually have any leads regarding Manukan's murder, then running them past Vocat would be smart. He was high enough in the Knights' command structure for it to be worth me putting him away, but lowly enough that it didn't immediately cause a hit to be put out on me.

Burns lifts his right foot onto his left knee and leans back, his belly straining the buttons of his shirt. I sit bolt upright with my hands in my lap. There isn't room for me to do much else.

'You can talk to him,' Burns groans. 'I'd just take anything he tells you with a sea-full of salt.'

Entrapment

I also did my damnedest to prevent anyone else from arresting Kamla. That's another of the reasons she's pissed off at me, because I promised her I could and I failed. In some ways, I wish we had arrested her. It would make this kind of thing much easier.

I'd also have a chance of stacking the odds in her favour when it comes to negotiating her release. We wouldn't be having to resort to bribes, for a start. Of course, it might have come out who we were to each other, which, on balance, might have just made things worse.

Burns doesn't know any of this. That's why he's assumed I'm here to see Vocat.

'That's a shame.' I try not to betray any of what's whirring through my head. 'I was kind of banking on this. I'm...'

'Desperate?' laughs Burns.

I pull a face.

'Not desperate, but not exactly blessed with options. You don't think there's any point? With Vocat?'

'He's remarkably lucid sometimes.' Burns laughs. 'Considering.'

The Tweak tends to get to you if you have nothing to absorb it. Hallucinations and paranoia are the mildest effects that Vocat is going to have to worry about.

'How's his memory?' I ask.

'Short term? Shot.'

Burns raises his arms and clasps his hands around the back of his head. His armpits reveal wide, dark, damp patches. I shrink even further into myself, painfully conscious of the alcohol seeping from my own pores.

'Faces?'

I don't know why I asked about his ability to recognise faces. I don't have any faces to show him. It's a hangover from the dream. I dreamed I was face blind. What did that mean?

What am I failing to see?

'No, not faces.' I correct myself. 'Would he recognise names? People. Contacts. I...'

Burns is staring at me. He can see that I don't know what I'm talking about. That's because I don't. I don't know what I want from Vocat because I don't want to talk to Vocat.

'We've prepped a room for you,' he says. 'I'm not sure what you're going to get, to be completely honest, but he's on his way to Visiting Seven.'

'Visiting?'

I thought I'd have access to the Interrogation block. I need access to the Interrogation block.

'We had...' Burns winces. '...some trouble. Yesterday. Interrogation is off limits for the foreseeable. All interviews are taking place in Visiting. All visits are off.'

I don't want to talk to Vocat; I want to talk to Kamla. If they're bringing Vocat down to Visiting, then I'm screwed. I have no way of getting to her.

I don't know what to do. I can't let Burns know. *Fuck.* I can't think, it's like I'm frozen. I can't see a way out of this. I'm going to end up interrogating Vocat and leaving. That's not what I had planned.

Drinking before I came here was a mistake. At the same time, mind you, not drinking would have been a mistake. I don't have a good option here.

I would, I think, on balance, be worse without a drink. That's a very comforting thought, so there's a very good chance it's not true.

Maybe I can get something from Vocat. It doesn't sound like I can get anything from Vocat. I think I've already got everything Vocat has to give.

Shit.

I shut up. That seems to be the best thing to do. Maybe

Entrapment

Burns will offer me something. I don't know what; he doesn't know what I want.

Burns stands. That didn't work, then.

'Well, give it your best shot,' he says. 'I know you don't have anything but your best shot to give, Sim.'

That's like a knife in the gut. I'm trying to con a friend, an old colleague. How did I become this person? Was it worth it?

I'm a mess. I'm making a mess of this situation right now.

Without knowing that I've done it, I'm on my feet now. I don't know how. I can feel my head reeling with the effort it took to stand up.

Burns slaps me, hard, across the back. It's meant to be a friendly gesture, I know, but I almost vomit.

This is a terrible state of affairs. This is all my fault. I swallow. Hard. It burns, it shouldn't burn like that. I can't talk to anyone like this.

'I need to go to the toilet,' I say.

It's an act of desperation, an act of self preservation. It turns out to be a stroke of genius.

It's the decision that turns this whole situation around. This is why I drink.

It doesn't happen straight away, though.

Burns follows me to the toilets. I think he's showing me the way, which isn't necessary because I know where they are. I suggest that I'm going to be fine from here and, as the door swings shut, I can hear his footsteps retreating down the corridor.

I need to give him enough time to get back to his office and get distracted by the next thing so that he doesn't see where I go when I come out.

I need to pull myself together first.

I lean on a sink and take a deep breath. In the mirror, I look green. I turn on the tap and, keeping my left hand in place for support, I scoop some water into my face. It doesn't do much.

I don't think the way I'm feeling is entirely down to the drink.

I rub my face on a fistful of paper towels and stand up straight. I need to make something happen. I've talked my way in. If I don't make something of this opportunity, I might not get another one.

And Kamla knows things.

The door swings open and a man comes in. A civilian, dark hooded top, a bit of a shuffle to his movement. He's carrying a plastic bag which looks to have clothes in it. He doesn't look up, just disappears into a cubicle.

My mind spins. Now I'm out of Burns's office, I'm feeling a little better. I've got a bit more space, a bit more leeway. I need to use that to my advantage.

I need to get Vocat sent back to his cell. I need to go with him. If I can get into the main block, then I'm confident I can find my way to Kamla.

She's in a different wing, obviously, but the main security sits between Visiting - where I am - and Detention - where the prisoners are. Movement between wings is comparatively easy.

So how do I make that happen?

Get him to attack me?

That's the most obvious thing and, to be honest, probably the easiest, but they will not let me take him back to his cell after that. They're going to send me to Medical and send him to Solitary.

I could plant some drugs.

If I was Vice, that would work, but I'm not and I don't have any drugs on me, anyway.

Something else, something that Vocat might have, that he

could have got from Kamla. Something I already have that I can pass to him and convince the keepers that I found.

Information. Kamla knows things. That's the plan.

It's a terrible plan. I need a new plan. I'm not going to find it hiding in here.

I take a deep breath and ready myself to leave the privacy and sanctuary of the toilets. I take my hand off the sink. It's shaking. I quickly put it back.

Shit, I'm nervous. I didn't think this would happen, but I should have known better. Kamla, the prospect of Kamla particularly, has a way of unsettling me. I'm apprehensive. Kamla and I have history.

I don't even mean that we used to have a thing, although we did. A romantic thing, a sexual thing, at least. But it was a long time ago. I think we're both over it.

The history is deeper than that. It's over thirty years deep, when Trinity was a different place. Maybe it wasn't, maybe nothing has really changed in all that time.

I was different. My life was simpler. Authority was simpler, before Chaguartay, before the Black Knights, although the seeds were there and we should have seen them coming well before they got the city locked down.

All our crooks back then were small time. At least that's how it felt, and it was easy to take them down. My monthly arrest rate was more impressive than one in seven years and made a significantly bigger difference than it does now.

I spent a lot of time undercover. I was young. I would have spent my time in those places anyway, mixing with those people. I thought it only made sense to turn it to my advantage. I crafted a persona, skirted as close to the law as I could without crossing the line.

That's what I told myself, anyway. I crossed the line plenty of times, legally, morally, emotionally. I just got away with it.

Kamla moved in the same shadows. She spent a lot of time being flattered by questionable beaus, men with connections, men of danger, of violence. But Kamla wasn't a moth to a flame, she was the flame and when things got too hot, because there wasn't any other way they could get, she turned to me.

I was pleased to help. It was part of my job. And I enjoyed her gratitude. Together, we took down half of the gang leaders in Docklands.

I was well on my way to cleaning up The Alleys. I was headed for great things, and that was attractive to Kamla. All she ever wanted was power, and I was on the cusp of taking it, in a way that was final and definitive. So much less precarious than that held by her gangster lovers.

I wasn't just her weakness for power, though. She loved me. I know she did. I certainly loved her. For a time. For that time.

That time came to an end. It happened gradually but, looking back, it's clear when it started. No one expected the outsider from Ashuana to win the election. Chaguartay was nobody's first pick.

He didn't even get a party nomination, didn't even hold a seat in the Dome. He came from nowhere with his big promises and his disruptive ideas, and everyone was convinced that he had all the answers, that he could fix Trinity.

Trinity wasn't even that broken. We couldn't understand it back then. It felt like we were wading through treacle, that things could only get better, that brand new thinking from a brand new type of leader was exactly what we needed.

We didn't know what broken looked like, not like we do now. We were just in the doldrums, a bit down. But that vulnerability was enough, and we've spent all our time since fighting what got in.

Entrapment

Suddenly, the gangs were protected. Before long, they were working together. The beast had enough heads that it was a fool's errand trying to cut them off because, as soon as you did, two more grew back.

My career stalled. That was much less attractive to Kamla, let's be honest, but it was more than that. It was a lot less attractive to me.

I spiralled for a few years. I'd always drunk, always got high, but it had been relaxation and socialisation until it wasn't. My coping mechanism, ironically, rendered me less and less able to cope.

We stopped seeing each other. We kept in touch, hooked up occasionally when neither of us had the willpower to prevent it, but we pretty much went our separate ways. I'm better on my own. Maybe not better for me, but better for everyone else.

I stopped spiralling for a while, but I never got better. I just bounced along the bottom. On my own.

Until earlier this year, when I needed someone to get close to Eamer. This was after Staunton - the Cadet who didn't make it - and before Bjorn Barlow. I should have mentioned this earlier. It wasn't just Staunton getting hospitalised that led to the Barlow plan - it was Kamla, too. One in Asylum and one in Detention was as much as my conscience could bear.

I would have done it myself, gone undercover, like the old days, but of course I was known, and too old and drunk for any of that. Kamla, on the other hand...

Kamla knew Eamer from when he was a General in a crew that used to hold up vans on their way to the docks, loading up on gold and machinery and liquor and fish. Pre-Chaguartay, pre-Knights, pre the connotations that Eamer's name now holds.

I didn't warn her. I didn't think I was putting her in any

danger. For her part, she was more than happy to rekindle our friendship and to do me a favour for old time's sake. "For the soil and the soul," she joked, like we were making some big move to reclaim the city.

It didn't take her long to rekindle whatever fire she had burning with Eamer, and then to direct it where she needed to for me to get what I wanted. I didn't ask too many questions, but I can assume how that went. I wasn't jealous, too much had happened for that.

She seemed to be having fun, so I didn't spend too much time thinking about it. I had someone on the inside. I was just going to sit back and wait for the intel. And then boost my arrest rate. I didn't think I was going to get Eamer, but sometimes I dreamed.

Somebody knew, though. Somebody - maybe Eamer, maybe not - knew and didn't like it. Before she could get me anything useful, she was fitted up and in deep shit.

I avoided her arrest for all I was worth. I deliberately screwed up investigations, trashed crime scenes, ordered Cadets to ignore what were perfectly good policing instincts.

My Division wasn't having a lot of success before, but that was due to how well organised our foes were. We were the best in Authority and even we couldn't take down the Black Knights.

My Division had little success after, the consolation prize of Vocat notwithstanding. That was because of the mistakes I made. That was because of my arrogance. That was because I felt guilty for putting Kamla in that position and would do anything to keep her out of this place.

Vice got her anyway. I hate Vice. They're all hypocrites.

That's why I'm not supposed to be here. I can't risk making it worse for either of us. But she needs me to get her out, which is going to involve me showing my hand. I don't know how that's going to go. Which is why I'm not showing it, yet.

I have to face it, though, I'm running out of people I can ask for help. I have to make some progress and if Black Knights are behind Manukan's killing then she's the last person I can think of who might be able to help me.

She will not help me for free, though. This is going to require a you-scratch-my-back type arrangement.

I can't make any sort of deal if I can't talk to her. I contemplate going back to Burns, telling him why I'm really here. We go back far enough that he'd understand. He knows me, in every incarnation, and he's accepted them all.

But I don't know what he'd have to do, what he'd need to record, who he'd have to report my activity to. If I know Westley Burns, and I do, at least as well as he knows me, then he'd play it by the book. He's never been one for bending rules.

Which leaves me with a problem. I don't want to put him in a difficult situation. I don't want to fuck things up for somebody else. But I don't know what to do.

I'll go back to his office. Hopefully, he won't be there. I have an unusually high level of security access attached to me, for reasons that I won't go into but are definitely a mistake. Not enough to get into the main block, but I could get into Burns's office. Maybe I could hack his desktop Com. Maybe I'll get lucky and he won't have locked it.

No. Burns will have locked it. Burns will lock it every time. And what if he is there? Distract him? Threaten him?

Nothing is jumping out at me here. There is no plan. There's certainly no good one. I grip the sides of the sink harder until my fingers ache. *Think, Sim, Think.*

The door of the cubicle swings open behind me. In the mirror I see the man emerge, no longer in the dark hoodie, but wearing a grey all-in-one Detention Keeper's uniform. And in the blink of an eye my prayers are answered.

I spin on my heel to face him. I narrowly avoid falling over. He looks shocked, taken aback by my sudden enthusiasm for his presence.

'Just the man I need to see!' I grin. I need to think fast. 'Burns told me I could find you in here, Keeper…'

I realise that there is no name patch sewn onto his uniform. This guy must be new. This could have been a tactical error. How new? New enough to be useful? Still on probation, obviously, but first month? First week? First day?

'Breck,' says the man. 'Thurstan Breck.'

'Keeper Breck,' I say, nodding. 'Of course, yes. That's what Burns said. "Keeper Breck can help you, he's just popped into the toilets to get changed…".'

I wait. That was not convincing. I don't think I'm going to pull this off. The keeper eyes me suspiciously.

'Yeah, OK, fine,' he says, surprising me. 'I can help. What do you need?'

Now I get a good look at him. I see that he's older than I thought. I had taken him for some green, callow, youth, maybe around Jo Jo's age. He is in his thirties, I'd say, at least. He looks worn, tired, the way that you do when you've lost the stretch and give of youth and start to harden.

'We need to change the prisoner,' I say. 'You need to send Vocat back to his cell. There's been a… clerical error.'

'A clerical error?' He pulls a Com out of the pocket of his uniform and examines the screen intently. 'Vocat is… on his way to Visiting.'

'Yes.' I try not to sound impatient.

I don't want him to think I'm trying to push him into doing something that his senior officer would not sanction. Although that is, of course, what I'm trying to do. I just don't want him to think it.

'But he needs to go back,' I emphasise. 'That's not who I want to talk to. Burns said you could sort that out.'

Breck looks confused.

'I can send a message and get Vocat returned. But who do we need to bring over? Who do you want to talk to?'

'I don't think you need to worry about that.' I smile.

Breck looks up from the message he's part way through composing. He appears concerned.

'I mean, I can sort that out. Burns said it would just be easier for me to go straight to her cell... So if you could...?'

'*Her* cell?' asks Breck, with an emphasis on the personal pronoun.

'Yes, I just need you to take me through security and I'll sort it out from there.'

'And Burns is OK with that?'

'Burns said it was fine.' I find it's helpful to follow up a lie like that with something that's very true. 'We go way back.'

Breck nods slowly. I don't think he believes me. It turns out not to matter.

'OK,' he says, hitting send on his message and sliding his Com back into his pocket.

He turns to the door.

'Thanks,' I say. 'I'll just finish up and I'll be out in a moment.'

I turn back to the mirror. I think I need another splash of water in my face. That, or to throw up. I just need Breck to leave so that I can figure out which.

Breck pauses and turns back.

'Just to check. Who are you going to see? Just in case someone asks, you know? I mean, if Burns has OK'd it then it's not a problem, but if someone else asks me. If my Section Leader asks me...'

'Yeah.'

I get it. I was trying to avoid this, but it wasn't an unreasonable request. I could make up a name, I suppose, but my knowledge of the inmates on the women's wing of Detention isn't the strongest. I decide to tell him the truth.

'Jeffman. Kamla Jeffman.'

He nods and leaves the room. I vomit into the sink.

CHAPTER 9

Kamla lurks at the back of her small cell. She's leaning against the wall, sat on her bed, staring at me. There's a reinforced glass screen between us.

She says nothing. She's looking at me expectantly, but she says nothing. I'm going to have to open the conversation.

'How have you been?' I ask.

That wasn't the right opener, but then I knew that. She snaps. It didn't take much.

'*Where* have *you* been?' Her tone is hard.

I didn't expect her to be happy to see me, but it's going to take a lot of persuading for her to be cooperative. I have some damage to repair.

'I've been busy,' I say. It's not untrue.

'Working a case?' she says. She sneers it. There is a lot of emotion in those three words.

'Yes. I told you I was,' I say.

'That was two days ago.' She rattles the words back at me, like machine gun fire.

It hasn't been two days. *Has it?*

'It was yesterday,' I retort. 'You called me yesterday.'

I am ninety per cent sure that is correct.

'Whatever. Are you getting me out of here?'

Our relationship has soured, somewhat, since I failed to prevent her from being arrested, then did nothing to thwart the investigation, then didn't stand up to be counted when she went to trial.

In my defence, I was trying to find out *why*. Why had Vice gone after her, what did she have, what did she know, that meant she was a threat to Eamer? Because Eamer has Vice in his pocket. Something about the scheme we cooked up had stood out to someone. I wanted to know who.

In her defence, that's not much of a defence. In her defence, it has all been for nothing. I am none the wiser, haven't found out anything. No names, no arrests. If anything, I am more confused that ever.

Now, here I am. But I haven't come to help her. I've come because I need something - something else - from her.

As if taking her liberty hadn't been enough.

'I'm working on it,' I say. It isn't, actually, a complete lie.

She makes a scoffing noise, throws her head back, and stares at the ceiling.

'That's what you've come to tell me, is it?' She keeps her head back. She's not looking at me. 'That you're working on it?'

'Don't be like that. I need your help.'

'I need your help, you bastard. I asked first.'

There is a hint of something in her voice that tells me all is not lost. It's not exactly warmth, or affection, more of a playfulness, a flirtation. I don't think I'm imagining that. I'm not sure I'm ready to play yet, though. Her games are wicked.

'I'm sorry,' I begin.

I'm trying to apologise, genuinely apologise, and not just because I think it will de-escalate things. This is all my fault.

She doesn't seem to want to hear it yet, though.

'How's Jo Jo?' she asks.

'Jo Jo's fine,' I say.

Jo Jo is our son. Well, her son. He might be mine. I wouldn't mind if he was, and I generally behave as if he is. He's a good kid. All the more so now he's not a kid anymore.

'He's pretty tight with Clar these days. He's got his head screwed on.'

She nods, slowly. She looks at me again. *Is that a smile?*

'Takes after his dad…'

I'm not going to let her change the subject. I'm not going to be sidetracked.

'I need your help,' I say again.

She stands up from the bed, walks slowly across the cell. Her eyes bore into me. I feel like she's stripped me naked and can see it all. Not in a good way.

'You're sorry?' she asks. She heard me.

'I'm sorry,' I admit. 'This is my fault. I should have done things differently. If only I'd…'

'Sim,' Kamla says. She places her finger on the glass in front of my face, as if she were placing it on my lips. 'Stop. You always do this.'

'Always do what?' I ask, confused.

'It's the past,' she explains. 'It's done. You did what you did for the reasons you did them. Your apology isn't going to change that.'

'But if I'd done things differently, then you wouldn't be in this mess. I regret…'

'You can only regret the way things happened,' she said. 'If things had played out differently, there's no reason you wouldn't be regretting those things instead. It's pointless, Sim, it gets us nowhere. I need you to stop living in the past and do something. Now.'

I know what she's saying, and I know she's right. *Head, heart, gut* be damned. I don't believe it, don't feel it, but I do have to do something.

'I can help,' I say. 'I will help, I promise. But my stock's a little low right now and I really need a breakthrough. If you've got the information I need, then I can do that, and I can get you out.

She sighs.

'That sounds... speculative,' she says.

She's right, it is. But I can't get anything done in my current position. I will not plead with her, though. I leave a prolonged silence. She holds out for seven seconds. She caves on eight.

'Hit me. Although... I don't know what help I can be. I don't get out much these days.'

Her smile is cutting. I can ignore it.

'Manukan. Ralph Manukan.'

'Chaguartay's puppy?'

She looks confused. But she knows him. That's a good sign.

'That's my case,' I say. 'He turned up dead. Three weeks ago.'

'That's your case?' She looks more confused. 'Why would the Black Knights...? That makes no sense.'

'I know!' I get excited at this point. I have to rein it in. 'I know. It doesn't make any sense, but I can't get Borate to see that. So I'm digging. But I'm not getting anywhere fast. I think it's...'

I stop talking.

'You think it's...?'

I mouth it. You don't know who's listening.

'Opposition?' She laughs, loudly. I guess we're not whispering it after all. 'Now that would be something. But I doubt it. What makes you think that it's Opposition?'

'I have my reasons.'

I don't, not really. I've got a hunch. And I've had some dreams about it. I don't think those sound rock solid, so I'm not going to mention them.

'But that's not the point.'

It's entirely the point.

'Let's just say, for argument's sake, that it was. Them. Who would have those contacts?'

'Fuck's sake, Sim. Who do you think I know from Opposition?'

'No, that's not what I mean.' I shake my head. 'Think about it from the other side. Who would take on a job like that?'

'You seem very sure that it was a job.' She shrugs. 'How do you know that's what happened? How it happened?'

'It was too professional to have been anything other than a contract kill. They did their very best to make it look like the Knights. We almost didn't see through it.'

In actual fact, I didn't see through it. I have Parker to thank for that.

'I know these guys don't just work for anyone. Someone felt comfortable enough to carry out a hit - a risky, high-profile hit at that - for Opposition. They were also prepared to blame the Black Knights. Which doesn't seem like a sensible career move.'

Kamla is shaking her head slowly, thoughtfully.

'You've spoken to Mouse, I take it?'

'Of course,' I say.

'What did she say?'

'She said to talk to Bennett Holman.'

'Bennett Holman?' She laughs. 'And did you?'

'I did.'

'Straight away?'

'Straight a..? No. The next day. It was late. I was tired.'

'So he knew you were coming then?'

'No, I...'

She laughs again.

'He knew you were coming, believe me. Holman doesn't do anything without Mouse telling him to.'

'I...'

I'm lost for words. James seemed so sure he was significant. Parker thought he knew something. That's why I ended up following Deleon all the way to an alleyway down the side of the Citadel. *And how did that go for you?*

'Dear, dear, Sim. What has become of you? You've lost your edge. I can see it. Whatever's the matter?'

She mimes picking up an imaginary shot glass, knocks back the imaginary shot and then throws her head back, a shudder disappearing from her shoulders down through her hips. She looks back at me. She looks pleased with herself.

'You can't tell me anything, then?' I say, standing up.

'I can't help you, Sim.'

She pulls a face. I think it's meant to appear sympathetic. Mock sympathetic, anyway. 'I think you might be beyond help.'

'It's a shame,' I say, turning away. 'It took all my powers of persuasion to talk Justice Cawooll around.'

A pause, a hesitation, I don't look around.

'Cawooll is going to agree to a deal?' she asks.

He's not. He doesn't know anything about a deal. But I might persuade him, if Kamla's intel is good enough, and I get myself back into Borate's good books. It's a risk, but I'm out of options.

I think I said earlier that I had the money that Kamla needed. That was a lie. I don't have those kind of funds. I can't afford, financially, to bribe anyone. And I can't afford, professionally, to admit what I've done.

'I drive a hard bargain,' I say cryptically. 'But I *can* get you out of here. If what you tell me is worth it.'

She stares me down.

'I can't talk here.'

I stare back.

'Yes, you can. I disabled the feed.'

Of course I disabled the feed. I'm not supposed to be in here, I don't want Burns clocking me on a screen and coming down here to turf me out. I rewired this cell's input to the one next door. We're good.

Unless he spots that he appears to have the same prisoner being held twice, which, as I know Burns, I know he won't. Not for a while.

We're good.

She nods, slowly.

'Of course you did. You're not meant to be here, are you?'

'In Detention? Yes. In your cell? Absolutely not.' I shrug, as if it's no big deal.

Kamla smiles at me. It's alluring. We had a thing. I'm remembering why.

'Shall we sit down?' I ask. 'Or should I go?'

She pulls up the chair on her side of the glass and sits down. I follow suit.

'You need to be careful where you share this.' She drops her voice, even though she's not being recorded.

I lean in, my forehead nearly touching the screen between us. Her breath fogs the surface.

'I lied,' she says. 'This is going to directly contradict many aspects of the story I've told everyone, including you, up to now. But I do know something about Ralph Manukan. I've met him.'

I'll be honest, I can't believe my luck. This was a shot in the dark. I didn't expect it to pay off.

'I knew it.' She's not the only one who can lie. 'I need you, Kamla. Help me. I can get you out of here.'

I'm breathing heavily, the glass of the screen pulsing with the mist from each breath.

'I don't think he was ever interested in the politics, or the power. It was the connections that working for Chaguartay could give him that got him excited.'

'Connections?'

'Drugs, gambling, sex… he was in love with a lifestyle that is, shall we say, Chaguartay-adjacent. If you're Chaguartay's man, then the Black Knights will roll out the red carpet and welcome you into their bloated bosom.'

I furrow my brow at the tortured metaphor.

'You know what I mean,' she scoffs. 'He liked to live it up. The high life with the lowlives. He was rarely out of Eamer's. Upstairs, downstairs, he liked to call that shithole home.'

'So what happened?'

I worry that I've got this wrong. That he'd pissed off his new friends, and they'd despatched him, as is their wont.

'He made a new friend.' Kamla grins, leaning back in her seat. 'You'll never guess who.'

I lean back as well. Obviously, I won't.

'Jack White,' I say, picking the most unlikely person I can think of in the moment.

His employer's estranged daughter's husband. The man who is going to, if the campaigning is to be believed, save Trinity from his corrupt cesspool of a father-in-law. I think we've established that there isn't an Opposition connection. There's no way it's Jack White.

The look on Kamla's face is staggering.

'You knew?' she says.

I pull a face which is supposed to come across as quizzical. I laugh. This is obviously a joke.

'You knew?' she says again.

It is no longer obvious that this is a joke.

'Fuck you, Sim. What do you want from me?'

She screams the words at me. This isn't a joke. She's on her feet now.

'That wasn't a joke, was it?' I need this clarifying.

She stops screaming. Her mouth hangs open.

'That was a guess? You…'

'Yes, that was a guess. He genuinely got to know Jack White? This is…'

'Nooooo.' She sits back down again. 'No, no, no, no, no… No. You don't know the half of it. When I say *new friend*… I mean, they got really close. Really close.'

The penny drops. Shit. They were fucking. I'm sure that's what she means.

'Sexually,' she adds, just in case I haven't got it yet.

'That's not a good look, is it?' I say. 'Cheating on Evie White? So it was Opposition? They killed him for that?'

'No, I don't think they killed him for that.' She shakes her head definitively. 'But being close to Jack White gave Manukan access to certain information that could be used to undermine their leader.'

She stops there, forcing me to ask the obvious question.

'What information?' I take the bait.

'Debts, gambling debts. And the crimes undertaken to service them. Jackie boy is in deep. He's avoided borrowing from the Knights because… well, because he is who he is. But, you know, eventually all trails lead back to the same place, especially where money's involved. And for Jack, it was loverboy Manukan who led him there. Just a little favour from just someone he knew and…' She pauses for dramatic effect. Then she grins. 'Bam!'

I jump. She laughs.

'The Knights know he's in trouble, so Chaguartay knows he's in trouble. So…'

'So Opposition have him killed to protect their man?' I don't buy it. 'It's a stretch, isn't it? Nothing's normal in this place but, even in Trinity, politicians don't murder people to keep their secrets…'

Even as I say it, I hear how ridiculous that sounds.

'Don't be so naïve, Sim,' Kamla says with a weary sigh.

'I know, I know…' I say.

My Com vibrates in my pocket. I pull it out, glance at the Breaking icon flashing across the screen. Something's happened. My Com explodes with alerts in my hand.

That's the moment that it all changes. That's the moment I learn that Jack White has gone missing.

CHAPTER 10

Borate's office is busy with Coms beeping and people sticking their heads through the door with updates. The briefing he's trying to give me is therefore taking twice as long as it needs to and is broken up to the point of incomprehensibility.

'So you don't want me to link it with the Manukan investigation?' I repeat, for the third time.

'It isn't linked with the Manukan investigation,' he says.

I can tell he's getting exasperated. He's looking quite flushed and his brow is dripping profusely. Even his moustache appears to be sweating.

I could make things easier by divulging what it is I actually know. I shouldn't do that, though, because it would raise too many questions I'm not prepared to answer. So I'm trying belligerence.

'But two high-profile incidents involving politicians of opposing sides…'

Borate cuts me off with a sigh.

'Manukan wasn't a politician,' he points out, which is technically correct.

I shake my head.

'Semantics.'

He doesn't say anything. He doesn't like it though.

'There may be a link between Manukan and Barlow, as well.'

I don't think I've established such a thing yet, but my gut is punching itself, trying to tell me they're linked, and that the link's name could well be Lukas Deleon.

Head, heart, gut. Whatever the holes in this one, it feels better than the Sara Chaguartay theory. I think I'm on firmer ground. Some evidence might help.

Borate puts his head in his hands.

'Focus on White,' he says. 'Talk to his wife, find out everything you can about his movements today, this week. Where was he going, who was he meeting, what precautions was he taking, what risks…?'

Borate's Com vibrates its way towards the edge of his desk. He slaps a palm over it and it goes silent. I see the name on the screen before his hand covers it.

'You're blanking calls from Chaguartay?' I ask. 'That's a career limiting move, isn't it?'

Borate shakes his head.

'It won't be Chaguartay, it will be a lackey. I'm not scared of the new Manukan.'

But are you scared of Chaguartay himself? I wonder.

'Chaguartay's not delighted by his principal opponent going missing mere weeks before the election?'

He won't care. It's not like he wasn't going to rig the election anyway, but…

'It's his son-in-law,' Borate says. 'He's not a monster.'

'Well…'

I leave it at that. I stand up to leave. Then I think better of leaving it there.

'I'm going to need James to stay on Barlow. If I'm right,

and there's a link to Manukan, then there could be a link to White. I can't risk missing any leads. I could be the difference between life and death.'

Borate looks confused.

'For Jack White.' I clarify.

'They're on opposite sides,' complains Borate. 'The people who did Manukan won't work with the people who have got White,'

'Unless it's someone who hates both of them.' I let that hang for a moment. 'As I say, I'll need James to…'

'We let Barlow go,' says Borate, folding his arms.

'You what?' I genuinely think I've misheard for a moment.

'Barlow's a free man,' says Borate. 'We had no grounds to hold him, so we let him go.'

Fuck, we're never going to see him again, are we?

James is standing outside, apparently minding his own business, or lurking within earshot, minding mine. It's hard to tell as I storm past.

'With me!' I sweep along the corridor, down the stairs at ankle breaking pace, and round into my office on the floor below.

I kick my bottom drawer open and swipe the bottle, which I put to my lips and take a deep swig from before hooking two reasonably clean mugs from a table and sloshing generous measures into them. I spin and press one into James's hand.

'Drink,' I order him.

He drinks.

'You need to find Bjorn Barlow.'

'The Chief just told me to stop looking,' he protests.

I shake my head, drain my mug, pour myself another.

'You shouldn't pay any attention to what the Chief is saying. The Chief is… isn't making sense.'

I suddenly realise that accusing Borate with no evidence might result in me losing my position, which might make it difficult to follow up any leads, sanctioned or not. Whatever is going on here, I need to get to the bottom of it. For Kamla.

'We need to find him,' I say.

'Barlow?'

'White. But also Barlow. Barlow might lead us to White. Barlow might lead us to Deleon, who might lead us to Manukan's killer. Which might lead us to White.'

I can see that James is thinking.

'That's... that's a stretch,' he says, eventually.

I sigh. Drink again.

'It is a stretch,' I agree, 'but I think I'm onto something. Opposition did Manukan...'

James splutters his drink. He's still on his first. Amateur.

'You all right, Junior Oficier James?'

'Opposition?' he rasps, his vocal chords fried by the liquor. 'Opposition? Killed? ...'

'Manukan,' I finish for him. 'Yes, correct. I mean, I don't think anyone actually got their hands dirty, but they arranged it. Manukan knew too much, knew secrets that would make Jack White's life very difficult if they became known. So they shut him up.'

'They shut him up?'

'If you keep repeating every I say as a question, this is going to take longer than it needs to.'

I pour another drink and pace. I pace when I'm thinking. I also pace when I'm giving a speech and showing off. All of those things are happening right now.

'Opposition got Manukan. Don't know who. Might have been Evie White herself - like father, like daughter - but it doesn't really matter. They made it look like it was the Knights to throw us all off the scent. But the Black Knights aren't stupid and they knew it wasn't them. Somehow, they figured out who it was.'

'And this is their revenge?'

James is cottoning on. But he's also interrupting me and I don't like that. I knock back the rest of my drink. It burns. Not surprising that James is struggling.

'They wouldn't move on Jack White directly, so they used a go between. Bennett Holman. Bennett Holman brings in Lukas Deleon. Bam!'

James jumps when I shout this last syllable. It amuses me.

'So you were on the right track?'

'The right track,' I agree, 'but the wrong part of the plot. I was missing a piece. An old friend gave it to me.'

'So what's Barlow?'

I spin around to face him.

'That's what you're figuring out,' I say. 'But you were onto something. He appeared from nowhere, suddenly, days ago. You can tell that he doesn't know how this place works, all that Brotherhood stuff… He's taken the name of a Black Knight as a cover. He's practically handed himself in. We were supposed to take one look at him and go "that's the man who killed Ralph Manukan, case closed"…'

'Taking the bait, believing it was the Black Knights,' breathed James. 'Only we missed it, because he picked the name of someone we knew didn't exist.'

'We had them both. Barlow and Deleon, they're the keys. Two sides of the same coin. We have to find them.'

'Before something happens to Trinity's last hope,' says James.

He makes a determined fist. *Bless.*

We have to find them because then we'll be in credit. In credit, I can get Kamla free. James can have a steak or something. I don't care what he does, I just need his help. And if it's going to take an appeal to his sense of social justice, then I'm fine with that.

'Don't get me wrong,' I say. 'Jack White is probably dead already. Dead or alive, he's not going to change anything. No one ever does. No one can. But we can't just give up on him. We can't just give up on people.'

'I didn't have you down as a moral crusader.' James is sipping at his mug. He still hasn't finished his drink.

I shrug.

'I'm really not. But if nothing's going to change, even if we find him, then sure as hell nothing's going to change if we don't.'

I glance up. Lomax Churchill's head is poking through the door. *Well, I never.* Lomax Churchill, on his feet, away from his desk.

'Can I help you?' I check.

'Sorry, Sim,' says Lomax. He doesn't sound very apologetic. 'Borate sent me down. You weren't answering your Com.'

I glance at the equipment on my desk. It's flashing. I must have put it on silent.

'Right.' I'm not apologising for that.

'Evie White is free,' says Lomax. 'Ready for your interview.'

Evie White can wait. I have other things on my mind.

'I've already spoken to her,' I say.

Lomax looks confused, uncertain. He knows I'm lying. I ponder whether I care. I feel bad for Lomax, but if he will work for Borate, he has to expect people to lie to him occasionally. It's an occupational hazard.

'Right, well, there's no one with her now,' says Lomax.

'I'm sending Solzinger down for follow-ups.' I made that up on the spot. 'He's fully briefed.'

'Right,' says Lomax, with a tone that betrays him.

He doesn't believe me, but he doesn't have enough to challenge me with. Lomax wouldn't attempt to contradict me if he didn't think he could win the argument.

'Is that all?' I pick up my mug and drain it.

Lomax says nothing, but his head retreats through my door and I hear his footsteps shuffle back down the corridor.

I pick up James's mug from my desk and drain that, too.

'You need to find Solzinger,' I say. 'Tell him to talk to Evie White. No need to brief him, there's nothing to brief him on. I haven't actually spoken to her yet. But give him some pointers. Then track down that Monk.'

'Where are you going?' he asks.

'I'm going to go solve some crimes,' I say. 'What else?'

CHAPTER 11

Evie White can wait until the morning. Borate, in his wisdom, has asked Mortimer and Oda to look into the case as well, so there's a queue of Cadets for her to repeat the same information once Solzinger has finished. Given what I think I know, I don't expect it to be the whole truth. Better I catch her in the morning when she's tired and bored with her story, and more likely to let something new slip.

I can't rest on my laurels, though. I'm going to need more information. I don't have time to waste - both Barlow and Deleon are out there somewhere - so I need to set some hares running.

I get most of my information from two places, Mouse and Clar. I'm pissed off at Mouse. I came to find Clar.

Clar and I have been working together for nearly five years. It started as a mutually beneficial arrangement that I kind of tricked them into. I never threatened to have them deported, but I think they thought I did. I've only recently seen fit to introduce them to Mouse. They seem to get on like a house on fire.

Phil Oddy

I don't think I'm a fan of that. I can't control a house on fire. But that doesn't matter right now. I need them.

The foolproof method of hiding in The Alleys until they turn up, on the heels of a story, has paid dividends as always. Which is as well because it wouldn't be a good idea for an Authority agent to hang around here too long.

It's cold, as well. It goes dark early at this time of year and despite the heat generated by a busy and densely populated city, there's a chill in the air that I haven't accounted for.

My coat is large and heavy and serves me in most weathers, but I could do with some gloves. I can't feel my fingertips. Or my nose. I'm glad of the week of growth covering my cheeks, keeping off the wind that whistles from the docks, funnelled by the high walls of the labyrinthine passages.

Clar is talking to Mishka, the assassin. Mishka was in the middle of a game, and he does not look impressed with their intervention. Small plastic animals are scattered across the paving.

I'm scanning the group for faces I don't recognise, taking mental notes for future reference. Anyone not known to me could be useful. You don't get into Mishka's game unless you're already in some kind of trouble, the kind of trouble that makes you vulnerable to being sucked further into the Black Knights vortex of corruption.

There might be someone I can save. There might be someone I can use. I recognise Deakin, Ort'a's weaselly little lickspittle. That's interesting. Ort'a is a significant figure in Opposition - their previous candidate for mayor. This could be another link between them and the Knights that I wasn't aware of.

Maybe it's just Deakin's dirty little secret. I have to say, I never bought him as a politician.

'You can't do that,' snarls Mishka, indicating the disruption that Clar has caused with their boot.

'Just did,' shrugs Clar. 'Tell me what I need to know.'

It is a cool response, but Clar looks anything but cool. They look like they're sweating inside, their breath short, every hair on end. They're on high alert, ready to run.

If this alley - a stone's throw from Eamer's, but only accessible through a series of turns and cutbacks that even the most experienced Alley rat would have to think very hard about - is not a safe place for me to be then that goes double for them. They don't even have a gun. I don't think.

I check for mine. It's tucked into my belt. Looks like I'm their backup if this all goes south, then. It would have been nice to have been asked.

These aren't safe people for Clar to be talking to, especially not Mishka. But safety is rarely high on their list of priorities. Getting the story, on the other hand, is a different matter. I wonder what they're looking for, whether it's something I'd be interested in.

I'm sure they'll tell me soon enough.

I push myself back against the wall, trying to get sucked into the shadows. Mishka is baring his teeth now, showing off his fangs. Clar doesn't seem impressed. They shouldn't be impressed, they should be scared. They don't *seem* scared.

'I don't know what you're talking about,' grins Mishka.

Mishka's grins drip with threat. Clar remains unmoved.

'Just give me a sign,' they say.

Smart. I love to watch them in action like this, it's like a ballet.

'None of these fine gentlemen…'

These are not fine gentlemen, but no one here thinks that they are. This is a phrase that Eamer uses with regularity. Directed at you, it means "I know who you are and I know where your weak spots are". When Eamer says it he often means it literally. Physically.

I'm sure Clar has dirt on every one of them that would make it equally true, and potentially even more devastating.

'...will be any the wiser as to what you told me, or why. Hell, they didn't even hear the question, did you fellas?'

There is a rumble of agreement from the group. They haven't heard Clar's question, because Clar hasn't asked it, not here, not today. I have to respect the lengths to which they're prepared to go, taking their life in their hands to come here to piss Mishka off, all in the name of the story.

I wonder again what the story is.

'Fine,' spits Mishka. 'You really want to know? Yes.'

'All I needed to know,' grins Clar, turning on a particularly high heel.

They stoop to pick up a plastic horse that they flip to Mishka. He catches it and snarls before returning his attention to the game.

I step out of the shadows and nod to Clar. They see me, but don't show it as they pass and disappear out the other end of the alley. I don't follow. Being seen to do that would compromise both of us.

Fortunately, there are many ways back to Eamer's.

Somehow, I get to the bar first. This is a good thing, because I need to have words with Mouse.

'Bennett Holman,' is all I have to say.

Mouse pulls a face.

'I'm sorry, Sim. I couldn't risk it. You know what it's like. I wanted you to know, but I couldn't tell you myself. I trust you but... if you're quoting me, you might sound like me, and then someone is going to know it was me who told you. I've got to be careful, I've got to watch my back.'

Head, heart, gut. I get this. It feels like it makes sense.

'Why send me to Holman, though?'

'What did he tell you?' She looks concerned. 'I was very clear with him what he should tell you…'

'He told me nothing. Nothing of use. I…'

I look hard into Mouse's eyes. I see nothing I shouldn't believe.

'For my ears only?'

Mouse nods to affirm. *Damn it!* We got interrupted. Deleon turned up. Then Parker and James. There wasn't time.

'Can you tell me now?'

Mouse shakes her head. It's subtle, but I see it.

Damn it!

'You'd better give me a beer, then,' I say with a sigh. 'And something for Clar.'

'Here…' Mouse pours a measure of Green into a glass. 'They'll love this. You should have one…'

I think I've had my fill of apple liqueur. My fill being an entire bottle, swigged on the miniTram like a vagrant. It must be new in town. Everybody's pushing it. I'd literally never seen a bottle before today. Now it's all anyone wants to sell me.

I turn her down, receive my order, and slide into a booth to wait for Clar. It only takes a few more minutes before they slide in opposite. I've nearly finished my ale.

'What's this?' asks Clar 'It's green.'

'It's Green,' I say. 'That's what it's called. Mouse thought it was very you.'

They pull a face at Mouse on the other side of the bar. Mouse waves.

'Would you drink this?'

'I have. It's appley.'

'Appley?' Clar takes a sip. They don't seem entirely offended by it.

A server I don't recognise arrives at the table.

'Impressive...' I drain my glass. 'This is not the service I have become accustomed to in this place. What's your name?'

'This is Kashka,' says Clar, meaningfully. They turn their head to Kashka and smile. Kashka looks nervous.

The penny drops. Kashka. She's Toun's daughter. Dear Creator, what has the old man got himself into now? He was always so good at keeping his nose clean, always played the game that is Trinity corporate politics with poise and grace and, if not actual integrity, plausible deniability.

If his daughter has fallen into Eamer's clutches, then things have gone wonky for the old bureaucrat. Unless this is an act of rebellion on little Kashka's part, but she doesn't look very rebellious.

'I'll have another.' I look expectantly at Clar.

'This is good,' they shrug, looking at the Green, 'but maybe it could do with a splash. Bring me some vodka.'

Kashka goes to get the drinks, scurrying away, head down, in a way that does not shout "rebel".

'You heard everything out there?' asks Clar, once Kashka is out of earshot.

'In The Alleys, yes. What was it about?'

'Manukan,' Clar smiles.

That should make me feel better. If Clar is positive about something, then it's usually a good sign. But I don't know when I last updated them and I don't know which version of my theories they're working on.

'Right,' I say. 'There have been some developments there...'

'Have there?'

Clar pauses. I think they're going to give me a hard time about sending them on wild goose chases and not keeping them in the loop, about letting put their life on the line when I already have the information I need.

But they don't, because they're Clar and Clar doesn't think like that. I didn't actually ask them to dig around Manukan's death. That's just their journalistic instincts at play.

'It would be interesting to know if you've collected some corroborating evidence, then. Do you still think it wasn't the Knights?'

I ponder this. Do I?

'I think we're meant to think it's the Knights,' I say. I say it slowly, allowing myself space to think between the words. 'But I think they knew. Not just in the way that they know everything that happens in this city, but in the way that they were actively involved in its planning…'

'…whilst actively staying out of its execution?' Clar finishes my thought, which is impressive because I hadn't figured out what I was thinking yet.

'Something like that.'

I drain the rest of my beer. More thinking time, while I lubricate my brain.

'Jack White, though,' I say.

I wonder how they'll react. I assume they know he's missing. Of course they know.

'It's connected,' says Clar.

They're way ahead, evidently. I wonder if they know what Kamla knew.

'Is that what Mishka confirmed?' I ask.

'Mishka put his hands up pretty quickly,' says Clar. 'I didn't have to exert a lot of pressure. Not for something this big.'

'You think Mishka did it?'

Clar shakes their head, looking doubtful. Music to my ears, although a lot less soothing music than it would be if I hadn't lost the guy that I think did.

'I think they brought someone in from outside,' says Clar. 'I think that's why Mishka was so ready to spill the beans. His nose has been put out of joint. Professional pride, you know.'

I've seen a lot of Mishka's work. I don't consider it to be anything to be proud of.

'Damn it.' I snarl, picking up my empty glass, realising that it's empty and putting it back down.

Kashka appears with our fresh drinks and looks taken aback at my outburst. Twitchy. I wonder again what has happened.

'Don't mind him, he doesn't approve of an empty glass,' Clar tells her, mixing the vodka with their Green.

Kashka says nothing and scampers away again. Clar watches her go, following her across the bar.

'Nice girl,' they say.

'Quiet,' I observe.

'Not your type, then.'

Clar sips from their drink. I can smell the sickly apple. I bury my nose in my glass, smother it with hops.

'So what are you going to do?'

'I don't know,' I say. 'Borate sent me after Manukan's killer, but I don't think he actually wanted me to find them. Borate does *not* want me to link it to whatever has happened to White. I don't know if he knows something or knows nothing. Someone's putting pressure on him. I assume it's Chaguartay.'

'That would make sense.'

'Something has to,' I say. 'I think I'm close. I just need to track down the suspects again and then I can prove it.'

'What if Borate gets in the way?'

'I plan to make this so watertight he can't,' I grin, putting my glass down. 'Not without exposing himself.'

'Good luck, you're going to need it.'

'What about you?' I ask. 'What are you going to do?'

'I don't know,' they parrot back at me. 'But I have a sense that I know what you want me to do.'

'Publish and be damned. Always, always publish and be damned. I won't pretend that you laying the groundwork for me wouldn't be helpful, but you also deserve it. You've helped me out enough times. Take the scoop. Quote "Authority sources". It'll put the shit up Chaguartay.'

'I can't say that's not tempting,' smiles Clar, chinking their glass against my empty one. They take the last sip of vodka and Green and signal to Kashka.

'Another drink? To celebrate?' they ask with a wink.

I would never, ever, say no to that.

'What are you..?'

A slight shape slides into the booth to my right. A familiar, grubby face.

'Sami,' Clar sighs, not finishing their earlier question. 'What?'

'I saw you,' hisses Sami. 'In The Alleys. I was hiding. But I saw, I heard. He's lying.'

Sami always adopts a ridiculous stage whisper in these situations. We lean in to hear his breathy secrets. Clar drops their voice.

'Who? Mishka?'

Sami nods, taps the side of his nose.

'He won't tell you the truth,' he insists. 'He can't.'

'Why? There's no….' Clar splutters. 'How do you know?'

This seems fair. They seem unsettled, less by the idea that Mishka would lie, that's a given, more by the idea that Mishka would lie *to them*.

If I'm completely honest, I'm unsettled by this. I know what Clar has on Mishka. If he's lying, then he's in trouble. If he's lying, then we're all in trouble.

'Because that was the wrong answer,' explains Sami, in the most irritating way possible.

I can see that Clar wants to punch him. He's very punchable, to be fair.

'He's protecting someone. He's protecting the person who arranged all of this...'

Clar shakes their head.

'Mishka working for someone else? He wouldn't live to tell the tale.'

'I don't know.' Sami holds his hands up. 'I don't know nothing...'

Clar's hand shoots to his neck, pins him against the bench seat. Sami's eyes bulge, his face shades a little more purple.

'Of course you know something, Sami,' they snarl.

I'm not sure I've ever heard them snarl before.

'You wouldn't be here if you didn't know something and you wouldn't be here if it wasn't something significant. You wouldn't be here if it was something that I wouldn't figure out for myself. So spill. Before I lose my patience.'

'I don't know,' squeaks Sami through his constricted windpipe. 'You're very clever, Clar...'

Clar squeezes harder. Sami looks like a beetroot right about now. They realise they might have gone a bit far and ease their grip. Sami gasps for air, swallowing it down with a wince, rubbing at his bruised trachea.

'It's Sim's theory,' Clar says. 'Although I think he's probably right, for what it's worth.'

It's worth quite a bit. I clear my throat.

'It's not complicated,' I say. 'Someone in Opposition had Manukan taken out for... compromising reasons.'

I glance at Sami. He knows what I'm talking about. It seems that the association between White and Manukan was common knowledge, if only you knew who to ask. I did know who to ask. It surprised me I hadn't thought to do so.

'Do you know who?' asks Sami.

'No,' I say. 'Do you?'

'Do you know who they contracted?'

His tone is almost demanding now. I feel like I'm being interrogated. *Little shit.*

'No,' I snap. 'Do you?'

Sami says nothing. I wait. Then I wait some more. He has some stamina, this kid.

'Sim has a suspect,' says Clar, who doesn't appear to have my patience.

'You're wrong,' says Sami. 'It's not who you think it is. Any of it. Who ordered the hit on Manukan. Who carried out the hit on Manukan. Who wants White dealt with. Who…'

This doesn't go down well with Clar, who is out of their seat and has Sami pushed back, flipped and face down on the floor in seconds. Being who they are, living in the world they do, has meant that they've had to hone their survival instincts and build a very special skill set. It's impressive to see it in action.

'Eww,' complains Sami, 'do you know what's smeared on this floor? What did I ever do to you?'

'You're being oblique,' says Clar, 'and I'm tired. And I have to be clever about how I get Mishka's attention, but you're easier to push around.'

Sami can't deny that. He attempts a shrug and, although it's difficult whilst being pinned to the floor, he pulls it off.

'Look. I don't really know anything. I just hear whispers. People talk and they forget I'm there. And I spend a lot of time in here.'

'Get on with it.' Clar, loosens their grip slightly.

Sami's right, the floor stinks of something unpleasant.

'It's all connected,' Sami talks more rapidly. 'But it's not simple and the connections are hard to see, even if you're looking for them. It's like a web… but there's someone in the middle. Someone pulling the strings.'

'Who?'

'I don't know!' protests Sami. 'Not for sure! But it's the same person. That much I heard. Manukan, White, all of it. It's one person and…'

'Chaguartay?' I ask. 'Ort'a? *Eamer?*'

I'm not sold on any of these guesses. I can instantly think of counterarguments, reasons none of these people could be the mastermind behind this plot. Assuming there is a plot, and this isn't all some flight of fancy, or massive sleight of hand, on Sami's part.

There's too much noise, too much happening. I need some space to process this, need some time to think.

Clar groans in frustration.

'Get to the point! Who am I looking for?'

Sami answers that question with another question, but it's barely audible, each syllable shaped by his gasping breath.

'What is the elephant for?'

My blood runs cold. *What the hell is this? I fucking dreamed this. And that's not an answer to the question.*

But I don't have time to worry about that now. As Sami squirms his way out from underneath Clar, sending them flying into a table, rendering them unable to stop him scampering out the door, I recognise a face at the bar.

What is the elephant for?

What the hell does that mean? Why didn't Sami just answer the fucking question? He was the one who posed it.

I catch Mouse's attention and hold up two fingers. She pours a couple of shots and slides them across to me.

Entrapment

Could there really be one person pulling the strings on all of this? If there is, there's only one name in the frame. But we're talking about Chaguartay's aide and his son-in-law. Why would he have both of them killed?

'Refreshments for Clar once they've got themselves back off the floor?'

I shake my head. I motion towards Lukas Deleon - that's who I spotted - who is slumped against the bar at the far end.

Why am I trying to second guess Chaguartay's motives? And it is his motives I'm examining here. Morally, he'd have no problem with bumping off either, or both of them. But he's a deliberate man. He wouldn't do anything like that, anything at all, without a reason. If I can uncover that...

'Him? Suspect?' asks Mouse.

'I think he could help me with my enquiries.' I knock back one of the drinks. 'I'll need another one in there.'

Mouse pours it, then leans in.

'Fuck it,' she grumbles. 'I'm trying to keep you safe, Sim. I'm trying to keep you out of things that are no good for you to be involved in. But I heard all of that, with Clar and Sami and... I'm worried about you because you just won't leave it alone. So here. This is what Holman was meant to tell you. There's more than one Bjorn Barlow.'

'I know,' I snarl back. 'One that exists, and one that doesn't. That I made up.'

'No,' insists Mouse. 'It's more complicated than that. There are more than two. I don't know how many but... Look, Eamer's clever. Cleverer than you appear to be giving him credit for, but I know you know this. I don't know what you're playing at...'

'But?'

'*None of them exist*,' whispers Mouse. 'You're chasing shadows.'

143

She stands up straight, takes a step back, busies herself with polishing glassware. I stare at her in disbelief.

Suddenly everything falls away. I know nothing. I don't know who Barlow is, I don't know who Deleon is. He was a suspect. I had a hypothesis. I nearly had a case. Now it's evaporating in front of me and I don't know what's going on.

It's not just Mouse, it's not just Barlow. Sami. Fucking Sami.

It frustrates me greatly that what's left of my entire theory now rests on the cryptic say so of that little gutter rat. It wouldn't be the first time, though, and that's what makes it all the more irritating.

We have history. Me and Clar and Sami, it's not the first time that we've stumbled across the truth because of his intel. He has a habit of getting into places no one else can, literally, a lot of the time. He lives in the drains and the crevices that are even darker than the shadows either myself or Clar can use to hide ourselves.

There's always a crack, and that's where Sami gets in. I have to take him seriously, even when he talks in fucking riddles. *Head, heart, gut* be damned. He's usually right.

But the elephant. I don't know what it means, but I've heard it before. I dreamed it, obviously, but I'm not credulous enough to believe in messages magically passed to me in dreams, so I must have heard it before. Someone, somewhere, sometime... it's buried deep. I can't locate the memory.

I will. Then all of this will make sense. Until that time, I have found one of my leads. I'm not letting him get away again.

'I was going to stop serving him,' says Mouse, indicating Deleon, who has slumped such that his nose is almost in his glass.

It's appears that it's safe to talk to me again now.

'He's a mess,' she says. 'I don't need a moon.'

'I'll look after him,' I grin. 'Especially if he cooperates.'

'He's fallen on hard times. Couldn't get a word in between his sob stories earlier.'

'That was quick…'

He seemed twitchy back in Tunnel, but that was only a few hours ago. He appears to have spiralled since then, and this character is a distant relative of the man who arrived in Trinity this morning.

You know what he doesn't look like. He doesn't look like a man who has had time to abduct and possibly murder the leader of Opposition. Which is a thorn in the side of my earlier theory. But not one, it seems, that bothers me. I guess Sami's intervention, and Mouse's, has already caused me to throw all my loose ends back up in the air.

'He's only just arrived in town,' I tell Mouse.

Mouse gives me a funny look, like what I just said doesn't make sense. I want to ask but she turns to face another customer and so I don't get a chance. I take my drinks down to Deleon and pull up a stool.

'You look like you could do with this,' I slide a glass towards him.

Deleon lifts his head from where he has further slumped onto his arm and looks me up and down. His shirt is stained, grimy, greasy. His skin sags, shadowed and slick with sweat. He does not look in a good way.

He also does not look like another drink is what he needs. But I need him to talk. I hope he can still talk.

'Who are you?' he asks.

This is good. I was half expecting him to run, although I don't think he'd be able to run very far before he stumbled, or tripped, and fell. He doesn't look like a man with much remaining balance. But I was worried that he'd recognise me.

He doesn't seem to. That means that I was wrong about the glances exchanged at Tunnel this afternoon, or he is now too drunk to remember. Or too drunk to see.

I thought that he'd run away from me but, crucially, I *hadn't* been drinking at that point, so I don't know that I can trust my recollections either.

'Me?' I knock back the drink, wince, wave at Mouse for another. 'I'm not anyone. I just don't enjoy drinking alone.'

'If you're trying to hit on me, you're barking up the wrong tree,' he says, eyeing the drink. 'I'm not into guys.'

'It's OK,' I reassure him, sliding the drink closer. 'I'm not either.'

That's a lie, but I do have higher standards, so it's all the same as far as he goes in his current state. Sober and clean might be another story, but he doesn't need to know that.

'I just like to talk while I drink.'

He takes the drink, stares at it for several seconds, then knocks it back. Mouse arrives with the bottle and refills us both. We have a routine in situations like this. She knows her role, which is to keep the drinks coming.

I think we have a rule that if I'm losing control of my basic bodily functions, she switches me to sugar syrup. I'm not certain, though, we've never needed to enact it.

'I've not seen you here before,' I say. 'What's the accent? Ashuana?'

Like I don't know. That name couldn't come from anywhere else. He might as well *be* an elephant. But he doesn't know I know his name.

Deleon laughs and nods, but he doesn't seem amused.

'I've not been here before. I only arrived this morning.'

'Staying long?'

'Staying longer than I planned. I lost my bags.'

My eyes go wide, but he's staring into his empty glass

again so he doesn't see. This is potentially very important. He seemed very keen to know about the whereabouts of his apparently empty bag, was not about to entrust it to the idiosyncrasies of the Trinity transport network systems. But now he has, in fact, lost it.

Maybe this is my chance to find out what was in it?

'What happened?' I ask.

'Confiscated by the police,' he groans.

This isn't what I expected him to say. I didn't do it. That is, if anything, the opposite of what I did. So why is he telling me this? Has he even lost it? Or is it still sat in Tunnel waiting for him?

Does he, in fact, recognise me after all, and he's trying to make me reveal my hand, or to go back to Tunnel to check so that…? What would I find? The bag was empty…

I'm reeling. Surreptitiously, I slide my Com from my pocket and ping a message to Parker. CHECK STATUS OF DELEON SUITCASE, I type with one thumb. That will have to do. I don't want Deleon to notice what I'm doing.

For now, I'm OK. Deleon is leaning over the bar and waving at Mouse himself. Guess he's in the chair this time. I knock back my drink to empty the glass for another. Perhaps I should slow down.

'What was in it?' I ask.

I don't expect him to tell me. Not the truth, anyway. I know he's lying to my face about pretty much everything else. I bet he's not even drunk.

I did not expect him to laugh at this.

'That all depends on your point of view,' he chuckles. 'A memory of home? A promise of the future? There is only one way to find out…'

He fixes me with a stare and points at me. I hold my breath.

'You wouldn't believe me if I told you,' he says.

I think again about the noise the suitcase made. *But there was nothing in the bag.*

Mouse pours me another drink, but doesn't fill Deleon's glass.

'I said I didn't want a mess,' she says, sternly.

That's not a tone I'm used to Mouse taking with me. I look to my left and Deleon is collapsed on the bar. I guess he was drunk, after all.

'Ah,' I say. 'Might be helpful, though. I need him to stay put.'

I do. If he's not in possession of his case, then I can't track him after all. I could arrest him, but I'm sceptical about what he's been telling me and I don't think that's just the drink. I don't need to hear what he has to say. I need to see what he has to do.

'Can you find him a room?'

'It's that or dump him in the dock,' shrugs Mouse.

'Keep an eye on him,' I say, downing what really needs to be my last drink. I need to sleep this off.

CHAPTER 12

ESTREL

It wasn't the first time I'd used the Research complex to pass under the city walls and find my way into Trinity. The last time, which wasn't due to happen for several years - this timeline thing was going to get very confusing, very fast - I'd been leading a band of new Resistance recruits from the Armpit.

It felt like yesterday, but it also felt like a different time, which is what it was. We'd set up a barricade around the Dome, tried to keep the Black Knight cliques from breaking down the doors, but my band hadn't been fighters. I wasn't a fighter. We got overwhelmed, and the Dome fell before we'd got Ort'a to safety.

That was the night that Mouse stepped up, the beginning of a very inevitable end for her.

All of that was about to change. I was here to make things different, to use my past future self to solve Trinity's problems once and for all.

Once it was done, I'd have no memory of coming back.

I wouldn't remember the plan.

I wouldn't even remember there had been a plan.

If you could call it a plan. It read more like the ravings of a lunatic. I'd said that to Lek, when he'd laid it out for me, before he'd introduced me to Venn who had tried, and failed, to explain the science of it to me.

This was the plan: I had to come back in time, to three weeks before I'd arrived for the first time. I had to find Venn and tell her who I was. I had to set up a machine that would allow me, when I eventually arrived in Trinity - in three week's time, remember - to put that version of myself in a time loop. A loop that would only break when that other version of me figured out that he had to kill Evie Chaguartay. I couldn't help him, or I'd create a paradox. He was on his own, with only his instincts and moral compass to guide him. He'd go on living the same day, until he got it right. He had forever, he would figure it out eventually...

As for me, I wouldn't know any different. I wouldn't even know that it was me who'd changed the course of history. I'd wake up ten years in the future with no recollection of any of it, all the memories I had before replaced by a new timeline.

I'd have no memory of putting myself in a time loop and forcing myself to live every possible iteration of the same day until I managed to live the right one.

I'd have no memory of everything I'd had to do to put things right.

Because none of that would have happened. It would all be undone, leaving only the day that should have been. The day I stopped Evie Chaguartay.

White. She was still Evie White. I hoped I'd get used to this soon.

I wouldn't know any different once it had all happened. I

couldn't imagine losing everything that had happened to me since that day. It was a special day, my first day in Trinity, my new home. The day I met Mouse, the day I fell in love.

But I would lose it. It would be gone. It would never have happened.

I'd give it all away in a heartbeat. Every memory, every lesson learned, for a chance to wake up in her arms again.

Venn had showed me the maps when I first met her. I hadn't been able to take it all in. There, in a computer, was every iteration of my life for that one fateful day, all the possibilities, all the probabilities, every choice I could make, every choice I would make. It was all mapped out for me.

I understood little of it. But I didn't think I needed to. As long as it worked, I would never know. I didn't want to know. I just wanted Mouse back.

But now, in the present, which was also my past, Venn - not my Venn, a younger, less confusing Venn - was telling me something. I wasn't really listening. My head was still a bit scrambled from the jump back. I leant on the shiny metal walls of the huge service elevator for support.

'What are you smiling at?'

I hadn't realised that I was smiling.

'I… dunno. I'm just feeling a bit strung out. This is all a bit trippy. I can't quite believe I'm here.'

'No,' agreed Venn, 'I can't quite believe you're here either.'

She pushed her thick-rimmed black glasses back up her nose. That was a familiar gesture, and I felt a little bit more settled.

'I've only just sketched out the theory.' She looked a bit annoyed. 'And suddenly, here you are. I don't know how I'm meant to help you. I'm delighted that my future self has such a high opinion of my abilities, but… I may be looking back with rose-tinted spectacles, somewhat.'

'You don't know how to put me in a time loop?'

I tried not to sound too disappointed, but I obviously was. This whole thing was Venn's idea. If this version of Venn wasn't on board, didn't know what to do, then I was damned if I did.

Maybe that was a relief. I was feeling... something... about this whole thing. Maybe it was guilt. It felt a bit like guilt. Guilt at what I was about to put myself through.

But that was the thing. *What I was about to put myself through.* It was hard not to think of this younger, more innocent, version of myself as a different person when he wasn't. He was me. A more miserable, less fulfilled, more annoying me, but he was still me.

He - I? - didn't know what he - he, it was still easier to think of "him" as "he" - was about to walk into, and he wasn't exactly consenting, but I was. I knew he needed to do this. I knew that his future happiness depended on him doing this thing.

If anyone knew what was good for him - me - then surely that someone was me?

It didn't feel great, though. I couldn't even meet him and explain or apologise. He was going to have to figure it out on his own.

Would he even know what was happening to him? Venn, the other Venn, had been vague about that. *"Maybe,"* she'd said, *"the theory isn't completely clear..."*

It was her theory. It felt like she needed to theorise harder before getting me to go through with this.

'I don't know how to put you in a time loop... yet,' replied Venn, in that clipped, stern way she had when you questioned her abilities, even if you only did it because you were agreeing with her.

'You've got three weeks. I've just arrived a bit early in

order to prepare the ground.'

I tried to make it sound light-hearted. It was meant to be light-hearted. It was encouragement, not a deadline. I could tell from Venn's face that it hadn't landed that way.

'If you say so.'

The lift bumped to a stop. We'd reached the bottom of the shaft.

'You know, I never knew this existed. This lift…' I was still trying to make conversation. 'You could fit an elephant in here!'

Back where I'd come from, ten years in the future, Venn hadn't necessarily been any easier to talk to, but I thought we'd become friends. I was struggling with the lack of warmth between us.

This wasn't my Trinity. It wasn't my home. It wasn't my time.

Venn shrugged as the elevator doors slid open. It didn't matter to her. My credentials - the handwritten note and the photograph that her older self had handed me solemnly before I jumped - had made little impression, it seemed. Certainly not as much of an impression as I would have thought a message from your future self should make.

Venn operated on a different plane than the rest of us, I guessed. Intellectually, philosophically… it made it hard to be on the same wavelength as her emotionally. I couldn't rid myself of the feeling I was just irritating her.

Still, it was strange. I'd lived in Trinity for ten years, and it wasn't like I hadn't sneaked in and out of the city regularly. Increasingly frequently, since the patrols had got tighter and the restrictions on movement greater. We'd had to get ever more creative, find new and unusual ways through and under, and occasionally over, the walls that surrounded us. Trinity took its status as a walled city so seriously that they even extended out into the Middle Sea, enclosing Docklands behind their shadow and security.

But I'd never known about this. A huge service elevator that operated from a hangar next to the Pod tracks that ran beside the Northern Exposure, all the way back up the valley to the Highway. Was that a surprise? Not a lot surprised me about Trinity anymore, but I thought it was odd. Maybe it has been shut down, dismantled during the Transition.

'Are you coming?' Venn asked.

I followed her out of the elevator and down a corridor. It was familiar, but then all the Research corridors looked the same so I could have been anywhere. I wasn't, though. I knew where we were going. I'd spent a lot of time in that place, recently, in the future.

Venn let me into our lab. It wasn't our lab yet; it was her lab, her experiments in progress, her notes scrawled all over the wall screens. Her bed roll in the corner, her pile of discarded clothes and dirty plates on the floor.

'Have you been sleeping here?'

'A bit,' Venn said. 'I've been busy. I haven't had time to go home. I had a new theory. I've been working hard on it. I guess that's not going to stop.'

'Touché,' I said. 'I'm sorry to intrude.'

'Intrude?'

She seemed confused. I thought the note covered this. I silently cursed future Venn.

'I'm going to need some lab space,' I explained. 'I've got some stuff I need to get set up. I don't think I completely understand it yet, and I don't think you will for a few weeks, but I've memorised some pretty detailed instructions, so I'd like to get started before I forget them all.'

'Oh yes.' Venn was already back at work, scrutinising a feed of data as it streamed across her screen, grabbing the occasional reading and throwing it up to a list that was growing on the wall. 'Help yourself. The note said something about that. You're not intruding.'

I felt like I was intruding, but I had to take her at her word and I had things I had to get done quickly. The timeline was very specific. And detailed. And top secret, so much so that Venn made me spend a week committing it to memory rather than putting it down in writing.

I could start with the CabinCom. The familiar pod was sitting in the corner of the room. I approached it and searched for the calibration port on the back. Duly located, I tentatively placed my finger into the narrow hole.

The machine whirred, closing around my digit and continuing to close until it held me in a grip that was tighter than was comfortable. I felt my finger numb, although not quickly enough to stop me feeling the sharp stabbing of the tissue sample being taken.

I waited for a minute, which felt like thirty, until it released me and I retracted my finger, shoving it into my mouth and sucking it to relieve the pain.

It didn't appear to be injured at all. In fact, I only now realised that it didn't hurt anymore. I removed in from my mouth. The skin appeared intact. Exactly as Venn had said it would.

Step one complete, then. That had gone well. One less thing to remember, one less thing to worry about. I had a good feeling about this. Everything was going to work out. Everything was going to plan.

Welcome home, Estrel, I thought.

Part Two

CHAPTER 13

ESTREL

Lek's chambers were nestled deep inside the Citadel, but I hadn't come in through one of the gates. From Research I'd had to climb through The Catacombs. up ladders, through wine cellars and along some of the narrowest corridors I'd ever come across. They were long, and dusty, and saw more spiders and rats than they saw people.

I'd never done that before and it took a few goes to get it right. I got lost more than once. By the time I was banging on Lek's door, it was getting light again. I was tired. I hadn't slept in over two days and it was catching up with me. I was breathless and dirty, exhaustion taking a hold.

The door swung silently open. Inside was dark, with a faint green glow. Out wafted the usual aroma of damp moss and pipe smoke, mixed with toasted crumpets and butter, and a lingering tang of sulphur. I focused on the crumpets and butter. I found that if I tried hard enough, I could get to where that was the only part that I could smell.

This wasn't my first time visiting Lek in his chambers.

'Lek?' I stepped inside.

I stood still for a moment, to let my eyes adjust to the light. This was normal, despite the daylight that was now washing across Trinity, waking the city.

The Devoted seemed to have an aversion to normal light. This green was pretty usual. I could now make out a figure in the rocking chair, shrouded in smoke, underneath the shuttered window.

I waited.

'Well, come in then, if you're coming in,' said a curt, croaking voice.

'Lek?' I moved further into the room and closed the door behind me.

'Hello Estrel.'

This surprised me. This version of the old Cleric shouldn't have known who I was. Time didn't seem to work in quite the same way for him, though, as it did for the rest of us.

'You know who I am...?'

I wasn't sure how to say what I wanted to say. That was a stupid question, though. He obviously knew who I was.

'Ask away.'

The old man's face became more visible, the smoke now drifting up, away from him. In his hand he held an elaborately carved pipe, the length of my arm. I was fairly certain that this was where the aroma of butter was coming from.

'How?'

It was a dumb question, bluntly put. I'd possibly overstepped the mark. Lek was an old friend in my timeline. I didn't know if this Lek knew about that.

He sucked a large lungful of smoke from his pipe and held it deep within before slowly releasing it into the room in a giant cloud of butter.

'You know?' he said. 'I'm not entirely sure.'

'How does that work?' I was new to this time travelling

lark, but I did at least know who I was. 'You're still in the future, right?'

'It gets to you, after a while,' said Lek. 'I find it all blurs together. Memories merge. I know things I shouldn't. Things I haven't experienced, not in this body, not yet. I'm joining the dots. Before long, I won't need to travel, not physically. Not like you. I'll be able to jump with just the power of my mind.'

'I didn't realise that it worked like that.'

I evidently had a lot to learn.

'It doesn't,' said Lek, a dark, foreboding note creeping into his speech. 'It shouldn't…'

'…but it does?' I finished for him.

None of this was making me feel more confident about what I was here to do. The very last moments before I leaped were still fuzzy, still vague, but Venn had made me remember the plan. She'd drilled it into me, again and again, repeated until I didn't even have to think about the words to find them tumbling out of my mouth. She made sure I couldn't forget the plan, a coherent plan, a concrete theory. Venn's theory.

This was an extra wrinkle that Lek had thrown in, last minute. I had to find him, in this time, and tell him where to find the book. I wasn't clear how critical it was to my central mission, of killing Evie Chaguartay and resetting the timeline, but I wasn't going to take the risk of waking up without Mouse by my side.

I was itching to get back to the lab, though. I didn't have time to be wasting on one of Lek's tangential diversions.

'You aren't my Lek, though?' I checked. 'You didn't come back, like me? There isn't another one of you wandering around here, somewhere?'

'That's a lot of questions.' Lek, puffed smoke again. 'I think all the answers to them are "no".'

'You think?'

'It's all I can do. I don't think I *know* anything.'

He talked like my Lek. It was infuriating.

'I knew you were coming, though,' he mused, chewing on his pipe. 'I didn't have a clue who you were and then suddenly I knew you were coming. I saw someone who looked a lot like you the other day, but it wasn't the right one. You're the right one.'

The right one? I didn't know what he meant by that. He can't have meant the right me. I was the only one for now. The other me wasn't due to arrive for two and a half weeks.

'I came to…' I began, but he cut me off again. He seemed to know what I was about to say.

'You came to tell me about the book!' he exclaimed, sitting up straighter.

This was still frustrating, but potentially more useful. At least I'd skipped the bit where I had to convince him of my bona fides. Venn had been highly sceptical. That was the woman of science versus the man of faith, I guessed.

'I did. You found it, in the future,' I explained, eagerly, 'and now you need to…'

'I don't want to know!' shouted Lek, drowning me out. 'Don't tell me anything. I don't want to know…'

Damn it! Once I'd convinced Venn that I wasn't crazy, she'd taken all the information-from-the-future stuff on board pretty well. She was back in Research now, ploughing on with her work with renewed vigour, with a fresh certainty that it was all going to come to something. What scientist had that luxury?

I thought Lek would be the same. I was about to end his decades long search for the Book of Keyes, tonight if he could be bothered to put down his pipe and venture out of his chambers. But it seemed that he didn't want to know.

No, there was something more than that. I looked into his

eyes. This wasn't the Lek I knew, not quite, not yet. But I knew him well enough, *would know* him well enough, that I could tell when he was scared.

'Something's not right,' he muttered.

'What? What do you mean, not right? This is a message from you. You know what's coming next, you know how things pan out. How can you not be right?'

'You forget.' He fixed me with the stare that still made me shift uneasily, like a schoolboy trapped in a lie. 'I know.'

Did he?

'Kind of,' I pointed out.

'Tsh,' he dismissed me. 'That's not what I'm talking about. You're right, I don't want to find the book, not now. It needs to stay hidden. But that's because something is wrong. I knew you were coming. I knew what we needed. I went to see him.'

'Went to see who?' The old man had lost me now.

'Lagrange,' said Lek. He sat back.

'You went to see Lagrange?' This was the last thing I expected him to tell me. 'Why?'

Lagrange had nothing to do with this, with any of this. Not the loop, not the book… He was dead before I even arrived in Trinity. He was important to Clar, of course, but I didn't think that anything about what was about to happen depended on anything he did or didn't do beforehand.

'I wanted to see, wanted to check how things were going, wanted to see if everything was on track…'

'On track? On track for what?'

'For…' His face clouded, confusion descended. 'I thought it was important.'

He looked lost, weak, old. This was concerning.

'Something's not right, though,' he repeated.

'With Lagrange? Does it matter?'

'All of it matters,' Lek snapped.

This version of Lek seemed to lack the infinite patience I was accustomed to. Maybe I should take this seriously. He was rattled.

'He's got no focus. He's not even looking at Chaguartay yet and maybe he'll get there, but… he's chasing shadows. He spent half of today chasing Lukas Deleon.'

'Deleon?' I knew that name. 'Evie Chaguartay's bomber?'

'The same,' Lek nodded, 'Except that he's not behaving properly either. He might not even have brought his equipment with him.'

'Might not have? So he might?'

'He might, he might not. It's a possibility, one of many. A probability. Equally, he might have brought an elephant.'

Right, what was this? Why were we talking about mythical creatures now?

'An elephant?'

'I know!' His eyes sparkled. 'Infinite possibilities, infinite surprises!'

'You seem excited?'

'I can't be excited and concerned at the same time?'

I was supposed to intercept and stop Deleon. Well, the other me was. It was part of the mission that would lead him to Evie. The established facts said that Deleon planted the bombs for Evie White. If that turned out not to be true, I needed a new plan. But what was he going to do instead? Plant elephants?

'You can be however you like,' I said, 'but is this a problem? Lagrange will be gone by the day I arrive, and Deleon's in town. He's got nearly three weeks. Maybe you're wrong about what he's supposed to be doing at this point.'

Lek tapped the side of his face and adopted a pained look. He was on edge, conflicted.

'I know things,' he moaned. 'It hurts. I know things I

shouldn't know. I don't have the pathways for them yet. My brain is rewiring itself as we speak, at twice the rate it's meant to.'

I didn't know how I could help him. I wasn't sure that there was anything to help him with. I couldn't imagine that this slightly odd, squirming old man was the wise old Cleric that I knew from our futures. Maybe he was right, maybe the pressure of his constant meddling with the timeline, the extent of which I didn't know and had only been hinted at, was taking its toll.

Maybe it was the butter in his pipe, of course.

I stood up. I didn't think I was going to get any further. I didn't think I'd got very far as it was. I had far more important things to do back in the lab. Maybe I'd try again on another day.

'Look, I'm going to go,' I said. 'You try to sleep off… whatever this is, and I'll come back in a week. Maybe Deleon will be behaving himself by then, and Lagrange will be closer to figuring out whatever it is he figures out that gets him killed. I've got a future version of myself that I need to trap in time until he assassinates the next Mayor of Trinity…'

'Jack White's disappeared,' gasped Lek.

I stopped mid-turn.

'Say that again.'

'Jack White has disappeared,' repeated Lek.

'What, like, properly? I don't remember this. When does he come back?'

'I don't know that he does.'

'B-but…' *But he had to.* 'He comes back. You know he comes back. He only disappears for good on the day of the bombings. It's all part of Evie's plan.'

'I don't know that he comes back, because he didn't come back before.'

The old man was making less and less sense by the sentence.

'If he didn't come back, how could he disappear for a second time?' I demanded.

'He didn't disappear for a second time.' I saw the haze fade and a steely focus appear in his eye. 'He only disappeared the once, on the day of the bombings. This didn't happen before. Things are taking place that shouldn't be taking place. Things are in the wrong order. Things are true and not true at the same time. I'm worried, Estrel…'

'What's going on?' I was panicking. 'Was this us? Have we… I don't know, broken the timeline or something?'

'I don't think it's you. It's sure as damnation not me…'

'Then who?'

'I don't know.' Lek shook his head. 'But we need to find out, Estrel. Quickly. I don't think I can promise that you're not in terrible danger.'

CHAPTER 14

LAGRANGE

'The first time that we met, we were both drunk, you know.' Evandra White twists her fingers together, her eyes cast downwards, her brow furrowed. 'Laying eyes on him for the first time was the only thing that I can clearly recall from that night.'

She seems tiny, right now, closed in on herself, her shoulders hunched, her head dipped. I don't think she recognises me. There's no reason that she would. She was six years old the last time we met. I remember her, though.

I don't trust her.

I have her statements from yesterday on a screen in front of me. I keep flipping them back and forth, scrolling past her words without reading them again. I don't need them. They're a crutch for when the conversation gets difficult, when she gets awkward, like now. I'm not really concerned with what they say. Those leads are covered. I want to know who she is, who her husband is. If I can answer who, then maybe I can get some idea of why.

Phil Oddy

My head hurts, though. My head really hurts. I didn't sleep well. I hate it when I drink too much and it doesn't even knock me out.

'He hadn't been long in Trinity. He came here to find someone, but it didn't work out. He stayed because he had no way of getting back. When I sat down next to him, all he had were the clothes he was wearing. But he wore them well, you know?'

She looks up at me. I don't know, but I nod, so that she'll continue.

'I spotted him from across the bar. He was doing this funny wave that was failing to catch the bartender's attention. It got mine though. After that, it was all over for me. We talked and drank and I offered him somewhere to sleep, which ended up being my bed.'

She blushes, looks up again, her half smile showing that she'd forgotten, for a moment, who she was telling this story to.

'That was that,' she finishes. 'After that, he stayed because of me.'

It's time to draw attention to the elephant in the room.

'What did your father think of him?' I ask.

She shakes her head.

'Didn't matter, From that day I ceased to be Evie Chaguartay. We got married a few months later, and that's when I actually changed my name, but it had never fit me and suddenly I had a reason to free myself. I'd taken a job in Administration, which I'd wanted more than needed, but now I could use it to build myself a career, an independence, to live my life in the daylight with the man I loved.'

She sighs and places her hand on her belly.

'Now, when our daughter is born, she will never have to bear the weight of that name. I didn't just free myself that night.'

She is staring at me now. The sadness has vanished from her tone and she sounds resolute, determined. That she is pregnant is not widely known - it's early days. It came out in questioning, though, yesterday. There are already leaks on some of the more gossipy Com streams. It will be in the news before the election, I'm sure.

'I don't talk to my father anymore, Oficier Lagrange,' she says.

She holds my gaze for a full minute, without either of us saying anything. I get nothing from her. She's not lying to me, but she's not telling me the truth, either. I don't know what to do with this realisation.

I get up and leave.

I come back and sit down.

'Can I get you anything, Mrs White?'

While I was out of the room, I tried to find James, but he's out somewhere. I hope he's out finding Bjorn Barlow, but no one seems to know where he's gone. I hope he's making progress. More progress than I'm making in here.

'No.' She indicates the pale and milky tea in the plastic cup on the table. 'I'm fine. Thank you.'

'That's perfectly all right,' I go on, 'but please say if you change your mind. You're here to help us find your husband, Mrs White, and we want you to feel comfortable.'

'Evie, please,' she asks.

'Evie,' I repeat, taking a seat. 'Evie, after the abduction you went to your sister…'

I flick the screen of the Com like I'm checking my information, but I know the name of her sister.

'…Sara… You went to stay with Sara?'

This is the one thread from yesterday that no one seemed

to have dug into. Sara Chaguartay is not a high-profile member of "that particular family", so it might not be obvious that this is an odd move.

I have connections, though. Sara Chaguartay is a pet project of Clar's and I know that they've not spoken in years. Sara remains close with her father in a way that Evie, deliberately, does not.

Evie's nod is vigorous.

'She's my sister. I didn't have anywhere else to go. It's closer to my father than I would prefer, but Sara is sensible enough and...' She seems to react to my expression, and drops into an apologetic mumble. 'I didn't have anywhere else to go. I'm sorry, it's all been a bit...'

'You've had a difficult few days.' I try to smile. I might pull it off.

'My husband is missing, detective,' Evie's tone is more frustrated, through teeth that are a little more gritted. 'They... someone... some people came to our house, armed. They burst in, firing shots. We hid. They took him. I want you to find him.'

'Of course, Mrs... Evie.' I put out what I think is a reassuring hand. Her recoil suggests it isn't received that way. 'We will do everything we can to find your husband.'

She wraps her arms around herself and nods without lifting her head.

'I think I want to go,' she says. 'Can I go?'

I don't think I'm going to get anything else that I can use. I'm not sure I've got anything I can use yet, if I'm honest, but there's no point in keeping her here. She has done nothing.

Head, heart, gut. Nothing I can prove.

'You'll be staying with your sister?' I check.

'No. Like I said, it's too close to my father. I have a friend.'

'Which friend?' I ask. 'In case we need to get hold of you again.'

'You have my Com.'

She looks up at me.

She doesn't trust me. Or doesn't trust us. And suddenly I have something. Suddenly I'm interested.

'Do I need to tell you where I'll be?'

'I have your Com,' I confirm, standing up. 'You're free to go. I'll get someone to see you out.'

She nods, and I leave, again.

I find Parker in the refectory. She's sitting at the far end, with a group of Cadets, drinking coffee. I don't know any of the others. I don't concern myself with Cadets until they cross my path. Most Cadets know better than to do that.

I try to attract her attention from the doorway, but she's focused on the people she's talking to and she doesn't see me. I don't want to approach them, but I do want to approach her. I don't want this to be a big thing, but I have little choice.

I sweep into the room, my bulk announcing itself with a sweep of an arm, causing my coat to billow behind me. She sees me out of the corner of her eye and her head snaps around. She's staring straight at me.

Job done. I could stop here, beckon, pull her away from the group. Except every other head, seven or eight of them, has done the exact same thing and now all eyes are on me. I have to keep moving. It would be weird if I stopped here.

I keep moving.

Parker stands before I reach the table, draining her cup and tossing it into the recycling. She fixes me with a stare. There's a hush that's descended on the group. Everyone is waiting, with bated breath, to see what I'm going to say.

I get a strong feeling that they all think I'm going to give her a bollocking. I wonder what she's done. She sent me a Com that the tracker on Deleon's case has gone dead, but even I wouldn't hold that against her. I try to be reassuring, try to flash a smile. I am very certain that it doesn't come off.

'What's up?' she asks.

No trace of nerves. She doesn't think I'm going to give her a bollocking. Either that, or she's already got a massive pair.

I put my hand on her arm and lead her away from the table. We're not out of earshot, but I need everyone to know that I'm trying to keep this quiet. Except I'm not. I think there's an opportunity here. I think I need to provoke some action.

I'm convinced that Parker is on the level after my earlier wobble. Maybe someone here isn't, though. Maybe they'll say something to someone who will react and give me a badly needed lead. On Manukan, on corruption in Authority, on fuck-knows-what. I don't care. When every case is stuck in the mud, I'll take anything that will pull me out.

'You need to see Evie White out,' I say.

Fourteen or sixteen ears prick up. I realise that half of them don't even know she's sitting in an interview room right now.

'Make sure she leaves the building. Make sure she sees you stay in it. Then you're going to jump over to Control and pull up the cam outside her sister's apartment. That's where she's going first. When she leaves, track her. I don't care how, use a drone, or relay the street cams… scramble a squad if you can find one. But find out where she goes afterwards.'

Something flashes behind Parker's eyes. I think she's excited. That's good. That's my Cadet.

'You got something, boss?'

'You don't need to know right now.' I don't know what I've got right now. It's just a hunch. 'Just follow her. I need to know where she's staying. I need to know who she's staying with. I need to know why she doesn't want me to know who she's staying with.'

'Juicy,' grins Parker, grabbing a doughnut from a plate on

the table and handing it to me.

I stand there, doughnut in hand, staring at it.

'You look hungry,' she says, taking another for herself and moving past me toward the interview room. She isn't, but I could almost imagine that she's skipping.

I grunt at the group of Cadets who are suddenly not looking at me, and walk out. When I get to the door, I go the other way down the corridor.

Evie White lied to me.

I have to assume that she knows I realise this. So what does she think I think she would do? It all depends on how clever she thinks I am.

I slip out of a back exit and around to the Divisional TransPod. It's unmarked, of course, but it's carefully calibrated to be as average as possible. Age, model, slate grey paintwork - it's the exact mid-point of every vehicle that can be found in Trinity. And, as a result, completely unlike any other vehicle in Trinity. It's a running joke about Authority. We're so average, you can spot us a mile off. On this occasion, it's perfect for my purposes.

I'm trying very hard to suggest that I'm not that clever after all. The obvious surveillance that Parker will run on her sister's place is part of that. I expect her to see it a mile off. If she even goes anywhere near Sara Chaguartay's flat. Which I very much doubt that she will.

Evie White, of course, has a private Pod, with a pilot, waiting for her outside the entrance. He's got the motor running. Maybe he thinks he'll need to make a quick getaway. That's good for me. If he's expecting a tail, then he's more likely to spot me. I slide into gear and get ready, my hand on the lever, ready to engage. I'm a couple of vehicle lengths behind him. There's another Pod between us. Not too obvious, just obvious enough.

I'm doing all the sensible things to prevent them from seeing me following her. But I hope they do, so I'm not doing them very well. I want Evie White to think that's the limit of how clever I am.

I'm going to have to work quite hard to make sure that her estimation of me doesn't go any higher. I'm going to have to fight every instinct I have, years of training and practice, all my best moves sacrificed.

I see Mrs White leave the building. Parker holds the door for her. That's good, she gets it, she's playing her part. Extra helpful, extra effusive in her warm wishes for the safety of her husband.

With a kind smile, she steps aside and Evie's gaze sweeps across the forecourt. I make sure we lock eyes before I look away, drop my head. I need her to know that I'm watching. I'm confident that she does.

Parker acts like she doesn't have a clue. She hurries inside; I assume to get down to Control quick-smart. I'm going to go easier on her. I don't think she's corrupt. The suspicion, the cynicism, it eats you. I have to hold on to some hope.

Evie White scuttles across to her Pod and slides inside. The doors close and the passenger windows go black. I can't see her, but it seems she's talking to her pilot, as I can see him lean back, head half turned, whilst he listens to instructions, nodding here and there. I don't see him say much. I don't think he's paid for his opinions.

I almost get caught out when he takes off at speed, aggressively crossing several lanes of traffic as he pulls onto the TransWay. On instinct, I almost flip on the siren, which would have been fatal. As it is, I pull around the parked Pod and give chase.

He's helped me out, somewhat, the pilot, because a lot of

the Pods ahead of him braked hard when he cut them up, and I'm quick enough to dart ahead of them before they can re-engage. Most of them are too shocked to react, but I get a few irate horns. I don't know what they expect. They should know where they're driving past. It's not like vehicles coming out of Authority at speed is a rare occurrence.

At first, the pilot adopts a modest speed. It isn't possible to do much more than that on the busy TransWay, but he avoids much of the weaving in and out that might have bought them a few extra vehicles in between us. I hold back, not as much as I would do normally, but enough that I avoid his mirrors. I don't want to be too obvious about the fact that I want them to spot me. I have a reputation as a competent detective. I'm trying to strike a fine line, remain believable, not look like I'm altogether inept.

Then he catches me out with a sudden right, just before the signal changes. The Pod in front of me isn't looking to go the same way. He's hanging back to avoid blocking the junction when the traffic comes the other way, like a good Wayuser.

This means that I almost lose them, but also means that I can pull the arsehole move of squeezing up the inside and swinging around the front. I narrowly avoid the oncoming traffic and, with only the slightest of skids, join the flow of traffic on the correct side of the road.

That's put a bit more distance between myself and Evie's Pod, but there's no way she's not looking back at the kerfuffle behind her, no way she hasn't seen the sparks. She might even smell the grinding gears, but that's a fancy Pod she's got, so it's bound to have a filter fitted. Mine doesn't, and I can taste burnt metal at the back of my tongue as I pull past another vehicle and narrow the distance.

Good, Evie's pilot responds. He knows I'm following. The right he pulled at the last minute was a test to make sure I was.

Now he's going to get away. And I'm going to let him. But not yet. I need to make this look convincing.

He takes another right, which is reassuring because that means that he's doubling back on himself, which means I'm not wrong about where they're headed. I make the same turn. It's narrow. I'm not even sure this alley is meant for traffic, and certainly not for traffic moving at the speed we accelerate to.

This means we have to hover. I've not driven for a while. I've not flown in forever.

He's quite the pilot, ahead of me, not your average executive chauffeur. He keeps the Pod just high enough to avoid the street furniture, just low enough to avoid blowing exhaust in through the open first-floor windows. I'm not as good as he is, but I can send chairs and trashcans flying with impunity because, well, because I am Authority.

Still, I feel compelled to wave an apology to a small, elderly woman, who has to flatten herself back inside a doorway to avoid being mown down as we pass. I glance up at the second floor level. There isn't even a ramp to the PedWay from this street. This is old Trinity.

I take an ancient lump out of a wall as I corner too tight. That will not look pretty when I drop the Pod back to the garage. The impact robs me of some of my momentum and in the split second I take to get back up to full power, Evie's Pod has reached the end of the passage.

This could be the perfect place to lose them, or rather, for them to lose me. If they fly straight out across traffic, they're going to cause an accident which is as likely to stop them in their tracks as it is to allow them to escape, so I have to assume they're going to turn left.

I have to assume that they think I'm thinking that. So if I just stop then it's obvious I'm giving up and, depending on how much they're second guessing me, it might be obvious that I was never serious about tailing them. I'm going to have to keep going, aren't I? I'm not sure how long I can keep this up.

And then I'm saved, as a trash container backs slowly out of a side alley, even smaller than the one we're flying through. It's timed to perfection, just as Evie's Pod passes, getting out into the street just enough that I can't viably pass it, and I don't have time to bank and get over it. I slam on the air brakes, and sit, catching my breath, as Evie and her wonder pilot disappear on the other side. The container completes it emergence into the alley and I see the driver. He's grinning at me. And waving.

I pull out my Com, hit a suggested contact. Clar answers, a tiny hologram of them appearing on my dash.

'Who's the kid?' I ask about the over excited teenager who is now punching the air and giving me a thumbs up.

'That's Miguel,' replies Clar. I can see their holo chuckle to themselves. 'I didn't think you'd come that way.'

'They spotted me early. Glad you had all bases covered.'

'Not a problem.' I can hear them grin. 'Don't arrest Miguel. Mouse has got a broken generator he's meant to be fixing.'

'Miguel who?' I ask, before disconnecting and backing up the alley.

I know where she's going. And it's not to her sister's apartment.

CHAPTER 15

I'm about to swing back out on the main TransWay when Parker gets on the Com. The holo stays off because I'm moving, but she sounds somewhat pissed off. I probably should have trusted her enough to let her in on what I had planned.

'Boss, did you follow Evie White?'

It didn't take her long, did it? I decide to play it off as innocently as I can.

'Hey, Parker, yes, yes I did,' I say. 'Lost her too. They clocked me pretty quickly. They doubled back on themselves before they gave me the slip, so, to be honest, it wasn't any help. I've got no idea where they were headed. You got anything?'

She declines to answer that question. Damn her. I think she knows.

'Why am I trying to track her if you were planning to follow her?'

Blunt and to the point. Awkward. And completely justified.

'I didn't know I was going to follow her.' I don't have a lot of confidence that she's going to buy the lie. 'Got a hunch that she was going to do something that gave her away. It was a spur-of-the-moment thing.'

'Bullshit,' says Parker.

Ouch. She's not stupid. I mean, to be fair, it is bullshit. It doesn't feel good to be called out on that, however. I'm supposed to be her superior officer. I'm not sure she should talk to me like this.

I park up the Pod, tucking it against the wall on the left. It's in trouble if someone else attempts a high-speed pursuit down this alley, but otherwise it will be fine.

A message flashes up asking if I want to switch the Com mode. I decide to leave the holograms off.

'Have you got anything?' I try the question again.

'Have I got what..?' Parker pauses, says something inaudible off-mic. 'No, we have nothing. Evie White did not, I'm sure it will be of no surprise to you to learn, return to her sister's apartment to collect anything, or anyone. We have a drone on standby, but that's not picking up anything yet, either. On account of not being able to follow someone who isn't there. No one has come out, either, if that's at all relevant to whatever investigation you're conducting here...'

To be fair to me, although I was very aware that Evie White was not planning to return to Sara Chaguartay's, it is useful for me to know that Sara Chaguartay hasn't left to meet with Evie somewhere else. I will not give Parker the satisfaction of knowing that, however, not if she's going to take such a difficult tone with me.

'Keep it in the air,' I say. 'She could still be coming.'

She won't be coming. I'm pretty sure I know where she's going now. I just need Clar to confirm it for me. That shouldn't take too long. If I'm right, then it won't take her long to get there.

In the meantime, Parker can fly a drone around Sara

Chaguartay's place and stare at a monitor, waiting for something that definitely will not happen. That will teach her to get smart with me.

Except I can't be arsed to drive the Pod back to Authority and I can't leave it here.

'Is there anyone who can take over for you?' I ask. 'Is Solzinger there?'

'Take over from me staring at nothing on a screen for the next hour? Sure. Solzinger's clocked off, but I think I can persuade Johnson.'

I know Johnson. Johnson isn't in my Division, so I don't care if Johnson wastes the rest of his morning staring at nothing happening. It's perfect. I switch the conversation to my personal Com and get out of the Pod.

'Fine, get Johnson on it. I've left the Pod in a sidestreet, I'll send you the location. Come and pick it up.'

I hear her sigh. I get petty. I hurry down the alley and around the corner I took a chunk out of earlier. I drop the pin from there. The quickest way here from Authority is from the other direction. If she comes that way, it will take a while before she figures out where I've left the Pod.

I think it's been a while since I had a drink. I'm not in a good mood. Things are going well, plans are coming together. I should feel better about all of this.

'You got somewhere better to be?' asks Parker.

'I've got a new hunch...' Which is kind of true. I cut the call.

I walk while I wait for Clar to get in touch. I need a moment, anyway. My head is still spinning from trying to second guess Evie White.

She's up to something. I know she's up to something, but I need to be patient. I need to let Clar come through. In the meantime, I walk.

I grab a drink from the corner vendor, which helps to relieve some of the pressure the moment the liquid touches my tongue. I should worry about how easy that was. I don't. I'm just glad that it is easy. Something needs to be easy.

I replay Evie White's interview as I walk, trying to find the holes, trying to see what she avoided saying. Every pause she didn't fill was a potential clue.

I don't believe that her husband is missing, for a start, or at least not in the way she says he is. She talked about armed men bursting into her apartment, forcing him away. The scene report did tally with that up to a point. Intruders did burst in, shots were fired, there was definitely a commotion of some sort, neighbours confirmed all of that.

But then they would. She mentioned that bit so she would have made sure that there was something to corroborate her story. Nobody saw anyone leave. There were no witnesses to the getaway. And none of the shots that were apparently fired seemed to have hit anyone or anything, not even walls or doors. There were no casualties, there was no damage. Not so much as a dirty footprint on her nice white living room carpet.

What didn't she say? What did she leave out? Where is the gap? If I can find the gap, I can fill it in for myself. I take another swig. I don't know what the alcohol is, but it's mixed with ginger, which doubles the burn.

My Com beeps. I check the image that Clar has just sent me. It's Evie White's Pod, parked up outside the Citadel.

It's hard to tell because there are dozens of them all around the outside of the ancient structure, but it looks like the alley she's parked up in front of is the same one I lost Deleon down earlier. That would be something, wouldn't it, if she's collecting something he left for her? That would cause one pet theory to land right in my lap.

Entrapment

Head, heart, gut. I'm suddenly excited. I'm very glad I asked Clar to surveille the Citadel. I'm very glad that Evie White thinks I lost her and have no idea where she is right now. I will be very glad when I know where she goes next, and with whom.

I reply to Clar's Com, asking them to stay on her tail for the time being. I then switch over and send a decent chunk of credits their way. They're from my personal account. Clar doesn't need the hassle of appearing on Authority's books.

Satisfied, for now, I look up and take stock of my surroundings. My feet have been moving, but I haven't been paying attention. I realise that I'm heading towards Docklands.

I feel a pang of guilt but then I realise what my subconscious has been up to. I have an itching for a drink, another drink, but, for once, that's not the reason my feet appear to be carrying me to Eamer's.

I check the time. It's nearly midday, which is more than a little fortuitous. Grabbing a drink may not be the reason that I'm going to Eamer's, but it will certainly serve as an excuse.

What I really need to do, though, is to check in on Deleon. I need to find out what he was doing in the Citadel, if there's an Evie White shaped connection there, after all. Hopefully, he's awake and recovered from last night's excesses. Not too recovered, though. I'd like him to be relatively pliable.

I wonder what he knows. I wonder if I can use him to get to Evie. I wonder if Mouse knows anything that might help me bring him onside, or at least to blackmail him. Mouse has a keen ear for that kind of gossip.

A drink or two while I'm there won't do me any harm, either.

I turn right onto the dock front. A large delivery truck blocks my view of Eamer's further down the street, but I can smell it from here. I am a little ashamed to admit that it smells like home.

I walk into Eamer's. It's busy, so I don't initially notice that Mouse is giving me wide eyes from behind the bar. That's not good. I furrow my brow, look inquisitive, but I keep walking.

I'm here now. Whatever Mouse is trying to communicate to me, she can tell me over the drink she's going to serve me.

'You shouldn't be here,' she hisses, as soon as I'm at the bar.

'Don't,' I say. 'I was getting impatient. And I needed a drink.'

'There's someone wants to see you.' She doesn't move to get a glass. She hasn't asked me what I want to drink, either, but she should be able to guess and I'm not fussy.

'Good,' I say. 'I'm at a loose end. It would be good to chat. Why are you being weird?'

'I'm not being weird. I'm trying to persuade you to not be here.'

'By being weird,' I clarify for her. 'Also, I don't have a drink yet. You're a very poor bartender.'

Mouse growls under her breath. I'm quite enjoying myself. I shrug. I'm not leaving.

'Here.'

She bangs down a tumbler slightly harder than is strictly necessary. Uncorking the bottle with the familiar squeak, she sloshes whiskey into it. The sight of it immediately calms me, like the alcohol is getting to work through my eyeballs, before I even lift the glass.

I pick it up; the vapour hits me, time slows down. Suddenly I'm invincible. I open my eyes. I hadn't realised I'd closed them.

'Who is it?' I ask, although I assume the answer is

"Deleon".

Mouse is shaking her head, slowly. I don't think that's the drink. I think she's trying to say something without words. I don't know what it is.

'It's Deleon who wants to see me, right?' I check.

Then I realise what I've just said. This is bad news. Deleon shouldn't know who I am. He didn't know who I was last night. Now I'm worried that was temporary, alcohol induced, amnesia. If he remembers me now, then maybe he did see me at Tunnel yesterday. Maybe he was running from me. He'd better not do that again.

I don't want to have to arrest him, just so that I can keep him in one place. I don't actually have anything on him yet. Mouse is still shaking her head.

'No. Mr Deleon is not currently at liberty to request an interview with you.'

'Deleon is..? What?'

That doesn't sound any better. That sounds like Deleon has had some kind of accident. The type of accident that silences a man. The type of accident that it is all too easy to befall in this fucking place. I groan.

'Mr Deleon is not currently at liberty,' Mouse says. 'Eamer has got him tied to the generator in the cellar. It's quite a good job that Miguel hasn't got it going yet, or I'd be worried about his wellbeing.'

I incline my head. Not Deleon then. *So who wants to see me?*

'More worried about his wellbeing,' she clarifies.

The penny drops.

'Eamer wants to see me?'

I avoid Eamer, if I can manage it. Most people do.

'Eamer wants to see you. Hence me trying to persuade you to just go the fuck away.'

'Appreciate that.'

I knock the drink back. It burns, but not as much as the scorch of anxiety down the back of my neck. Still, this might be OK. I have problems. Many, many problems at the moment. Barlow, Deleon, Manukan, Jack White. Evie White. *Kamla*. Can adding Eamer to that list really be that much worse?

I nod, slowly. Mouse's eyebrows shoot up.

'Still, you're here,' she observes. 'You were supposed to get up and leave.'

I'm thinking. Something is brewing. *Head, heart, gut*. Kamla. I don't have a proper solution to Kamla's problems. I can't think of a way to get her out of Detention without revealing the link between me and her. There probably isn't a way to get her out of Detention without revealing the link between me and her. Not a legitimate one.

There's one place you go if you're looking for illegitimate ways of doing things. Only one, if you want it to work. And Eamer is fond of Kamla.

I think.

'Still, I'm here,' I say. 'Maybe I want to see Eamer.'

The noise that Mouse makes does not bear much similarity to a laugh, but I assume that's what it's meant to be.

'You don't want to see Eamer.'

I will not let her tell me what I want.

'I want to see Eamer,' I say. 'I have something to ask him.'

Mouse shakes her head, takes my glass and uncorks the bottle of whiskey again. She sloshes another unmeasured measure into the glass.

'Drink that,' she says. 'Drink it and leave. You're being an idiot. Stay clear of Eamer. You're an Authority Oficier, for fuck's sake. An Authority Oficier with responsibility for investigating and dismantling his criminal empire. He's in a terrible mood. This would be a terrible move.'

'I can handle Eamer.' I'm almost sure that's true.

Entrapment

'Do not meet him.'

I pick up the glass, shake my head.

'I'll just pop out back. He's in his office, yes?'

Mouse looks horrified. I down my whiskey.

I'm going to need that. I haven't got a clue what I'm going to say to Eamer.

CHAPTER 16

There's a dance that plays out here in Trinity. It has rules and conventions and niceties that should be observed at all times. It takes a lifetime to learn them all, and they shift and bend over time, so you never stop learning. If you pay attention, and get lucky, you can avoid stepping over the line, breaking a rule.

You can avoid ending up like Manukan.

Eamer and I, we've been dancing for a long time. I think we have a good understanding of the rules and conventions and niceties, at least as far as they apply to us. We're about to break the first one.

We don't talk directly to each other.

We've met, of course. From the start, our paths have regularly crossed, and we've spoken - in person, over Com... We have a regular dialogue. It wouldn't be possible for either of us to achieve anything without it.

But we don't *meet* meet. We don't sit down. It's against the rules.

The thing is, I always knew we'd break this. I always knew that at some point, one day when all the alternatives had been exhausted, we'd have to meet face to face, to sit down man to man and tall it all out.

I always imagined that day would be more dramatic than this one. I don't know what I thought the crisis would look like that would rock the world to the point where one of us would crack, but it was more than... nothing?

I also always imagined that it would be me who asked for the meeting. I'm very confused that it's Eamer.

I don't think Jack White's disappearance would register on Eamer's radar. He's got a direct line to Chaguaray himself. There is nothing political that could touch him, surely? So what could it be?

Is it me? Maybe I found something that makes me a threat. Barlow? Perhaps he knows about the plan with Barlow. Barlow, the fake one, the Cleric, could be one of his men. Was this whole thing a setup?

Well, yes, it was a setup, but I thought I was the one setting things up. I thought I was holding all the cards. My hand feels pretty empty right now.

Unless it was Deleon. Unless he'd got information from Deleon. What could be so significant that he'd need to talk to me? I have to decide; I need to know, before I go in, on which side my bread is buttered - whether this information, extracted from Deleon, painted me in a negative light, as a threat to Eamer.

It might be for my own good. He could have information that he needs to share to save my skin. No, that doesn't feel right. But our interests could be aligned. This might be a mutually beneficial thing.

Head, heart, gut. I can't imagine what we have in common.

Apart from everything.

I try not to think about that.

I can't imagine what he might have got out of Deleon. I haven't had a chance to get anything out of him myself. I wonder if Eamer knows about his luggage. I should warn Nolan. Although Nolan might not even have it anymore.

That probably won't matter to Eamer.

I'm worried now. The bravado I'd felt in the bar, the confidence that I could use this situation to my advantage, has evaporated quicker than a puddle of piss in the sunshine.

I feel bad for Kamla. If I'm her only hope, then she's screwed. She's never getting out.

I'm wondering if the second drink, maybe either drink, was such a good idea. I should probably have more of my wits about me than I do at this precise moment in time.

I stand outside Eamer's door, drawing myself up to my full height. We're dancing, then. I need to make sure that I don't let Eamer lead.

'Come.' Eamer's voice barks from the other side of the door. Which means it's too late to regret my choices now. I suck in a lungful of air. It's foetid. This isn't a nice place. I want to throw up.

I close my eyes and push on the door.

When I open them, I can't see a lot more than I could with them closed. The room is dim, the only window looking out into the side alley has the blind pulled down. Clouds of smoke surround the big man.

Did I mention Eamer is a big man? Physically big, I mean, not just big in Trinity. He dominates the room, making the two Black Knights lounging in the chairs in the corners of the room look slight and sly. Neither of which are adjectives you would use to describe them in any other situation. Not if you wanted to leave with the same number of fingers as you came in with.

'Oficier Simeon Lagrange,' booms Eamer. It's like he's announcing me at a ball.

'Eamer,' I nod.

'What brings you into the lion's den?' he chuckles.

I stop nodding. *Mouse said*...I have a sudden panic that Mouse was having me on, which leads to a further panic as I scramble to figure out what I did to Mouse for her to stitch me up in such a definitive and probably fatal way.

Mouse told Holman that I was coming to see him. Maybe I shouldn't be trusting Mouse as much as I do. That hurts. We're almost family.

'Mouse said you wanted to see me?' I say.

My voice is strangled, high and whining. I hate the sound of it. I don't want Eamer to know that I'm intimidated by him. Without even trying, I'm telegraphing it.

'She did,' Eamer smiles.

It is not a welcoming smile. I note he didn't confirm what he wanted, merely that Mouse had said what I reported. It's a mark of the confidence of the man. He knows that's what Mouse told me, because that's what he instructed her to say.

'Sit down.'

I sit down.

'I believe you may know something about the man in my cellar?'

I swallow, hard. Straight to the point, no courtesies or niceties. No coded references to the fact that he knows who I am. No sidestep, no promenade, no chassé.

'I was at Bridge when he arrived in town,' I explain, sticking to the facts. 'I followed him.'

'Here?' asks Eamer.

I sense he already knows the answers. He is dancing, after all. These questions are his opening steps. I'm not yet certain that I understand what our purpose is, but I need to be patient, to follow his lead.

I wasn't going to let him lead.

'No, to the Citadel,' I say. 'Then I lost him.'

Entrapment

'I found him here,' says Eamer, raising a meaningful eyebrow. 'In my bar.'

I nod a confirmation.

'I know,' I say. 'I saw him here last night. I don't know what happened in between.'

I have a theory, though.

'You were here, in my bar?' asked Chaguartay, a mocking surprise inflecting his tone. 'Is that a safe place for a man of your vocation to be spending his leisure time? Or was it business which brought you here? In which case would it not have been polite to inform me of your presence and intentions before commencing your investigations here, on my premises?'

I know he doesn't talk like this all the time. He knows how frequently I drink, and that I rarely drink anywhere else. This is an unnecessary fleckerl, but I resist the urge to cut him off, because that might be considered suicidal.

'Purely social,' I say, in my most reassuring tone. 'I like your bar. I like your bartender.'

'Employee of the month,' nods Eamer, apparently satisfied that whatever point he was making is now made. 'Most months.'

'Purely social until I saw Mr Deleon at the bar,' I clarify. 'I didn't think I would get anything useful from him, so I thought I'd wait until today. I asked Mouse to keep an eye on him.'

I realise what an amazing stroke of luck I've been granted. I hadn't planned it this way but me returning today, me coming to see Eamer - even if it was at his invitation - is the perfect development. Showing due respect to the Godfather-of-Fucking-Trinity-Over whilst trying to get to the bottom of the presence of the mysterious stranger. A stranger who, apparently, is acting suspiciously on the streets of the city that, in our unique ways, we are both committed to keeping safe.

We might have quite different definitions of the word "safe", mind you.

'She's good like that, Mouse,' muses Eamer. 'Kind-hearted sort.'

This doesn't sound like Mouse.

'Right,' I say.

He's waiting for something more from me, I can tell. It's probably not "right".

'She was a bit busy though, so I had to step in,' he says, appearing to move on.

I'm left two steps behind, trying to catch up. What's happening here?

'She takes on too much, that woman.'

'I, uh…'

I have to say something. I'm losing my advantage, which I now suspect I only imagined, and never actually existed. I'm lost for words.

'So Deleon, he's OK?' I check.

Eamer smiles. It's unpleasant. I know he's not OK. What I mean is, "will I ever get to talk to him?".

'Mr Deleon is alive and intact,' Eamer says.

Those are not reassuring words to hear. "Alive and intact" should be a minimum expectation.

'But he's not helping himself, particularly. He is, if anything, jeopardising his current state of aliveness and intactness. Mr Deleon refuses to answer my questions.'

'What questions are you asking him?' I ask.

I need to know if he has anything to do with Jack White's disappearance. The window is tiny, only a few hours between me losing him at the Citadel and him turning up here last night. I'm starting to doubt my own theory. It might be about the get disproved.

Head, heart, gut. Evie White went to the Citadel, used the same door. Just like I knew she would. I can't ignore an instinct like that. *Fuck you, Eamer, you'd better have been asking the right questions.*

'Basic stuff,' smiles Eamer. 'Who he is, where he's from, why he's here... Why he's carrying several crude but potentially devastating explosive devices?'

'He's...?'

I don't know why I feel so disappointed. I was right.

Bombs? I was right to follow him.

Bombs? I knew he was up to something.

Bombs? He had nothing on him when I lost him outside the Citadel. He had left his bag. He was carrying nothing.

'Carrying explosive devices?' I ask.

Eamer nods, slowly.

I think about the suitcase. *There was nothing inside.*

It had made a noise. *There was nothing inside.*

I may never know what was up with that bag, but I am certain it didn't contain bomb making equipment.

And then I remembered. At Bridge, he had another case.

Had he already left it at the Citadel? Are the Devoted building bombs now? I know that there are dissenting elements within the ranks of the Clerics. Of course there are. It's hard to live here without getting a bit radicalised, but this seems a step too far. Maybe in the days of the Brotherhood, but not now. The Superious wouldn't stand for it.

'What did he plan to...?'

I stop. I should say nothing more.

I fail.

There's another conclusion that I'm struggling to come to, but this one makes more sense. I also don't think I want to play my cards right now. I've only just realised that I'm holding any.

'Who was he...?'

Evie White went to the Citadel.

'I can see, Oficier Lagrange,' Eamer says, 'that you and I are on the same page here. I can tell you no more, but I can see that we seek the same answers. We have the same gaps in our knowledge that we wish to fill.'

'I, uh...'

I do want to know. The thing is, I think I do know who is helping him, who he's working for. Not that it makes much sense. Not that I can even start to guess at why.

'Yes.' I finish, weakly.

'Good.' Eamer spreads his arms wide.

A cloud of expensive scent drifts my way. I sneeze.

'Bless you,' grins Eamer. 'As you have blessed our little endeavour, here.'

He nods to a figure that I hadn't noticed, stood in the shadows of the left-hand corner behind me.

'Mishka, you may continue. Do not stop until you have the answers. I... we...' At this point he points to me, then back to himself, then backwards and forwards a few more times. '...seek.'

I twist round in my chair to see the wiry shape of Mishka Karpov slip out of the door. He doesn't seem to open it, or close it behind him, and yet it is very much closed and he is no longer in the room. My heart is pounding in my boots. I am anxious about what I have agreed to here. I am certain that it won't be good news for Lukas Deleon. I turn back to Eamer, who is filing his nails.

'You will understand, Oficier, that there is no way I can have explosive devices deployed around Trinity. Think of the chaos. Thing of the disturbance. Everyone will panic, knowing their lives are in jeopardy.'

What Eamer means, of course, is that he can't have those things happening without him being in control of them. People would panic. He isn't wrong there. Because if bad things happen without Eamer's say so, if Eamer loses control of Trinity by force, no one wants to meet whoever wrests it from him.

'It is nice when there is accord between reasonable men.' Eamer stops filing and beams at me. It is chilling. '…and I do not want you to think that I am ungrateful, so I am going to do you a favour in return.'

A favour from Eamer, unasked for? This is unusual, to say the least. And whilst I don't want to look a gift horse in the mouth, a "favour in return" could easily become a debt to be repaid. I don't want to be in Eamer's debt.

I should get out of here. This was a bad idea. I should just ask for something minor, something that's not going to become a problem for me.

'I just need information,' I say, tentatively feeling my way.

Eamer inclines his head, as if in thought. He's not thinking, he's playing with me.

'What sort of information?' he asks.

'Ralph Manukan,' I say.

'Never heard of him.'

'Bjorn Barlow,' I say.

There is a pause. The corners of Eamer's mouth twitch. I think he's about to burst out laughing, but he contains himself and maintains a serious demeanour.

'Never heard of him,' he says. 'Probably because *he doesn't exist.*'

I remember what Mouse said last night. Eamer's not stupid. He's playing with me.

'But he does,' I say. 'He was in my cells the day before yesterday.'

No twitch this time. If anything, he frowns slightly. His brow certainly knots. I didn't realise he had so many tells. I don't think I've ever made him uncomfortable before.

'That isn't possible, Oficier Lagrange,' he snarls, 'is it?'

'And yet it happened,' I insist.

I wait. He pushes his finger against the table, hard, until the tip goes white. He releases the pressure and watches as the colour rushes back to his digit. I don't know what's happening, but I know I don't want to interrupt it.

'I don't believe I can help you,' he says. His teeth are tight, gritted, his lips barely move. He's angry.

'That's a shame,' I say, easing myself up out of my seat. I turn, ready to leave. I feel that it's getting progressively less safe for me to be here the longer I go on talking. 'Never mind, I…'

'Your friend,' says Eamer.

I look at him. This is a mistake. He grabs my gaze and holds it, staring me straight in the eye. I don't give him the reaction I can see that he's waiting for. In part, that's because I take a moment to realise who he's referring to.

Kamla.

Shit. He knows.

'My friend?' I ask, but this sudden realisation has strangled me, and my voice is again a thin, reedy impression of its normal self.

Eamer laughs. He knows.

'Your friend,' he smiles.

It's even more terrifying than the grin.

'I think I should…' He takes a deep breath, leans backwards in his seat, spreads his arms again. '…put some wheels in motion. See what we can do about getting her out of her current confinement.'

Shit. He knows.

And now I'm in his debt.

'You enjoy the rest of your day, Oficier Lagrange.'

Entrapment

I catch the MiniTram from Docklands back up to Authority. The buzz from the drinks is gone. The buzz of feeling like I have any kind of leverage in my dealings with Eamer is gone.

My investigation is in tatters.

It's possible that I've managed to get Kamla out of Detention. It's possible I've landed her in more danger than she's ever known.

Eamer knows about Barlow. He knows what I tried to do. It's possible that I've landed myself in more danger than I've ever known.

I can't think too much about any of this, because of the violent jolting of the carriage. I can hear a semi-regular sparking noise, and there's a faint smell of burnt plastic. It's distracting. This is an old Tram. I didn't know there were still any of these on the circuit. I could have it impounded. Not my job, but I could.

I have zero leads. No, that's not true. I might have one.

Kamla could be getting out. Could be out already. She'll be delighted. Probably. And I couldn't have done it myself. But it might at least make her think better of me. And I can look Jo Jo in the eye again. This is all good.

But Eamer knows. Eamer *knows*. He told me he knows, to my face, and then let me walk out of his office. That cannot be a good thing. I am now in debt to the worst person in Trinity. And he's got a hold over an Authority Oficier.

'Fuck!' I shout.

There's no one on board but the pilot and he's evidently used to carrying crazy men cursing at themselves at the tops of their voices because he doesn't even look round.

What am I going to do? I don't have many cards left.

But I do have one. I think it's an important one. Evie White. I need to know where she's gone. I need to know what she's up to. I need to know if Jack White is still alive.

I just need Clar to get in touch. I toss my Com from hand to hand, agitated, impatient.

'C'mon, Clar. Come the fuck on. She must be leaving by now.'

Unless I'm wrong. Unless she has other plans. *Head, heart, gut.* I'm banking on my last hunch being at least vaguely correct. There's still a connection between Deleon and Evie. She still has a hand in her husband's disappearance. There has to be something there.

If I can't get information directly from Deleon, I'll have to infer it from what she does. I need to know where she's going to go next.

I stare at the Com, but it doesn't react. It knows I'm watching, it won't give me the satisfaction.

I should do something else.

I can't call Clar. That's not how this works. I have to wait.

I want to do something, though.

I need to do something.

I snap and I call Parker. She answers immediately.

'Sir?' There's no holo, and I can hear the traffic noise, the cough and wheeze of rush hour Trinity, even over the death rattle of the tram.

'You still in the Pod, Parker?' I check.

'Barely moved from where I picked it up.' She makes no effort to hide her weary tone. 'It's shift change, the TransWay is jammed. Every crossing is in use.'

'You heard from Johnson?' I get straight to the point.

If I can't get an update from Clar, maybe I can get one from Johnson. Who's to say that Evie hasn't gone back to her sister's place now? Even if she hasn't, ruling it out would be something. Maybe.

'Nope, have you?'

She has a point. Parker isn't Johnson's boss. She's a Cadet just the same as him. Why would he report back to her? I shake my head. She can't see that, of course.

I should have called Johnson. But my brain is pinballing around, trying to get a fix on something, anything, that will show me the way forward. Calling Parker was a reflex.

'How far from base are you?'

'I don't know.' She does sigh this time. 'I'm around the corner from the Palais. But we're stuck. This is solid. I could be hours.'

The Palais? She really hasn't got far. I'm going to make it back to Authority before her. That's annoying, quite frankly. I'm going to have to do my own donkey work.

'OK,' I say. 'Let me know when you get in. I'll let Johnson know that he'll need to stick around. I'm sure he'll appreciate the overtime.'

He will, in fact. Johnson likes a flutter, everyone knows that. It isn't healthy, and it's taking him into some rather undesirable company, but he is cultivating some useful contacts while he's wading in the filth of his maybe-addiction, so I'm not going to stop him.

What I'm actually doing here is giving him an opportunity to play with some slightly higher rollers than he could access without the overtime. This could be the start of something big for him. As long as he makes sure he doesn't get his throat cut prematurely, the road to Vice is wide open for him.

Good on him. We all have to find our way. Of course, Vice… well, everyone is going to hate him. Especially me. But I'd be disappointed if that was any influence on him going forward. I hate many people. Some of them don't even deserve it.

'Right then, out,' Parker cuts the call. Abrupt. Rude. I will need to have a word.

There's a loud bang as the Tram pulls into South District. It's lucky that this is my stop, because I'm not sure how much further this vehicle is going to get.

A brisk walk, and I'll be back in the office in less than ten minutes. At which point I'm going to have to figure out how to track Clar. I don't have a clue how to start. I was hoping Parker might have a bright idea.

CHAPTER 17

I don't have time to talk to Johnson. I mean to, but I need to drop into my office first to check for messages.

On the walk to the building, I suddenly wonder where James has got to. I need an update on what he's found out about Bjorn Barlow. I need to tell him what I know.

He's not in my office, of course, but he hasn't left any messages either. I drop into my chair, pull the bottle and mug from the bottom drawer, and put my feet up on the desk.

I just need a moment. I need to process what Eamer said, what he threatened in what he didn't say, and what exactly the consequences are likely to be. I need to compare notes with James.

Where the fuck is James?

I don't have time to spend long pondering any of this. Borate appears in the doorway.

Borate. Appears in the doorway. I can't remember the last time I saw him out of his office. Everyone thinks he has a secret elevator. Or that he sleeps in there. Yet here he is.

First Lomax, now the Chief. Maybe the bug problem isn't electronic. Maybe they're all looking for an excuse to get out and about.

This can't be good. I slide my feet off the desk and sit up, putting the drink to one side with as much nonchalant I-can-take-it-or-leave-it style as I can muster. I don't think I pull it off.

'Sir,' I say.

'Oficier Lagrange.' Borate steps in and closes the door. This is really not a good sign. 'This is not a conversation I want to be having with any of my team. Least of all one who is at what I hope is a critical point in their current investigation.'

First, *what the fuck is he talking about?* Second, *would he feel better about this conversation if he knew I was nowhere in this investigation?* Third, *if he doesn't want to have this conversation, then the answer is simple: don't have it.*

'Is something the matter?'

I am trying to sound innocent.

That should be easy because, as far as I know, I am. Not generally, but specifically. He's not actually accused me of anything yet, so that should be a straightforward position to take. I sound guilty as hell, though.

Borate takes a deep breath. He doesn't seem like he wants to say what he's about to say.

Don't fucking say it, then.

'It has come to my attention that you have been keeping company that may compromise your position,' he says. 'Your position here, at Authority.'

Shit. My stomach hits my bowel, my heart leaps into my throat. I guess there must be a massive void behind my ribcage right now. I don't know what he's talking about.

And yet I do know. Kamla.

Eamer moved fast. What has he done? Sprung her and left a trail back to me? That seems elaborate, and there hasn't been enough time. Also, that's way more subtle than he needs to be.

Something more direct, then. Does he have footage of me

in Detention? He has eyes everywhere. What about the guy I'd bumped into in the toilet, Breck? I had a weird vibe from him.

Maybe he wasn't even a keeper.

I suddenly realise that I've been thinking too long and I should have said something by now. If it were me accusing me of impropriety, I would take my silence as incriminating.

'I...'

Borate cuts me off.

'You had a call. While you were out. I understand you were chasing Evie White. That was a dumb move, Oficier. But not as dumb as giving your work contacts to prostitutes.'

Crap. Not Eamer, then. Laihla.

'Ah.'

I have nothing more to say. I will not explain myself. Especially not to Borate. I think that Borate is the sort of person I should protect Laihla from. There, I said it. I've not articulated that properly before now.

'I hope you have more to say in your defence than that in your disciplinary proceedings,' says Borate. 'I'm not a fan of you, or your methods...'

It's not a good thing that she's calling me. I would hope she's OK, but the fact that she called suggests that she isn't.

'...Or your lack of decorum.' He glances at the chipped mug on the floor. 'But I can't afford to lose an Oficier. If I could then, make no mistake, I would suspend you now. I'm not going to do that.'

Thank the Creator. I'm being stitched up here. Because I didn't give Laihla the details of my work channel. I gave her my personal Com. How did she get hold of my Authority channel?

'Thank you,' I say.

It wasn't her.

I'm very lucky that Borate isn't overreacting. But that's not as good news as it sounds. If I thought I had any leverage, any leeway with Borate, that's all just vanished. I'm hanging on by my fingernails.

'I've put a monitor on all your Com channels, personal and official,' Borate is saying. 'You should be aware of that. I don't want you making things any worse for yourself.'

'Appreciated,' I look down, with an air of humility. I think.

I'm going to have to watch what I say from now on. No time like the present to start. Borate grunts and leaves.

I pick up my Com, toss it between my hands. It wasn't Laihla, then. I can only assume this is Eamer. He's not using Kamla to get to me, after all. Maybe that means she's safe, maybe he's protecting her. Maybe he cares about what happens to her.

Maybe he's saving her for later.

I'm in trouble. I can't even imagine how much trouble I'm in. Not with Borate, I can handle that. I was right about Eamer coming for me. But I feel oddly calm.

I have too many things to do, too much on my mind, to worry about that right now. If I can make a breakthrough, then maybe I can head this off before it drags me down. I have to find out who Bjorn Barlow is. I need to know what Evie White is up to. Deleon's beyond my grasp, but I need to find out what he was doing. I need to…

My Com beeps. It's Clar. I answer. There's no holo, the signal's too weak.

'Sim,' says Clar. 'You were right.'

I punch the air. That is exactly what I need right now. I don't even care what I'm right about. But this line isn't safe anymore.

'Don't say anything else.' I say. 'We need to meet. In person.'

'I followed… The Alleys,' Clar's voice is breaking up. The

connection is poor. I don't think they heard me. 'We're deep. I'm surprised I managed… this call. Avoided… at Eamer's… with Jack. They've gone…'

'Don't say anything.' My mind is racing for a meeting place that I can communicate to Clar without giving it away to anyone listening in.

The call cuts out. Damn it. I swipe the mug from the floor and drain it.

Think Sim, think.

I'm standing outside the elevator, stabbing the button. I don't have a lot of time, and I have a lot to get done. Borate is giving me the benefit of the doubt, for now, but Eamer won't let up and this is going to keep happening. I'm going to get suspended, minimum.

I'm hoping I can spin it. It doesn't look good, but I was trying to do the right thing and I think that should count for something. I'm not so worried about that. But even if Eamer doesn't turn up the heat any more, Laihla works for him. I think that's what he's banking on.

Laihla leads to Eamer and Eamer leads to Kamla and Kamla leads to a misconduct charge that I don't think there's any coming back from. Eamer doesn't need to reveal my links to Kamla. They're going to reveal themselves.

But everything happens for a reason. Well, maybe that's not true, but every move someone like Eamer makes is for a reason. So if Eamer wants me off the board, then I'm onto something.

But what? Which of the many, many leads I've been following for the past few days is giving him cause for concern? Barlow? Deleon? Manukan? Evie White?

At one stage, I thought they were part of the same thing. What if they are, after all? All part of the web, with Eamer the great, fat spider, sitting in the middle.

What do they have in common? None of them seemed to be particularly connected. Most of them have nothing to do with my remit, yet they all landed on my plate.

Head, heart, gut. What if the connection is me? Eamer is most definitely my remit. If he's behind all this and he doesn't like what I'm up to, then I must be onto something.

The elevator doors open. It's empty. I get in and my hand hovers over the keypad. Up to find James? Or down to see Johnson?

Shit! Johnson. I didn't tell him to stay on, he's probably clocked off. My finger drifts down towards the basement, but before I can press it, a hand dives in over mine and hits the number nineteen. We're going up, then.

I take a step back and nod at the person who hijacked my lift. I don't recognise them, but they grin at me, as if they know who I am. Their lanyard suggests they're from Tech. I nod again.

'Oficier Lagrange, right?' he says.

He has a greasy air to him, his clothes don't seem to fit him. They don't look old. It's like he hasn't mentally updated his sizing and is still buying for a much younger version of himself.

'Mm-hmm. Yeah,' I confirm.

I don't want a conversation. Now I'm looking at him more closely. I think he's done this on purpose. His hair is meant to look unwashed and neglected, but it's been styled that way. The ill-fitting clothes don't make sense. His shirt's too tight, and I'm no stranger to the problems presented by a gradually expanding waistline but...

My trousers are still the right length. His are well above his ankles, skimming the tops of his socks. That makes little sense, unless he's had an adult growth spurt. Or he's wearing somebody else's clothes.

'I'm a fan,' he grins.

That's nice. I don't know what that means. I don't like people talking about me. I don't think that I want fans. There is something familiar about him, after all. I'm backtracking on not recognising him.

'Right.'

'I heard what they did, tapping your Com,' he says. 'That sucks.'

Fuck them. I don't need fucking Borate with his nose in my fucking business. I might as well throw my Com out the window, for all the use it's going to be to me now.

'Here.' He pulls a field Com from the back pocket of his too-tight trousers and hands it to me. 'They can't tap that.'

I stare at the boxy device in my hand. I've never seen one before. *Who the fuck are you? Resistance?* is what I don't say.

It's only Tech. They're bound to have loads of stuff like this hanging around the office in the basement. He's a fan. He felt sorry for me; he thought I could use it. Nothing to be worried about.

Because Resistance in the building would be bad news. News I should probably make sure that Oda is aware of.

On the other hand, my Authority career is about to get curtailed. I'm going to need something to do. Maybe I'll join up. I've always fancied getting out of the city. I bet the air up on the Northern Exposure is bracing. And I think they could use the knowledge I'd bring to the organisation. It might actually help them make a difference.

'Thanks.' I take it, dazed.

I don't really know what's going on. We hit the nineteenth floor and the doors open.

'You're doing important work,' says whoever-he-is. 'Resist.'

I try to speak, but no words come out. That seals it, does it? Are they recruiting me?

The Tech guy slips out of the doors and disappears from view. I step out of the elevator myself and turn right, the way they went, but the corridor ahead is empty.

Like I imagined the whole thing. I look down at the Field Com. It's bulky and heavy in my hand, and looks ugly with its green screen and block text. But I'm not imagining it.

Every turn I take, this thing gets weirder. I still need to figure out what's next. I still need some answers. To get some answers, I think I need to ask some relevant questions.

Where the fuck is Sergey James?

Sergey James is not in the Operations Room. His jacket is here, hung over the back of a chair which is blocking the aisle. Wherever he's gone, he got up suddenly.

I cast my eyes around the office, but there's no sign of him. I mash the control pad in front of the nearest desktop Com. It comes up with a message to tell me it's locked. By user Sergey James.

'Here!' I shout at a pair of Cadets bent over a screen a couple of desks down.

They look up.

'James,' I bark. 'Where is he?'

One Cadet straightens up, wrinkles her brow. I recognise her from earlier, downstairs, in the refectory with Parker. *This morning, was that only this morning?*

'James?' she asks. 'The guy who was working there? I...'

She looks around, lost. It is very apparent that she doesn't know who she's looking for.

'He was there a minute ago.'

That's not helpful. I need him now.

'Maybe he stepped out for coffee? Or the toilet?'

I leave a heavy pause. To her credit, she takes it stoically, returning my steady gaze, but I see her fellow Cadet squirming on her behalf. One of these two is going to make it. I'm impressed.

I grunt, which Parker's friend rightly takes as a dismissal, and march across to the small kitchen in the alcove at the far end of the floor. My march is swift and sweeping and paperwork floats to the floor in my wake. A Cadet literally scuttles away, out of my path. I appreciate my previous interaction all the more. Why is a backbone such a rare commodity these days?

When I reach the kitchenette, there's a half-full jug of coffee on the hotplate, the end of a banana loaf, a box of biscuits, open and with only crumbs remaining and a dozen unwashed mugs. There is no Sergey James.

Where next?

The toilets are in the same place on every floor, so I know to come out of the alcove and take the right turn into the corridor. A Cadet, another Cadet, a different Cadet flattens themselves against the wall, of all things, to avoid being crushed by my advance.

I shake my head with feeling, and plough on through the swing door. Someone at the urinal jumps, and is going to have to contort themselves in front of the hand dryer to save their trousers if they want to show their face back in the office in the next half hour.

I kick the cubicle doors. The first two swing back violently, smashing against the partition with a snapping bang. The state of the pans is disgusting, but there's no one in either of them.

The third door resists my flying foot. The lock rattles and holds. There's a surprised yelp from inside.

'James?'

'No, it's Melton!' comes the thin, reedy reply,

Melton? I don't think I know a Melton. Could be one of Mortimer's lot. They have a tendency to stray from their floor...

'Do you know where James is?' It's worth a try.

'James Kapstan?' asks the voice of Melton, over the sound of a flush and a fly being zipped up.

Who the fuck is that? Why would he...?

'Sergey James,' I clarify. 'My Junior Oficier.'

'Oh, right, sorry.' I can hear a quiver introduce itself into Melton's tone. 'Sorry. Oficier Lagrange, I didn't realise it was you.'

Who the fuck else behaves like this?

'No,' he says. 'I haven't seen him.'

But I'm not really listening anymore. There's a vibration coming from the pocket of my coat, the right one. I stick my hand in and pull out the field Com the Tech guy gave me in the lift. There's a call incoming.

One guess who it's from.

'James!' I answer in a tone that is meant to suggest a mixture of enthusiasm and impatience. 'I need an update, stat!'

'I think you should come out of there, sir.'

It's not Sergey James.

'Lomax?' I ask.

It's not a complete surprise that Lomax is behind something elaborate occurring in Authority. But I didn't have him pegged as Resistance.

'You should come out of there, sir,' he repeats.

'Why are you calling me from James's Com? How have you even got this Com? It's...'

'...a Resistance device. I know.' Lomax is using a voice that I recognise is specifically designed to placate me.

I won't have it. Eamer, Borate, even fucking Lomax Churchill... I'm being played. It's coming at me so fast that I can't untangle all the strings. But I will, and when I do...

Entrapment

'Just come out of the toilet, sir. There's something you need to see.'

If Lomax knows I'm in here, then he must have seen me barge in. Where is he calling me from?

'How do you know I'm in the toilet, Lomax?'

'Just come out,' he insists.

I leave the small room as Melton skulks out of his cubicle and creeps over to the sinks. I turn back towards the office, the Com still pressed to my ear.

'Not that way, sir.'

I turn.

Straight ahead is a window, which looks out onto the roof of the annexe which sticks out from the floor below. It forms a sort of balcony, albeit one with a view that is pretty much entirely TransWay.

There's someone out there.

It's James. He's standing on the edge of the balcony, his back to me, facing into the traffic fumes billowing from below. He has a Com pressed to his ear.

'What in the Creator's name is he doing?'

'Just come outside, Sir,' says James's voice.

It must be a conference channel. That's why it was James's Com that appeared on screen. I see he's holding it to his ear. He doesn't turn around.

Then he lowers the Com and gently tosses it over the edge of the building. It takes ten seconds, but the connection goes dead.

'Lomax?'

But Lomax is gone, too.

I put the bulky field Com back into my pocket.

There isn't a door, but the window opens fully. I pull it up and stick my head out. James doesn't react.

I don't want to startle him and cause him to fall, so I don't shout to him, although I want to. I want to yell all manner of abuse and reprimands in his direction. I should be worried, I suppose, but I'm not. I'm angry.

I climb clumsily through the window, catching my elbow on the frame and grazing my knuckles on the rough surface of the roof as I crawl out.

He turns as I drag myself through. He must have sensed my presence. It is weird, because he's smiling.

He's standing on the edge of a precipice, swaying gently in the breeze, staring at me, and he's smiling.

'Sim,' he says. Not "Sir" or "Boss" but "Sim".

'Sergey.' I drag my foot clear of the window frame and scramble into a standing position. I don't think I've ever called him "Sergey". Mostly it's "James", or "Junior Oficier" with an emphasis on the "Junior", or just plain "you".

'I'm going to jump,' he says matter-of-factly. 'Just so you know. There's nothing you can say to me that's going to change that so, maybe you probably shouldn't try. You'll only fail and I don't want to be on your conscience.'

We've been trained for this. James has been trained for this, so he must know I'm not just going to stand here while he jumps, or slip back inside and leave him to it.

'I can't do that, James.' It feels more comfortable calling him by his surname. I'm happy to fall back into it. 'I'm not going to do that.'

I put my hands up, keeping them where he can see them, and take a slow, exaggerated step forwards, towards him, towards the brink.

'I know,' he sighs. 'You should, though. I am going to jump.'

I don't understand. I don't see the path where he ends up here.

'What happened?'

He laughs and shakes his head.

'What happened? I saw the light. Suddenly everything snapped into place and I realised what I have to do. It's going to be OK, Sim, really.'

'Not if you jump,' I say. 'Nothing's going to be OK if you jump.'

'Nothing's going...' he repeats my words. 'Oh, man, you don't see it. I get that. It's hard, but, you know, I've seen the light. I *understand*.'

'Understand what?'

I'm trying to keep him talking, to delay the moment when he has to decide whether he is going to go through with it. But also I have no fucking clue what he's talking about. So yes, "*Understand what?*" Because I sure as hell don't understand anything at this precise moment in time.

'I found him,' he says. 'Barlow. I found him. He was expecting me.'

'Right...'

My guts drop to my feet. Something went wrong, something went badly wrong.

'You were doing your job. You were just doing your job. Whatever happened, we can...'

He cuts me off.

'Nothing happened, Sim.' "Sim" again. 'He was fine. We talked.'

OK, I'm missing something here. I don't see it.

'That's great,' I say. 'Did you bring him in? Can we go talk to him? Together? Now?'

He shakes his head.

'He left.' He offers no further explanation. 'You were right, though. His name isn't Barlow. He said he was trying to get your attention. He got mine instead, but... Thank you.'

Thank you?

'Thank you for what?' I ask.

I am not comfortable with the way this conversation is going. I feel that I've lost control. I feel like James is steering it somewhere that I don't want it to go, building to something. I don't want to admit that I know what, but...

He's standing right on the edge. I see his toes move in his shiny, shiny shoes. He's flexing them. Getting ready to jump.

'Sergey, I don't know what this is about but I know you don't really want to...'

'Thank you for letting me meet him,' smiles James. 'You didn't know what you were giving me but... I will always be grateful for that. And I'm sorry.'

'Sorry?'

I stay calm. It's the only tool I have left. I know, now, that I'm not going to be able to stop him. I'm too far away to grab him and I daren't get closer for fear of pushing him to that point quicker. I just need to find something, something to keep him here.

'You keep saying I don't know, and that I don't understand. I don't, you're right, but I'd like to...'

'You will.' The smile drops. 'Stay safe Sim. You're in more trouble than you realise. I'll see you. Later.'

And with that, Sergey James steps off the building and drops, like a stone, onto the pavement below.

CHAPTER 18

The traffic noise vanishes. The mouths of the people who are suddenly all around me - their faces masks of shock and horror as they look over the edge, as they recoil, as they grab me by the arm and by the shoulders and pull be back inside the building - those mouths open and close, lips making shapes, tongues flapping, but no sound seems to come out.

I allow myself to be led. I allow myself to be put in a chair and left. There are too many people here, now, too many eyes on me, too much discussion, too much action. It's all too much.

I go back to my office to wait. I take the back stairs, because it's quieter, slipping out through the door behind the chair I've been sitting in. I descend slowly, counting every step. My office is five floors down. There are forty-five steps. Counting them helps fill up my brain a little, so I don't have to think as much.

I assume that someone is going to want to talk to me. I know that's protocol. I don't think I want to tell anyone about what just happened, how it was for me, what led up to James jumping, but I should. I need to sort through the thoughts in my head, so that I can present them in a way that makes sense.

But I can't think straight. I'm no longer cluttered with too many thoughts, getting in each other's way, jostling for my limited attention. Now my mind is windswept and bleak. There is nothing there anymore except the image of James stepping off the ledge. His smile, before he stepped off. He said that he would see me later. He said that I would understand. He got that wrong. I don't.

He wasn't upset; he wasn't distressed, he was, if anything, peaceful. He is, now, none of those things. He's dead.

I rub my eyes furiously, slide open the drawer and reach for the bottle. I throw my head back and upend it into my mouth. Three drops strike my tongue where they sizzle and fade. It's empty now. I look at it in disgust and launch it across the room, where it thuds unsatisfactorily on the carpet.

I don't expect to understand why he did it. My sense of self-preservation is too strong. Don't get me wrong, I hate myself more than anyone, but I've made my peace with that. I've created my own personal torture chamber where I can make sure I get everything that's coming to me. Death would be too easy. I won't let myself off like that.

But James? I don't expect to *understand* why he did it, but I should *know* why he did it. And I have no idea. He was happy; he *thanked* me. What did Barlow say to him? Why did he seem to think that he was going to something better?

Barlow.

Bjorn fucking Barlow.

Bjorn Barlow doesn't exist. This is Eamer's doing, somehow.

Fear races up my spine. This has escalated quickly. But I know it, I can feel it. Eamer left me in no doubt that he knows what we tried to do with Barlow. He's already started fucking with me through Laihla.

Now he's showing me what he can really do.

I don't know what I'm close to finding out. I don't know

why he wants to scare me off. But this is a warning shot, one across the bows to slow me down and show me who rules the waves.

He's showing me that he's the Lord of the dance.

It's worse that he's using my subterfuge against me. I thought I was being so clever, in the way that only somebody doing something spectacularly dumb can. It's not too late, though.

I can feel a rage building, a sense of wrong having been done. I welcome it. This is my fuel, this is my fire. This is the reason that I do what I do. I need this.

Welcome back, friend.

My mind fills with plans, with motivations. Fills with a determination to find Bjorn Barlow, whoever he is. I thought he would lead me to Manukan's killer. Maybe he will, but only if that's also Eamer. Otherwise I don't care.

I reach across my desk and pull my tablet to me.

There's a knock at my door. I look up. It's Rey. I sigh. It makes sense. She's responsible for personnel. I had assumed that someone was going to want to talk to me. I had hoped that it would be someone else.

'Sim…' She pulls the pinched face I've seen so many times before. She thinks it expresses sympathy.

She takes a step inside the room and half raises her arms, as if she's going to come around the desk and hug me where I'm sitting. I don't respond, and she drops them.

I'm not going to hug her. That's what got me in trouble last time. I was a lot drunker last time, mind you. I'm not proud of that.

Rey takes the seat opposite me. She puts her head on one side. More performative sympathy. She must be forgetting that I know how empty her heart is.

'You should go home. You don't need to be working.'

On the contrary... I say nothing. She'll only tell Borate, who will decide that suspending me would be the best thing for everyone. And I need Authority resources if I'm going to find Barlow.

'It's a shock for everyone. I spoke to the rest of the Operations Room. No one had any sense that he wasn't feeling himself.'

I've worked in the Operations Room when I was a Junior myself. No one pays the slightest attention to anyone around them, unless they're banging. Or want to bang. It's very much an every-Cadet-for-themselves environment. You could take an overdose at your desk and no one would have any sense that you weren't feeling yourself.

Again, I say nothing.

Rey pulls another face, which I struggle to interpret, but I think she's trying to acknowledge that I'm not saying anything and communicate that it's OK and she understands. Without saying anything herself.

This is dumb.

'Apparently, he took a call, then left the room. The next thing anyone knew was you screaming from the roof.'

'I was shouting.' I break my silence.

This isn't important, this detail, but I want to make this point. I'm not altogether certain that it's true, either. I might have screamed. I don't want Rey thinking I screamed, though.

'I didn't scream.'

'Sorry.' She pouts a little. 'I didn't mean anything. It must have been very distressing. Horrific. Awful...'

'Who did he get a call from?' I ask.

I assume that was it, that was Barlow. That was the trigger. But I realise James said he met Barlow. I'd had the impression then that Barlow had said whatever he'd said in person. So the call could have been someone else. I do not know who. But I'd like to know.

'We don't know,' Rey replies. 'I…'

Head, heart, gut. Alarm bells are ringing now. Only in my head, but they're loud and they're impossible to ignore.

'Has no one traced the call?' I demand.

I'm standing up now, I'm pushing around my desk, I'm walking to the door, leaving Rey spluttering and lost for words. Not as lost as I am.

The Operations Room is on lockdown. I can't get past the door, partly because it's locked, partly because there's someone keeping me out.

I don't recognise them, but I rarely interact with Security. Not since I was a Cadet. There are a lot of very pissed off looking Cadets inside the room who aren't interacting with Security either. Presumably he's already told them they aren't leaving.

He is bigger than Eamer. I wouldn't have argued if I were in their position.

I notice a couple of Oficiers, both Junior and Senior, a handful of them over by the kitchen. I guess I was lucky not to be kept back myself. I wonder if it was seniority or trauma that saved me.

This is a problem, though, because anyone who might have interacted with James immediately before he went out onto the roof is in there. Anyone who might have interacted with James in the aftermath of what seems like a critical call, the Com device on which he took the call on, any possessions he had on him, all of it is locked away behind a door and a very substantial glass partition.

Clues, all of them just outside of my reach.

'How long until…?' I ask the Security guy.

He stares at me. The stare is as expressive as the shrug he

doesn't give. It's impressive how still he can stand. He's coiled, ready to spring, at the slightest provocation. I am in no mind to provoke him. He'd flatten me.

'Until they're done,' he says, eventually.

I wait, but it doesn't seem like he is going to say anything else. I don't see the point in further conversation. It doesn't feel like I'm going to get anything more from him. I press my face against the glass.

My mind wanders back to the roof, and my conversation with James. He'd said some strange things, some out of character things. He'd not seemed himself, but not in an agitated or anxious way.

He'd been calm. Serene, almost. He reminded me of somebody.

Bjorn Barlow. It was the same, superior, all-knowing air that Barlow had exuded in the interview room.

Why? Why would Eamer pick someone like that? If it was to confuse me, then he's done a great job. But I don't see why he needed to do that. I'd already contacted Laihla. He already had me on the hook. Why was he trying to turn up the heat?

Was the plan to use Barlow to brainwash James into jumping off the building and implicate me in his death because the Grey Knight plot was my idea? It's possible, but... *Head, heart, gut...* it really seems like there are too many variables at play there. Not enough guarantees that it would work. Too inefficient for Eamer. You can usually see what he's up to. Not from a mile off, but when you get up close. Like I am now.

And I can't see it. So what was the point?

I'm trying to connect all the dots here. I'm trying to make everything add up. But what if it doesn't? What if it never did?

I was so set on linking Barlow to Manukan to White and Deleon. It made so much sense until it didn't. What if it's the same here, in trying to link Barlow to Eamer? Except Eamer said he knew. He knew what we tried, and he knew that we'd spoken to Barlow and…

No. No, he didn't say that. He didn't say much. I play the exchange in my head a few times. He frowned when I mentioned Barlow having been in my cells. I glossed over it at the time, but he didn't give me any sign that he understood what I was saying.

He didn't know about that part.

What does that leave me with? Two Bjorn Barlows. One who doesn't exist, that I invented and pretended to embed in the Black Knights as an undercover operative. A ridiculous plot that Eamer saw through. Then a second Bjorn Barlow, who also doesn't exist, not really, but who has assumed the name and deliberately engineered a meeting with me. Then he convinced Sergey James to jump off the Authority building.

Mouse had implied there were more, that none of them were real. I thought that meant that Eamer knew about the Cleric. Maybe he didn't. Maybe she just meant that he'd created more Bjorn Barlows, turning our deception to his own ends, using the name as an all-purpose pseudonym.

No one has ever said that he knew about this one.

This theory is weak too, but there's something about it that feels right. *Head, heart, gut*, we're almost there. Someone else is trying to fuck with me. Until now, I don't think that I knew they existed.

Something makes me turn back towards the elevator - James's ghost whispering in my ear. There's nothing I can do here.

Parker is sitting, perched awkwardly on a plastic stool, next to the lift door. She has her head in her hands, but she hears me move and looks up, jumping to her feet when she sees me. Her complexion is pale, like she's seen a ghost. I'm not the ghost.

'You're back,' I say, as I approach.

'Sir…' She hesitates.

There are tears in her eyes. My own eyes prick. This is a mess. Now I think it's my fault, it's even more of a mess. I don't know what to say to her.

'Are you OK?' she asks me. That's what I could have asked her.

'No, of course you're not,' she continues, and bobs as if she's about to move towards me and hug me but then thinks better of it. 'I… I would have come to find you straight away, but I thought you'd still be… you know, questions. Or support.'

Funny, I'd had little of either. It was good of her to think of my wellbeing. It had taken me a moment to think of hers. I don't think of my subordinates having personal relationships with each other. I realise how little I know about the people I rely on.

'They let me go be sad on my own. But I couldn't stay away.'

I indicate the Operations Room. Parker nods her understanding.

'It's hard to believe he's gone.'

I have a sense that she wants to talk about it. I don't. I have things to do. I have things I want her to do.

Something stops me. I realise that this is a time to pause.

So here, in the quiet of the nineteenth floor corridor, with just a Security guy as a witness, I do something I don't think I can remember having done before. I ask Parker how she's feeling.

'Were you two close?' I ask.

I don't know what I mean by that. Friends? Lovers? Siblings? I realise that, other than the difference in names which could be easily explained away, they could be any of those things and I wouldn't know. I know nothing about those people's lives.

'I guess.'

Parker gives a little half smile. It's warm, affectionate, but casual. I recognise the look. It's very her, I suppose. I'd never tried to interpret it before.

'He was an idiot,' she went on, 'but he meant well. He's got this thing... had this thing...'

I know this. I've felt this before. I've lost plenty of people in my life and I'm not a monster. It's easy to lose track of the appropriate tense, and the impact of that is intense. It's as if talking about them brings them back for a moment.

Then you stumble and they're gone.

I should say this to Parker. It might help. I don't, though, and I don't understand why.

'He had this thing...' She picks up her thread, again, with a sniff. '...for Kassi. You know, my friend...'

I don't. One of the Cadets, I guess. I am ill equipped for this conversation, in all sorts of ways.

'...so he was always hanging around. He used to pop up in places where we were. Nights out and stuff, you know?'

I used to. These days, most of my nights out are spent propping up a bar, mostly on my own. Given how often that bar is Eamer's, those nights probably count as work, anyway.

'How about you?' she asks.

She thinks it's just her I'm distant from. Maybe she thinks it's because she's more junior, or because she's a woman, but she's assuming that my relationship with James was any different from the one I have with her. It hurts a bit. I like her rather more than I ever liked him. That sounds harsh, to say that now. I keep all of it to myself.

'Oh, I didn't really... we didn't really know each other outside of work.' I'm dissembling. 'But, you know. He was a valued colleague and... I can't help but think that if I said something different, if I...'

Parker cuts me off with a firm hand on my forearm. Her touch jerks me back into the moment. This is fine. I'm sure James deserved our thoughts and prayers, but what he really deserves is some answers to why this happened to him.

'Don't blame yourself,' she says.

I'm not, although I realise that's a reasonable interpretation of what I just said. But really, I was just saying things, the things you're meant to say, playing the mood music, reading the room. Or the corridor. I'm twitchy now. I've remembered about the things to do.

'Was it horrible?' she asks. 'I can't believe he did it.'

'It wasn't fun.'

I don't watch my tone this time, my brain is already descending in the elevator on the way to get some answers.

Terse. That's how I sound. Terse and dismissive, just like I usually do.

'And no, I can't believe he did it. Not on his own, anyway. Apparently, he got a call just before. I wanted to see if anyone knew who it was from.'

Parker's demeanour changes, suddenly. She straightens up, looking ready for something, looking pleased with herself.

'That's why I'm here.' She brightens, especially compared with moments ago. 'I know who called him. That's what I came to tell you. I was waiting for you to come out. When I thought you were still in there...'

I wish she'd get to the point. And then she does. And then I know who it is who's been fucking with me. I feel like I should be more surprised.

'It was Evie White,' she says. 'I came to tell you I found Evie White.'

Entrapment

I feel sick. All the way down in the elevator, from the nineteenth floor to Control in the basement, I'm repeating it. In my head, under my breath, on a loop.

'I don't believe it. It can't be right.'

If I thought I couldn't think straight earlier, then I don't know what state I'm in now.

I almost missed it. I almost convinced myself that this was all random, that there was no grand plan, no connection between all the things that have been happening.

But Evie White called James before. James jumped because of what Barlow said to him. That must connect them. And if Barlow is connected to Evie, then maybe that connects him to Deleon. Then to Jack White. Then back to Manukan.

My head is spinning, even if it's now spinning in the opposite direction from before. What I can't deny is that Evie White is very important in this.

The way she taunted me, like she wanted a reaction.

A thought hits me like a lightning bolt. Was it even Eamer trying to compromise me in the first place? I was quick to blame him. He's an obvious culprit. But I have no actual evidence that any of this came from Eamer.

There's a world in which I'm very useful to him right where I am. I'm a known quantity, and I'm compromised in his favour. He knows about my connections to Kamla. Nobody else does, yet, and I'm keen to keep it that way. That's quite a hold he has over me there. Does it make sense for him to throw all that away?

Shit. I've got this all wrong. But that's not the bit I've got most wrong.

I'm looking at the clip looping on the screen where Parker has pulled it up. The stream of Evie White. At her sister's apartment.

There are some rocks on which my certainty rests, some

things that will always hold. I can trust Clar. They are unimpeachable. They have never let me down. They would never let me down. Even making honest mistakes is not their style.

But Parker is showing me the stream and there she is, Evie White, arriving at her sister's condominium in the same TransPod I chased down a side street. It has a scratch up the side.

She gets out, goes inside and, ten minutes later, I can see the data log record a call from inside the apartment to Sergey James's personal Com.

The timing lines up perfectly with when I talked to Clar, the moment they tried to tell me she was deep in The Alleys. Almost to the minute.

Two pieces of information which can't both be true. And I'm looking at one of them with my own eyes.

'I don't have audio,' says Parker. 'On the call. I can't play you what she said to him.'

It's fair enough, if anyone has encryption that Authority can't break, it would be the Chaguartay clan.

'I don't need to hear it,' I reassure her.

That's not really true. If I knew what she said to James, then I might know why he jumped. I might learn what the connection to Barlow is. I might learn if there is a connection to Barlow or whether I'm just trying too hard to join dots that I'm not even sure are really there.

I don't want to hear it. I'm not ready

The call audio would be a dot, though. Knowing what Clar is playing at would be one more.

I find one of these dots. I think I've realised how I can track Clar.

'I need you to stay and monitor her. Evie White. If she moves, I need to know.'

Entrapment

'Where are you going?' asks Parker.

I'm not going to tell her that.

'While Evie's staying put, I need to lock down another moving piece.'

I think that sounds important enough, without committing me to anything. I still don't know who's trying to bring me down and whilst I don't think it's Parker, she's presenting me with some surprising, contradictory evidence about someone I definitely do suspect.

She doesn't look happy about it, though.

'I've worked a double shift here, and you're definitely the one who forgot to tell Johnson to stick around. Can't you pull him out of the bar? He can't be that drunk yet. He isn't you.'

I stare at Parker. I don't know what to do with her talking to me like this. Unfortunately, I can't argue with most of what she said.

'Sorry…' She speaks before I can form the words for my response. She rubs her face. 'I'm tired. I shouldn't have said that. Of course I'll stay on.'

I shouldn't let her do this. I want to, but I know I shouldn't. I don't need to punish her. She's not a suspect.

'I'll get someone else.' I actually mean that, although I don't know who I can get. Solzinger, maybe. Although he'll be shit at it. 'I'm not being fair. You need to rest.'

I see her shoulders drop as she releases the pent up frustration.

'Can you sleep onsite, though?' I ask. 'Just in case?'

There are cabins in the lower basement. They're horrible.

'I guess,' she says with a resigned shrug. 'You really need me for this?'

'I really need you on this,' I lie.

Better that she thinks it's her indispensability that is top of mind. I don't want her getting too far away. She's not a suspect, but I don't want her disappearing on me. I need to know where she is. I keep losing people.

I still don't believe that Clar is mistaken. So Parker might be.

I definitely don't believe that Clar is lying to me. So Parker might be.

She's not a suspect, but she could easily become one.

CHAPTER 19

I have a feeling that I'm going to need to employ advanced Clar-finding techniques tonight. Even though I think I know where they are, it won't be as simple as hanging around The Alleys until I bump into trouble. The Alleys are vast, and the only thing I got from their call was that they were deep.

I'm going to need some help. Fortunately, I know just the person.

I don't actually know where Jo Jo is living at the moment. I know, for a while, he was bedding down on Clar's sofa, because I remember a very heavy insinuation that I should take him in round about that time.

It was an insinuation that I resisted. Jo Jo seemed quite happy on Clar's sofa, and the last thing I needed was a flatmate.

Later on, Jo Jo seemed even happier in Clar's bed. I chose to see that as a vindication of my resistance. I was just lucky, I think. Still, they're good together, as far as I can tell.

Kamla's apartment has been vacant since she was detained, so there's a good chance Jo Jo has moved back home, without the need to make things up with his mother. He and

Clar are just a casual thing, they both claim. Who am I to judge?

I'm taking a chance on him being home. The lights blasting hot from every window suggest I am right.

This is a nice area. She's done well for herself, by which I mean Eamer did well by her. North of the centre, most of the apartments, Kamla's included, are two storeys. Twice as many windows to illuminate. Jo Jo has risen to that challenge admirably.

He takes a while to answer the door, which he does in person.

'Sim!' he says, with a brightness that contradicts his dishevelled, bleary-eyed appearance.

He's never called me "dad", even though we've both long accepted that's probably what I am. I don't think we need it.

He lurches forwards and pulls me into a tight hug. He smells of stale sweat and last night's alcohol.

'Are you OK?' he asks, into my shoulder. 'Haven't seen you in a while.'

'I've been busy.' I step back.

He scratches the back of his neck.

'Yeah, same.'

There's a pause. It's awkward. That goes without saying.

'Why are you here?' he asks.

My emotions suddenly deliver a gut punch, taking me by surprise. I feel guilty. This isn't nice. I'm no stranger to self loathing, but that doesn't mean that I want to feel like the bad guy. I don't want to feel like the bad guy in front of my son.

But I can't pretend I'm here for anything other than what I am, which isn't a father-son catch up.

'I need your help.'

Straight out with it, not trying to build up to it. Just there, *blah!* No attempt to make this look like anything else. Straight talking is a strength, in many situations that I find myself in.

Maintaining positive family relationship is not one of those situations.

Jo Jo sighs, with a strong hint that this was entirely what he was expecting.

'You'd better come in, then.'

He stands aside. I squeeze past him, down the hallway and into the kitchen. You can tell that Kamla isn't living here at the moment. Her aversion to dirt would send her running back to Detention before she set foot in this kitchen.

She doesn't cook, so this was never a functional room for her. In its current state, this isn't a functional room for Jo Jo, either, but for completely different reasons. There isn't an available surface. They're too crowded with precarious stacks of unwashed plates, glasses with an assortment of dregs - enough to make a punch for a small soirée - and grease. So much grease.

I look around for somewhere to perch, or lean, or sit, but I don't think I should risk any of it. Jo Jo shuffles into the room. He's wearing a grubby dress shirt and red striped boxer shorts. He has one sock on, the other foot is bare. He looks like he was recently sleeping.

'Did I get you up?'

'Kind of.' Jo Jo rubs his face. 'I wasn't in bed, but I wasn't awake. What is it now? Early morning, early evening, or tomorrow?'

'Early evening.'

'Thought so. It wasn't that big of a bender.'

He produces a kettle from behind a stack of plates, unplugs it with a tug and takes it to the tap. He has to angle it to get around the other stack of plates in the sink, but he needn't worry about spilling any water because nothing happens when he twists the handle.

'No tea,' he says, putting the kettle back down on top of

one of the stacks. 'You, er, you said something about helping you? Is this going to involve me having to get dressed? I'm going to need a shower if I'm going out.'

'I...' I shrug. 'It depends, I guess.'

I'm not sure I'm keen on taking him anywhere. Definitely not in this state and I'm not sure I have enough time to wait for him to get out of this state. I cut to the chase.

'Do you know where Clar is?'

'Ha!' Jo Jo exclaims.

This question seems to delight him, and he almost skips across the kitchen, to the fridge, where he opens the door. A wave of sour air hits me. It makes me want to retch and I'm not nursing a fresh hangover.

It doesn't seem to touch Jo Jo, though. The boy is made of stern stuff. I'm weirdly proud.

'Is that a yes?'

I'm not sure what the decaying contents of his fridge have to do with the answer.

Jo Jo doesn't reply, instead he takes a plastic bag out of what might, in another kitchen, be a salad drawer. Inside the bag is a bulky-looking piece of tech. It looks a lot like the Com I was given in the elevator by the suspicious Tech, who I now strongly suspect might have been working for Evie White.

I should get Parker on that. Maybe she can pull some footage, find out where he went afterwards. I also should get her to talk to Lomax. I need to know who gave him the contact for that Com.

'Is that a field Com?'

'That *was* a field Com,' nods Jo Jo. 'I hacked it a bit. Now it's a Clar Tracker.'

'A what? Why do you..? Can I..?'

I grab it out of his hand. It's cold to the touch, and a bit slippery. The screen is dark.

Jo Jo leans over and flicks a switch. The Com springs to life, a green map appearing on its green screen. A green dot pulses in the middle with an accompanying beep.

'There they are.'

Jo Jo lifts a milk carton from the still open fridge to his lips. He takes a large swig, before his face changes and he turns to spit a stream of spoiled milk into the sink,

'How come you have a tracker on Clar?' I ask, ignoring the disgusting sight of my son narrowly avoiding food poisoning and watching the dot on my screen move back and forth.

'I'm meant to have their back,' shrugs Jo Jo, wiping his mouth. 'It's difficult to do that if I don't know where they are.'

'So, where is this?'

I hold the Com out in front of me. He squints at it.

'Do you need glasses?' I ask.

Jo Jo ignores me and swipes the Com from my hand to hold it closer to his face. He does need glasses. He shrugs and hands it back to me.

'In The Alleys,' he says, picking up a packet of biscuits from the counter. He peers inside it.

'Can I take this?'

'Go for it,' says Jo Jo, throwing the packet down on the table. Something tiny scuttles out of the opening. 'Fucking ants, get everywhere.'

'Thanks,' I say. 'I need to go.'

'See you around,' says Jo Jo.

I feel bad. I got what I wanted, now I'm off. I wonder what he wants, what he needs. I wonder if I should give him a hug. I don't usually. I watch him pick a stray ant from his sleeve and squash it. He looks up.

'You still here?'

'I... yes, Bye.' I turn awkwardly. 'Get your eyes tested.'

'It was good to see you, dad.'

I half turn back. He's smiling.

'I won't leave it so long next time,' I mutter, before I scuttle down the hallway and out the front door.

Clar isn't moving anymore. I can see that dot deep in The Alleys, and it's staying put. When I say deep in The Alleys, I mean deep.

I don't think I'd venture that far voluntarily, even with mapping functionality at my disposal. I always like to be within striking distance of a way out. Sometimes you have to find one at short notice, and there isn't often much time for messing about.

So Clar is deep and stationary. That does not bode well. I approach the next corner with caution. If Jo Jo's tracker is to be believed, they're right around it.

I've thought this through, though. Deep in The Alleys, this deep in The Alleys, and not moving.

There's usually a reason for that.

It usually means you're dead.

I press myself up against the wall, just before it ends, and tip my head around, slowly so as not to catch the eye of anyone murderous who may be lurking. My right eye sweeps around until I can just about see around the corner. All my left eye can see is the brick of the wall. Around the corner I see…

Nothing.

It's dark. There is a phenomenon in The Alleys where, in some sections, the shadows seem darker for no reason that has anything to do with the light or the height of the walls.

Some sections just seem to suck in the light. This is what I'm dealing with here, apparently. I give my eye a moment to adjust, but it makes no difference. I can't make out shapes in the gloom, other than those I am pretty certain I've imagined.

I can't see anything, but that doesn't mean that there isn't anything to see.

There's two ways I can go from here. I can inch my way around until I *can* see something, with the attendant risk of the something I see being someone else, patiently waiting for me to make enough of myself visible so that they can stab or shoot me. Instead, I could leap out and hope to leverage the element of surprise.

I slide my hand to my hip, under my coat, and check the reassuring lump of my gun. It's nothing special, standard issue for Authority, but it will make a mess of anyone I fire it into. I just have to see them first.

I consider my options again. Careful or surprise?

I go for surprise and jump out from my cover into a crouch, my hand pulling out my weapon as I stand back up, which I raise to aim at…

Nothing.

There is no one here, dead or alive. There is just me, and the gloom and…

I feel the icy edge of a blade against the side of my neck.

This is exactly what I was trying to avoid, with the jumping and crouching and the element of surprise. Which hasn't worked for me at all.

The owner of the knife grasps my wrist and I drop the gun. It would not be much use to me, not when my opponent was behind me. I should have looked in the other direction. They must have watched me from the shadows. They always had the upper hand.

I shift my weight onto my right foot, lean away from the blade. They catch what I'm doing and push it against me harder.

I feel my pulse in my neck, imagine it cut, the blood pumping out. My stomach turns. I'm not good with the thought of my blood. I can handle anyone else's, but mine belongs inside my body. I try to think of how I can ensure it stays in there.

'I don't have any quarrel with you,' I say. 'I'm just looking for someone. I haven't seen anything. I don't want to see anything. You lose nothing by letting me go. If you kill me, you've got a body to dispose of. Maybe *another* body to dispose of. I don't know, I don't care. It's none of my business. I can save you any hassle, though. Just let me go. You'll never see me again.'

I hope beyond hope that I've caught someone in the middle of something they rather I didn't see, instead of someone determined to rob me of my worldly possessions. Not that those two things are mutually exclusive, but I can't afford whoever this is to go through my pockets.

Once they know I'm Authority, then there's no way they're letting me go, regardless of what I promise I haven't seen. I still have no clue of who they are. That's not altogether true. I can smell the whisky on their breath. His breath, I'm guessing.

'I don't know who you think I am, Oficier Lagrange,' he hisses, cold and cruel in my ear. 'But we both know that isn't true, don't we?'

Shit, it's Mishka. This will not end well for me. I'm good as dead. I close my eyes and pray.

I don't actually pray, of course. I don't believe in anything. Who or what would I pray to? Even if I did, I definitely would not be praying to my actual saviour on this occasion.

A noise, a clang of metal in front of me, causes my eyes to open again. Out of the darkness barrels a figure dress in black, camouflaged by the gloom. I throw myself sideways, to the right, and they thrust forward and take down the slight figure of Mishka in a flying tackle.

Entrapment

Taken by surprise, the knife flies from his hand to clatter to the floor on the opposite side of the alley.

Mouse pins Mishka to the floor. She must be half the size of the wiry assassin. I have never been so pleased to see her.

Mouse lowers her head, snarls something unheard into Mishka's ear. He spits back in her face. Mouse's voice catches in her throat, the shock of the disgusting assault catching her out.

She wipes her face on her sleeve, and then punches Mishka, hard, on the side of his head.

'That will keep him quiet for a bit.' She climbs off the now unconscious Mishka. 'What the hell were you playing at, Sim?'

'I was trying to find Clar.' I wave Jo Jo's device. 'They aren't moving. I'm worried they're dead. Doubly so now that I know Mishka's lurking.'

Mouse shakes her head.

'Not dead, no. AWOL, certainly.' Mouse holds up what I recognise to be Clar's Com. 'But Mishka's no threat. If I can take him down, then Clar would have no trouble. I don't know where they've got to, but I've a feeling they'll be OK.'

I'm not so certain, but that's not what is bothering me right now.

'Where did you come from, anyway?' I ask, picking up my fallen gun.

This is suspicious. I consider Mouse to be on the right side of most arguments, but the same can't be said for her employer. I haven't completely ruled out Eamer trying to screw me over. And this is a suspicious place to be lurking at this time of night. Or literally any other time that there is.

She gestures to the dustbin, lying on its side in a rare pool of light. That would be what the clang was.

'You were hiding? From Mishka? Because I think you just showed that you don't need to hide from…'

'No, not Mishka.' Mouse cuts me off. 'I was hiding from the Authority Oficier who suddenly appeared while I was on not altogether legitimate business…'

'Not altogether legitimate?' I repeat.

'For the soil and the soul,' she says, by way of a cryptic explanation.

'Resistance? You?' I'm surprised.

'You know me, I love to surprise.'

'But it's not something I should know about?'

'Am I still hiding?'

'No…' I'm not sure where she's going with this.

'It's not your beat. Don't worry about it.'

I look at her blankly enough that she feels the need to elaborate.

'Resistance needs to get information to Opposition,' she says, 'and vice versa. I… facilitate that.'

'Facilitate?'

She's right, it's not my beat, but I'd like to know how it works. If for no other reason that to hold something over Oda. I know he's baffled by how Resistance knows so much about what's going on inside the city walls. He's tried to intercept their dispatches, but there's very little Com traffic.

'They make drops.' She taps her breast pocket where a drive shaped box is snugly tucked. 'Here, in The Alleys.'

'How do they get into The Alleys?'

I think it's a good question. Mouse evidently doesn't.

'Ummm, where do half the Research tunnels come out in the city?'

'Ummm, I don't know?'

'Fuck me, it always amazes me how little you lot know,' she scoffs, 'and I already thought you knew nothing.'

'That's not necess…' I begin, but Mouse pushes me back into the shadows. Further back into the shadows.

'Shhh,' she hisses. 'Keep your voice down. You hear that?'

I listen. The grinding of gears, metal on metal, but dampened, muffled. I feel the slight vibrations through my feet. Something is happening under the cobbles.

'What is it?'

'They're coming back,' whispers Mouse, pulling my arm down. 'I'm not supposed to be here.'

I drop into a crouch.

'Who's coming back?'

'Agent Wright. That's who made the drop. He's an idiot. He probably dropped his Com. Or he thinks he's dropped his Com, but he hasn't. It'll be in his pocket...'

She pulls me deeper into the shadow. I didn't think that was possible.

'But whatever the reason, I'm not meant to be here anymore. He's not meant to meet me. And he certainly can't find you here. He's an idiot, but he's an idiot with a weapon. So fucking hide.'

A hatch opens up in the ground, shooting light skyward like a beacon. I see why Mouse was so keen to get as far back as we could, because the alleyway is suddenly flooded with light. It dramatically reduces the amount of available shadow, but it does make that shadow appear even darker. We are perfectly hidden.

Then I see who emerges and suddenly it all makes sense. I know who's been playing with me.

Except it can't be. I saw the footage myself. You can't fake an Authority screen. There are digital watermarks and encryption and fuck knows what else. That was not faked.

But if it wasn't fake, then the person I can see coming out of the open hatch, the person who Clar told me would be here... if Parker didn't fake the footage, then this must be the woman who did.

Because there she is. Even clambering out of a hole in the ground, she's poised. And even in the darkness, it's unmistakable who she is.

Evie White, I'd stake my life on it, is climbing out of the hatch and brushing herself down, looking around and walking with purpose, back up the alleyway past Mouse and me hiding in the shadows. She doesn't see us and we don't make a sound until a count of twenty after she rounds the corner.

I gasp. I was holding my breath. Mouse's splutters suggest she was as well. A silence hangs between us for a beat.

'What are you even doing here, Sim?' she asks. I can't see her face clearly, but her tone suggests confusion. 'This has nothing to do with you.'

'Oh, believe me, I think it does. Evie White has been leading me a merry dance all day. I had Clar tailing her, and now Clar's gone missing.'

'Clar can look after themselves,' she says.

'I hope so…'

I genuinely do. I don't have time to find out what happened to Clar, not right now. I have to trust that Mouse is right. At least she found their Com. She can get it back to them.

'But there's something strange happening. I had to see for myself,' I say.

I still do. I hook my Com out of my pocket, punch in Control. I don't care if someone's listening in on this one. I've got an actual, genuine lead here.

'And now there's something I need to check.'

Parker answers, she's not in the cabin. I doubt there's anyone else still around. Full marks for dedication.

'You were meant to tell me if she left.' I say.

'Hi boss. Nice of you to check in. I will tell you if she leaves, but as it stands, there's nothing to report. Evie White remains inside her sister's apartment. Drinking tea, maybe coffee, could be chocolate. Or soup.'

She must have a way into Research from the condo. It happens a lot. The foundations of most of Trinity's building are only a couple of layers of bricks removed from the Research labs. There are breaches all over the place. It makes you wonder why they even bother with security. My brain finishes processing the words that Parker said.

'What do you mean? Why would it matter what she's been drinking?'

'It doesn't,' admits Parker, 'not really. But I can see she's nursing a mug of something and there's no one here to talk to so I've been speculating. To kill time.'

'You can see..?' I'm confused. I stop.

'Here…' The screen of my Com flickers as Parker casts the drone feed from outside Sara Chaguartay's building to my device.

I can see her too, now, stood in the frame of a large window, staring out onto the street. Evie White is holding a mug in two hands, blowing the steam from the top.

I zoom the picture, hoping to spot something off. Maybe it's her sister. Maybe it's a decoy or a mannequin or just an unlikely reflection of a photograph, enlarged by some chance of perspective.

It isn't, though. It's Evie White. The same Evie White who has also, undeniably, just passed us in The Alleys. It's too far. There's no conceivable way that she could have made it back in such a brief space of time. There is only one conclusion that I could come to, but I am struggling to do that. Because it is preposterous.

There are two Evie Whites.

CHAPTER 20

I cut the connection and my screen goes blank. As the hatch slides closed, eclipsing the bright light emanating from underground, the alleyway falls back into pitch darkness.

Mouse has seen what I have seen. I heard her gasp.

'Two Evie Whites?' she asks. 'How does that work?'

I rub my eyes, put my Com back in my pocket.

'I don't know,' I say. 'I don't know how and I don't know why and I don't know what I'm going to do about it.'

I don't even know what this is. There can't be, literally, two of her, obviously. So one of them is a double, a decoy. Or one of them isn't really there. The Evie White who just appeared in the alleyway in front of us looked pretty real, so she must have done something to mess with the feed that Parker's monitoring.

Head, heart, gut. I know that's not possible. If there's one thing Authority is good at, it's watching people, usually without them realising that they're being watched. Doing anything about what we see them do is less of a strength, but watching people is our speciality.

I can't deny what I just saw here, though. Parker may be

watching something utterly fake and pointless. I should pull her off that. She's exhausted as it is. I need to be fair. I don't want to be that cruel.

I take my Com back out and tap a message. STAND DOWN. SWITCH TO PASSIVE RECORD. GET SOME SLEEP.

'Just so I'm clear,' I say. 'That was definitely Evie White we saw right there.'

I need to check that I'm not losing my grip on reality, because it feels like I am.

'You saw what I saw,' says Mouse.

'Not helpful,' I say. 'You know her better than me. How certain are you that was her? And not a very similar-looking person.'

'Unless she's got a twin that no one knows about, and the only features that distinguish them are hidden away in very private places, I'm very certain.'

'OK.'

That's all I can think of to say. I don't know what to do.

'Is this…?' Mouse stops, looking for the words to say something she knows I'm not going to like. 'Is this yours to do something about? It's not Black Knights. And it's very political. You might be better off…'

It's a very good question. It's a question I'm a little surprised that I'm not asking myself. This shouldn't have anything to do with me. I should be able to walk away.

Why can't I? Because she made it about me? Because she got James to jump? How certain am I that either of those things is true?

Head, heart, gut. Not very. So why aren't I walking away?

'I'm not staying out of it,' I snap back. It turns out I know the answers to the questions running through my head. Or I feel the answers, I guess. It amounts to the same thing for me. 'Whatever is happening here, it's her fault I'm involved. Too much has happened, too close to me. I am involved. I'm getting to the bottom of this. Borate wanted me in on the Jack White disappearance. That means she's a person of interest. And she…'

'But Jack White hasn't disappeared,' says Mouse, before I can tell her the real reason I'm so invested.

Before I can confess my guilt about what James did.

'No, of course, they'll be keeping this quiet, but believe me, Jack White…'

'Jack White hasn't disappeared,' says Mouse, again. 'Well, maybe officially, you'll know more about that than me, but in reality… That's my contact..'

'That's your what?'

'My contact,' says Mouse, again, tapping the box in her pocket. 'That's who I'm taking this to. I spoke to him an hour ago.'

I would imagine it's too dark for Mouse to properly discern the look of shock and disgust that passes over my face at this point.

'You didn't think to mention this?' I ask. 'Earlier? This wouldn't have been a helpful thing for me to know?'

'How was I supposed to know that? You didn't say why you were here. You only mentioned looking for Clar.'

I did. I'm snappy. For once, I don't think I need an alcoholic top up. I think I'm worried. I'm worried about Clar. That makes me worry about Jo Jo. And Mouse. I have a horrible feeling I'm about to drag Mouse into something complicated and deadly. I'm a toxin, poisoning my friends one by one.

I look at Mouse. Tiny, scrappy, scruffy Mouse. If anyone can handle herself, she can.

'Clar knew, though,' Mouse adds.
'What?'

'Clar knew. About Jack White. He came to Eamer's. Clar was keeping a low profile because they were tailing someone. Don't know who, they wouldn't say…' Mouse points at me and grins. 'Hey, what do you know? Maybe it was Evie White. She was there too. They took a booth. Thick as thieves, and a bit public if he's supposed to be missing.'

'Unless it was only us who were meant to think he's missing.'

'Us? Oh, you mean Authority. Not us, us.'

'I do mean Authority, yes. But maybe not us, or us, us. Maybe just me.'

'Paranoid much?' Mouse looks a bit concerned.

Maybe she's right. This is all feeling very personal right now, though.

'So where is he now?' I ask. 'Jack White…'

'No idea,' shrugs Mouse. 'I'm not due to meet him to make the exchange until tomorrow. He said he'd come to me. Said he had things to do, "wheels to set in motion".'

'Do you think they're in this together, whatever it is?' I ask.

'They live together, work together, hang out in sketchy drinking dens together. I would imagine they don't have many secrets from each other.'

'So, do you think he's down there?'

I wave my hand toward the closed hatch.

'Maybe.' Mouse seems open to the idea.

'Doing what?'

'Setting wheels in motion? You don't have any theories? You're the one who's been tailing Evie White all day. What do you think she's up to?'

I *have* been tailing Evie White all day. I know her every movement apart from the ones that matter. The ones that happened underground. What if she took her husband into Research and came out without him? What's he doing down there? Is he her partner or her prisoner?

'We should follow her,' I say. I shouldn't be letting Evie White get away. Not this one, not this time.

'We should, but...'

Mouse turns to look at the hatch. I've known her long enough. I know what she's thinking.

'But Jack White is probably down there,' I say.

'He's somewhere in a Research complex that reaches under most of the city, and quite a bit outside it, too?' she says.

She's right. It's vague. Mouse pulls Clar's Com out and places a call. She holds it to her ear so I can't hear the other end.

'Miguel,' she says. 'No, it's Mouse. Don't worry about that. They'll be fine... Look, Sim and I need a favour. Evie White is on her way out of The Alleys. She was heading East, so she'll have to come out by Eamer's. I need you to tail her. We're headed underground... Yeah. So I'll be a bit quiet for a while but I'll call you later for an update... Thanks...'

She goes to disconnect, then thinks better of it.

'Oh, and Miguel? If you see Clar, can you tell them to check in? I'm with Sim... yes, the Authority guy... He's fretting over here. Yeah, I know, but you know how it is... I don't know, lend them your Com...?'

I stare at Mouse through the darkness. She probably can't tell. It's probably just as well.

'She'll have to come out by Eamer's?' I ask.

I have no idea how Mouse knows her way around The Alleys so well. I've lived here all my life. This is my beat, yet I'd swear blind that new turns and dead ends breed in here like rabbits.

'It's an educated guess,' shrugs Mouse. 'Besides, we'd never catch her. Let's get ourselves down to Research.'

She puts the Com back in her pocket and pulls out a security token instead.

'This?' she says. 'Oh, this is just something I found lying around. Full disclosure, this is why I thought that Wright was coming back. He's not going to get far without it. I assume he left the hatch open while he made the drop, but once he got back inside he'll have been severely limited as to where he could go.'

'Do we need to be looking out for him?'

'We need to be looking out for most people.' She walks towards the hatch, continuing to talk to me over her shoulder. 'I hear rumours about what's actually going on down there these days, and who's actually doing it. Let's just say that some of them will not be happy to see you.'

'You mean Black Knights?' I ask, exasperated, following her. 'You didn't think to mention this, either?'

'I'm just trying to protect you, Sim,' she says breezily, removing a brick from the wall and flashing the token at a hidden reader.

The hatch opens, the light from below providing a creepy illumination of her face.

'I don't need protection,' I grumble.

She looks at me, sadly. I can see it clearly now. I don't know where it's coming from, but I feel it, a vice grip in my heart. She's worried. I don't think I've ever seen her look so sincere.

'We worry about you, Sim,' she says. 'One of these days, you're going to get yourself killed.'

I have never understood the design of the Research access shafts. There are hundreds of them, dotted all over the city. There are more than a few outside it, too, I believe, although I've never used them. They're all exactly the same, though, and I don't think they make sense.

I wait at street level for Mouse to reach the bottom. She'll exit through the hatch at the other end, which will then release this one for me. In the meantime I'm crouching in the darkness, staring at a small red light hidden in the wall, clutching the token that Mouse swiped from Resistance Agent Wright.

Don't get me wrong, I'm not desperate to share that confined space with someone else. It's tight in those shafts, and I'm not suggesting that we should descend together. But the fact that I can't even open the hatch until it's confirmed that Mouse is out of the other end is a strange arrangement. I've never understood what the point of that was. It leaves me kind of vulnerable up here.

I wait. The air doesn't move much in this part of The Alleys, and the night hangs heavy all around me, laden with the stench of rot and decay that I've come to associate with the worst of the city.

The symphony of The Alleys interrupts my silence at regular intervals. It's not for the fainthearted, but nothing sounds close enough to make me any more on edge than I am already.

Whoever that is who keeps screaming is in trouble, I feel bad for them. I do have an urge to help, really I do, but ultimately I stay where I am. I don't move. I'm never going to find them in time to do anything about their predicament.

Everyone is lost in The Alleys.

I lean back against the wall, taking the pressure off my ankles, which are stiff and complaining. My head dips out of the moonlight, the moon itself riding higher in the sky as the night gets later, eating the shadows, exposing the putrid underbelly of the streets.

A rat runs along the top of the wall, sending an uncomfortable shiver down my back. I'm not a fan of rats. Not that many people are, but. I have a history with rats.

I have a history with a lot of things. I have a history with

Trinity.

I certainly have a history with Research, although it's been a while since I had reason to venture down there. That's not a bad thing. There's something weird about the air down there. Weirder than the air up here, even.

The air in The Alleys isn't weird. It stinks. It coats the back of your throat like it's trying to smother you, but that all makes sense. If you spend any time in The Alleys, you will come across plenty of reasons for the stink. And it is trying to smother you. The Alleys aren't the sort of place that wants anyone to get out alive.

But down there, there's something else. There's an oppressive pressure that clouds your thoughts and crushes your soul. I spent some time as liaison between Authority and one of the labs. They were trying to develop advanced surveillance, something that could tap into the power network and allow us to plant a listener anywhere there was a socket.

It didn't work. Even if it had worked, we'd never have been able to deploy it. Too many powerful people have too many secrets to allow it. Their secrets matter. It wasn't the idea that was the problem; it was the execution. Not selective enough.

I got to know some Researchers, though. That was an eye opening experience. I don't think they're bad people. I don't think they start out that way, anyway. I'm sure that there are some who keep their perspective and their sanity and their desire to improve the world for humanity.

But locked down in the bowels of the city, cut off from the society they started out wanting to help? It's easy to wander off the path, to lose sight of the implications of your actions. All they can see anymore are the actions.

The resources at their disposal are ridiculous. No expense spared, no whim goes unfacilitated. It's a slippery slope from there, though, from "no expense spared" to "no ethical limitation considered", to "no moral objection sustained".

It's a trap they had fallen into. It's a problem you hear about too often.

That's what worries me about what Mouse said. About the Black Knights taking an interest. That kind of freedom of operation, unencumbered by anything as inconvenient as a moral code, is the default mode for the Knights.

The Knights aren't clever. Organisationally, I mean. There are plenty of intelligent Black Knights, just as there are plenty of idiotic ones, but the loose association of gangs doesn't lend itself to clarity of thought, or efficiency of process. There's no strategy to the way the Knights get things done.

But they get things done. Incredibly, frighteningly efficiently, they get things done. Usually by clearing obstacles out of the way that might prevent progress towards whatever their goal might be in any given situation. That's usually a goal whose outcome is very favourable to them and, at best, neutral for anyone else. But it's usually worse than neutral.

Their method for clearing things out of the way is whatever causes the most chaos and violence. There's plenty down in Research that could be used for chaos and violence. I suspect that the Black Knights' involvement will be like pouring petrol onto a fire.

If Research explodes, we're all in trouble. It doesn't matter whether the explosion is physical or metaphorical. Which makes me wonder about Evie White's possible involvement with Lukas Deleon. Until today, Trinity blowing up is something I would have been certain she would actively work to avoid.

Now I'm not so sure.

The light turns green. I use the token to open the hatch cover and disappear into the ground.

I drop out of the shaft into a crouch. I wonder where we've ended up. I've never accessed Research from anywhere other than the Citadel. That takes you down into the centre of the complex. Technology, accommodation, a few detention cells, that kind of thing. Not a huge amount of science in that bit.

I don't know what is underneath The Alleys. This place is so vast that I can't picture which arm snakes this far out. I'm not sure anyone could. I look around for one of those plans of the complex that appear at regular intervals on the walls all over this place. No one has a clue how to navigate it without one.

The walls are uncharacteristically bare, however, unfinished with rough concrete splashed all over. Further up the corridor, there is no light. That doesn't seem right either.

There's also a smell which brings tears to my eyes. I stand up, coughing as the miasma hits my chest.

'It's something, isn't it?' says Mouse, seeing my distress. Her voice is muffled by the scrunched up undershirt she's got clamped to her face. 'Glad I wore layers.'

I grunt, which quickly turns into another cough. I'm not stripping off in a corridor, though.

'Where the fuck are we?' I ask, looking around.

The corridor disappears in the other direction before turning a corner. As usual, in this infernal place, it looks exactly like every other section of corridor in every other part of the complex. In that direction, anyway.

Behind me is a different matter. I have a very strong suspicion that's the direction we're interested in. The bit that only looks half built, the bit that disappears into the darkness. The bit that, in any other situation, you would walk briskly away from. That kind of bit is very familiar to me.

'Don't know what's down here,' admits Mouse, 'but I'm

suspecting something zoological. That ungodly smell has to have come from the digestive tract of something with a significant appetite.'

I nod as I turn around. Together, we both stare into the darkness.

'What do you make of that?' asks Mouse, vaguely gesticulating at the obscurity with their spare hand.

'I don't know,' I say. 'It doesn't look finished. It could still be under construction, but I thought that the Research expansion finished years ago.'

'It did. On time and under budget, if Administration are to be believed. Which, obviously, they're not. It was one of Clar's first stories after they arrived here.'

'At least five years ago, then,' I say. 'It looks like there might have been some creative accounting going on.'

'That was their second story,' Mouse adds. 'Regardless, no one's meant to have been building down here since then. The boring equipment was all surfaced and retired.'

'If Administration is to be believed,' I echo. 'And yet...'

'Maybe they just never finished? Maybe they ran out of funds? It looks like it's abandoned, rather than a work in progress.'

'Maybe.' I say. 'But Evie White chose this point to exit the complex. It's not like it's a convenient access spot above ground. I get that it's helpful to come out in The Alleys from the point of view of avoiding surveillance, but it's not close to anywhere useful. And it's pretty nasty.'

'This feels like it's a long way from anywhere useful underground as well. She went to great lengths to throw us off the scent.'

'Except she didn't know we were watching her,' I say. 'We didn't know we were watching her until she turned up.'

'So, not evasion tactics? This is where she came?'

'I think so…' I glance back over my shoulder, towards the light, before turning back in the direction we're both facing. 'We don't know which way she came from, but I think if we were forced to, we'd both place the same bet. I hate to say it, because I'm thinking that it's where the smell is coming from, but I think we have to check this out.'

Mouse seems unconcerned about this choice of action, setting off briskly down the darkened corridor. I follow behind her.

The corridor slopes slightly upwards and when you get out of the brightness, you find that the darkness isn't quite as dark as it seemed a moment before. There's light behind us and something very faint coming from somewhere up ahead. It's enough for our dilated pupils to utilise. It's more than there was in The Alleys.

'So what are we looking for?' asks Mouse. 'What are we going to find?'

'If I knew that, we wouldn't need to be looking,' I say. 'More Evie Whites? Her husband? Whoever the hell she's working with?'

I don't really think we'll find "more Evie Whites". I still think there's only one. She's not Bjorn Barlow. I don't know how she's doing it, but that feed we're receiving back at base is not real. It can't be.

'Working with? That's Opposition, surely?'

'I don't know,' I sigh.

I've been trying to avoid jumping to any more conclusions, trying to go only where the evidence leads me, but there's precious little of that. What I've found is confusing and contradictory.

Head, heart, gut. My subconscious, however, reliable as ever, seems to have been working overtime on this one. And I don't think it's Opposition.

'It's not Opposition,' I say, 'not in any official capacity. Can you imagine Ort'a standing for any of this? He's just looking for an excuse to stand on a podium and denounce the pair of them, Jack and Evie. This is something else. It's cloak and dagger, conspiracy stuff. Slipping out of half built tunnels into The Alleys. At night. Faked video feeds.'

'Who then? Black Knights?'

I hope to damnation it's not.

'I have no intelligence that the Knights are working with Evie White. It's very hard to imagine, given how close they are to her father. And how distant she is from him.'

'I just told you they'd infiltrated Research. Are you sure your intelligence is that good?'

She's trying to rile me. I'm not sure why, other than that it amuses her to wound my professional pride. There's a time and a place, though. I don't think this is it.

'Mouse, you are a major source of a large part of that intelligence, so yes, I think it's robust. Do you think the Black Knights are working with Evie White?'

'No, I don't,' she admits. 'I think I'd have got wind of that.'

'Right.' *So what was the point of that little exchange?* 'So who, then?'

'Well, Resistance maybe. Everyone else is run by or in league with the Mayor.'

'Including Research, and yet here we are…'

'I don't know, though. Is this Research?' She gestures at the rough walls and the lack of lighting. 'It doesn't look like Research, doesn't feel like Research…'

We are approaching a bend. Instinct makes me veer towards the near wall, ready to press myself up against it, readying myself to peer carefully around.

Mouse does not share those instincts. She breezes on around the corner, disappearing from my view, just for a moment.

I hear a gasp, a scuffle of feet moving fast. Mouse is in trouble. I leap forward, ready to reach for my gun again.

There's no one around the corner. No one except for Mouse.

'What the fuck was that?' I demand. 'I thought someone had got you.'

'If someone "gets" me, Sim,' Mouse says, a weary note of admonishment in her voice, 'I will make damned sure you won't be in any doubt about the fact. It would be the most unambiguous scream you have ever heard. Nobody got me. I found something, though.'

There's a smaller corridor leading off this one. It's narrow and dark. I might have missed it if I'd been walking briskly past. As it is, I've got Mouse grinning and pointing at it to make sure that I can't possibly fail to notice it.

'You found something?' I ask. 'What's down there?'

'We have a door.' I can hear the excitement in her voice. 'A secret door.'

CHAPTER 21

The door isn't locked. I'm not sure it's all that secret, either.

The room on the other side of it is small. It's also barely a room. It's more like a cave; the far wall and half of the ceiling are exposed rock. I can see claw marks left by the excavation machinery.

All around, along both sides and on the rocky back wall, there are banks of small screens. There are dozens, maybe a hundred, of the things, each one showing a fuzzy, black-and-white image. Each one that's working, anyway. I realise that half of them are blank, or showing a snowstorm of interference. I peer in at the closest one.

'What is this tech?' asks Mouse. 'It's primitive. We were literally just watching a high definition stream from an airborne drone directly to your Com. This is what? It's shit, that's what it is.'

I tap the screen with my knuckle. The image wobbles. I'm not sure how that works, but this is handmade. Someone has rigged this up.

'It's basic,' I say, 'and yes, it's a bit shit. I also think it's not official. Look at how many of these screens there are.'

I stab my finger at one, where the grainy shapes of people in lab coats pipette liquids, then another where another lab coated person seems to be recording the vital signs of a what might be a wombat.

'These are all from the labs. But they're not from the main security network. If it was tapped from there, the quality would be better, but also, look at the angles. There are cameras all over this place, but they're all up high in the corners of rooms. None of these are filming from there. The position is too low, the range is too narrow. These are additional cameras, hidden, probably in innocent items around the place. No one wants anyone to know they're watching.'

Mouse peers into another of the grainy portals.

'If they were from the security network, it might be more obvious what was going on.'

'I don't think there's much going on.' I move from one screen to the next. 'Just people going about their business. Doing their jobs.'

'So what are they watching for? Why the covert surveillance?'

I don't know. But I'm scanning the monitors, trying to figure it out. They're not all the labs. I find one that looks to be at ground level, above where we are, in Trinity itself.

It a bedroom. At first glance it looks fancy - luxuriously upholstered, lace and silk. Perhaps a *boudoir*, rather than a bedroom. But on closer inspection, I notice signs of age - the bedclothes are frayed, possibly grubby. It's impossible to tell at this resolution.

Someone drifts past the camera in a state of undress. I take a moment, but I recognise her. It's Laihla. My heart thumps in my chest, my breath catches.

Again, it circles back around to me.

I peer closer. This isn't Eamer's. I wonder what Laihla's got herself into, but I also worry about what it means for me. Except I can't. I don't have time for that. I squash it down, move on.

I stop on another screen, bottom row. There is a man. He's sat on a chair in the middle of a large, empty room. It's hard to tell, given the lack of colour in the picture, but everything around the room is bright. I think it's white, the entire room. I look a little closer. I notice he appears to be restrained in his chair. He's not resisting, or even moving much. I think he has his eyes closed.

'This guy,' I say to Mouse. 'I thought he was your contact?'

'Wow,' says Mouse, looking at Jack White on the monitor. 'She tied him up. I guess he is, kind of, missing, then.'

The image is frustratingly clear of any sort of clues as to where he might be. Underground, overground, this could be anywhere. It is nowhere I recognise.

I check back to Laihla's screen. Maybe I've got this wrong. She's no longer in shot, but there's a telltale shaft of light from a streetlight through a window just out of the frame. It's ground level all right.

That's not helpful. Jack White could be anywhere.

'Where do you think this room even is?' I ask. 'Is it part of the complex?'

Mouse leans in, but she doesn't seem to discern any more from it than I did.

'I don't know. It could be anywhere. Are you sure it's not in Authority?'

I'm not sure, to be honest. My clearance is pretty high but even I don't get to go everywhere. It has the look of a cell, I'll give her that, but we have nothing that large.

'That would be a ballsy move,' I say, 'reporting him missing and then locking him up in the same building. But you spoke to him, right? An hour ago? That was way after I chased her away from Authority.'

'You chased… who?' Mouse looks at me, confused.

'Evie White,' I explain. 'I followed her when she left Authority. They clocked me. Well, they were supposed to, I made sure of that. They tried to lose me. I chased her.'

The cogs are turning. Even as I'm talking, my mind is reeling. Something is nagging at the back of my head. Something about the Pod pilot.

'I didn't think you had it in you, old man…'

Mouse is laughing at me. I don't respond to that. I'm nearly there. *Head, heart, gut…*

Something about the way Jack White is sitting, leaned back, head half turned. It looks like he's listening to someone who is behind him.

'I think he was in the Pod,' I shout, suddenly.

Mouse looks around nervously. I forgot we aren't meant to be here.

'He was driving the Pod. I didn't recognise him at the time, but I'm sure it was him. He took her to the Citadel. I think he drove her here.'

'So he was working with her, at the point she reported him missing? So what? He's tied up in there voluntarily? Or did she double-cross him?'

'Your guess is as good as mine. We won't get to the bottom of that standing here. How do we find him?'

'Maybe there's a pattern to these screens?' Mouse walks along the wall, eyes flicking from one to another. 'Maybe the order they're in somehow represents where they are?'

'I don't know,' I say.

They look pretty random. The one that I saw Laihla on is in the top row. The scientists are all on the bottom two. So is Jack White.

Of course.

'The top rows are above ground, I think.'

Mouse looks sceptical.

'That one is, but I don't know that you can assume that. Most of them aren't showing anything useful. You might be right...'

She bangs one monitor on the top row a few times. The snow scene settles into another grainy image. A thin, ghoulish face looms into view, baring its fangs. Mouse jumps backwards in shock.

'What the..?'

I recognise the face immediately. Mouse should have, too. Although from this angle, his razor sharp nose is way more prominent. It looks like it is going to break through the screen.

'Mishka?' I ask. 'They've got Eamer's bugged too?'

There is a sizeable lump on the side of his head, from where Mouse clocked him earlier. I'm impressed he came to fast enough to get back to Eamer's.

'Eamer's bathroom, by the look of it. Gone back to lick his wounds' says Mouse, as we watch Mishka hook something from between his teeth with a blackened fingernail. 'Urgh, I did not need to see that...'

'But that supports our theory? High monitor overground, low monitor underground.'

Mouse shakes her head, pointing at another screen, this one in the bottom row.

'No, look, Evie White's on this one.' She points at a screen in the bottom row. 'Although I can't tell where she is. Is that Administration? Has she gone back to work?'

I lean in again. The flickering, grainy picture defies identification. It's a corridor. It could be in any of several buildings in Trinity: Authority, the Dome, Detention... Administration is the most obvious answer. She could have gone back to the office, although it's a bit late to be going back to work. And she's supposed to be concerned about the whereabouts of her missing husband.

We both know that he's not going anywhere, though.

She reaches the edge of the frame and the camera loses her.

'Guess we'll never know,' says Mouse.

'No, look…'

I point to the screen two along. The one in between is snow-storming, whatever feed it was meant to be showing is broken. But the next one is showing a grainy image of a corridor. Not another corridor, though, the same one.

'There, she's right there,' I say, as Evie White moves right to left across the screen.

'Interesting,' says Mouse. 'So does this entire row show the one corridor? And where the hell is it, that it's so important to track someone down every metre of it?'

I glance to the end of the row. It's still hard to make anything out, the picture quality is poor, and the lighting is terrible. The shiver down my spine tells me everything I need to know.

'We need to get out of here,' I say. 'we need to hide.'

'What?' asks Mouse. 'What happened? What's changed?'

I point at the latest monitor with the marching figure of Evie White on it.

'I don't think that's proof that our system is wrong. Those screens are in the bottom row, because that corridor is down here. It's not Administration. I think Evie White has come back to Research. And if she's come back so soon, that probably means she's worried about something…'

'And there's every chance that the something she's worried about is us?' From the expression on Mouse's face, I can tell that we're on the same page now. 'Shit, they've got surveillance everywhere. She probably knew we were here from the moment we dropped out of the shaft…'

Entrapment

We stare at each other for a fragment of a second, then both make a leap towards the door.

We stand in the small side corridor and peer out. The main corridor is empty, at least up to the corner we came around. I don't know what to do. I don't know where Evie White is, not exactly. Maybe five or six screens from the corner, maybe in a different section of Research altogether.

I don't know how far away she is. I don't even know that she's coming here. Maybe moving is the worst thing we can do. Maybe she's not looking for us at all.

'Which way?' asks Mouse.

I don't have time to talk through my uncertainty. I don't know that it would help to overthink it, anyway. *Head, heart, gut.* I gesture back the way we came.

'She's coming from that direction, I guess,. We should go the opposite way.'

Mouse looks down the corridor. A light flickers.

'I get what you're saying but… Doesn't that just take us deeper in? Further away from our exit point?'

'There are shafts all over the place. We'll find another way out.'

'Do we even know there's anywhere to go?' she asks. 'This place looks pretty unfinished. What if we just run out of corridor?'

'It crossed my mind,' I say. 'I don't think we have any other choice.'

'I think you're right,' Mouse sighs. 'I was thinking the same thing. I was hoping you had a different idea.'

She pushes past me into the corridor, turning both ways before glancing back at me.

'So what, we just run?'

She takes off without another word.

I pick up my heels and accelerate past her into the darkness. The floor is even and there's not much danger of tripping, even in the bits we can't see properly through. There also doesn't seem to be much down here by the way of equipment or stores. Just a long, dark corridor leading somewhere. Hopefully, somewhere safer.

It doesn't feel right, though. Quickly I can feel the strain in my legs, the ache of exertion I wasn't expecting. My shins prick and my calves burn. The corridor is sloping upwards.

It was hard to see in the dark, but it's a deceptively steep gradient. I slow to a trot, and Mouse catches up to me. Neither of us stops moving, but at least now we can hold a conversation.

'We're going uphill,' she pants. 'Are we going to surface?'

I'm wondering the same thing, but I don't know of anywhere that the Research complex hits the surface, even outside of Trinity's walls. There's always an access shaft, or a service lift. There aren't doors cut into the Northern Exposure. Well, there are, but they're all Resistance bunkers. Research is much, much deeper than that.

It's not the only thing that's bothering me, though. I hold up my arm and point in front of me.

'Is that daylight?' I am certain that it can't be. 'There, up ahead?'

'Can't be. It's dark outside. I…'

She slows to a walk. I do too. The further we get, the more obvious it is that there is, indeed, light up ahead. It has to be artificial, but it's dazzling. It also seems to come up out of the floor.

'What's going on?' asks Mouse.

We can hear something now, as well, the rumble of vehicles, the murmur of voices, the occasional shout. Bangs and crashes at irregular intervals. I take another few steps

Entrapment

forward and realised that the slope ends about a hundred metres ahead of us. From that point, the corridor levels out and it's from beyond that both the noise and the light are coming.

I make a vague motion with my hand to tell Mouse to follow me, and also to keep quiet, as I climb the rest of the slope.

Once it levels out, there isn't a lot of corridor left. It ends no more than a long throw ahead of us, and beyond that it's hard to tell for the brightness of the light. I walk slowly to the end.

As my eyes adjust, I realise what I'm looking at. My head spins and I have to take a dramatic step backwards, almost falling into Mouse as I do.

At the end of the corridor is a sheer drop, as beyond it is a vast hangar, brightly lit. We have emerged high on one side, with the drop below being the equivalent of at least four storeys. I'm not fond of heights. I don't know if I mentioned that.

Mouse slides up to the edge and takes a look herself. I hear her gasp. She should. It's huge. I prepare myself for another look. There are tugs and forklifts down there, moving pallets piled with boxes and barrels. The opposite wall looks like a massive retractable door, but it's closed, so I've no idea where it goes.

'So, we're in agreement that there's no way this is legit, right?' says Mouse.

'Completely.'

This, whatever this is, is what Evie White's doing down here.

'What do you think they're moving?' I wonder.

'No idea, but some of those barrels have some serious warning symbols plastered on them.'

She points down to one pallet against the right-hand wall.

It's covered in yellow signs, although we're too far away to tell what they signify. There are people milling about, some of whom are wearing hazmat suits, so I assume it's nothing benign.

A forklift scoots forward and picks up the pallet, lifting it a metre off the ground and then reversing with a beeping noise. There's a shout, and a man in a red cap runs over from the far side of the hangar, waving a tablet.

He runs in a wide loop so that he can approach the reversing cab from the side and, as soon as he has caught the driver's attention he tucks the tab in his armpit and moves his forearms up and down, palms down, in a definite "slow down" motion.

He stops as the driver takes heed and cuts his speed. The barrels on the pallet wobble a little less as the truck makes more steady progress across the floor.

The man in the red cap looks to the sky and appears to let out a sigh of relief. I don't think he's looking at us, but I see his face for the first time. He's a long way away, but I recognise him instantly, my suspicions confirmed by the shot of adrenaline from the sudden realisation that shoots up my spine to the base of my neck.

It's Lukas Deleon.

'Get down!' I hiss at Mouse, pushing her down so that we're less obviously framed, in full view of anyone who thinks to look upwards with more purpose than Deleon just did.

'You've seen someone?' Mouse is scanning the floor. 'Who? Oh, what the fuck? Is that the guy from Eamer's?'

'Deleon,' I confirm. 'He seems to be some kind of foreman. How did he get out?'

'I don't know,' mutters Mouse. 'The last I saw him, he was strapped to a generator. There's something fishy going on. Why would Eamer just let him go?'

Entrapment

A face flashes in my mind. Not a pleasant one, but a recurring one. Mishka was interrogating Deleon. Mishka attacked me in The Alleys. *Head, heart, gut.* It wouldn't surprise me to find he has divided loyalties. Multiple paychecks can do that.

It's obvious Deleon's in charge here, he's directing the various vehicles, taking an interest in all the activity. He seems to have a very particular order he wants these materials, whatever they are, to leave the hangar. They disappear, on his command, one by one, into a wide doorway directly beneath us. They're heading back into Research, or this strange add-on to Research, but deeper underground. Is there some kind of complex underneath the complex?

'Where do you think that opens out to?' asks Mouse, pointing to the giant doors opposite us. 'Are we close to the city walls here?'

I guess we might be. It's hard to tell how far we travelled underground.

'You think that's a door to the outside world?'

She might be right. I've lost my bearings. But we came down in The Alleys and surely it's more than a five-minute jog to the city walls from there?

'Could be,' says Mouse. 'A door in the escarpment would be easy enough to hide. Cover it in bushes and barbed wire and no one would ever get close enough to notice the joins.'

She is right. It makes perfect sense. But I don't think that's what it is.

'What about the Chaguartay line?' I propose.

The Chaguartay line is an underground train tunnel. It only has two stops. One is at the docks, the other is at the Citadel. It was meant to be the first phase of a huge project to revolutionise Trinity's transport infrastructure, to move all the traffic underground so that the surface could be redesigned as a pedestrian's paradise - green spaces, cushioned walkways, a healthier, happier population.

It didn't work. Construction halted before Phase One was finished. No trains ever ran. The TransWay got busier, and the pedestrians got stuck up in the sky, on the PedWay.

'No, it...' Mouse pauses while she draws a mental map. 'No, you know, it could be. Fuck me, has she built an extra station? That's more than her dad ever managed!'

I'm not sure that Chaguartay ever planned to build any more than he did. I've heard stories about the project and the whole thing smacks of corruption and lies. It benefited him, after all. If the greening of Trinity wasn't going to happen, there wasn't a lot of point in objecting to the factory expansions, was there? And Chaguartay has done rather nicely out of that, thank you very much.

I don't have time to say this to Mouse, although I think she is fully aware. I don't get a chance because I spot another figure I recognise, walking briskly across the hangar, towards Deleon. Mouse has seen her, too.

'Is that Evie White?' she asks, with a notch or two more volume than I'm absolutely comfortable with.

'Uh-huh,' I say. 'I wonder how she got down there?'

'We must have been wrong about which corridor she was coming down. It must have been down there, or we've got two of them wandering around.'

I hear a sound behind me and turn around to see a gun pointed at my face. Behind the gun is a Black Knight. He reaches out and takes my gun from my belt. His partner is pointing a second gun at Mouse. Behind them is a familiar figure.

'You've got two of them wandering around,' says Evie White.

CHAPTER 22

They march us back the way we came, down the slope, past the side corridor, into the light.

The corridors look more familiar, more finished. The light improves, the walls are whitewashed, the ceilings tiled. The floor turns to concrete, apart from the bits that are chequerboard. I always wondered what that was about. *Now is not the time.*

The first time I see one of the little map diagram things appear on the walls, I know we're into Research proper. We march past too fast to see exactly where we've emerged, but it's somewhere out to the East. We're closer to the centre than I thought we'd be, though. Maybe the section we've been in is, indeed, a separate set of tunnels above the main complex.

Evie White is leading the way. Mouse and I are being prodded along by the barrels of the Black Knights' weapons. They seem to prod harder every time we approach a map. It's almost as if they don't want us to know where we're going.

'Are you taking us anywhere special?' asks Mouse, as if she's reading my mind.

She yelps when, in response, her personal Black Knight

guard digs her in the middle of her spine with his gun. I wince, but to be fair to her, other than the yelp, Mouse doesn't flinch.

It's definitely as if they don't want us to know where we're going.

I decide it would be better for me to keep my mouth shut. Mouse is supposed to have a pre-existing working relationship with these people and they're still treating her like this. I definitely don't have that advantage. I'm lucky they're not dragging me along by my balls.

Eventually we're walking up a corridor, just like every other corridor, approaching a door identical to every other door we've been past. It's wide, thick, grey and metallic, and at first seems as resolutely closed as the rest.

However, as soon as Evie White reaches it, it slides open, as if triggered by her presence. She turns. This might be where we are going.

'Bring them in,' she snaps to the two Knights.

Mouse thinks to step forward so that the dig in her back is cushioned a little. I'm not so quick. My back is more brittle than Mouse's. I imagine I can hear my spine crack as I'm shoved forward. This guy knows who I am. I'm worried I'm not making it out of here alive.

As we follow her into the lab beyond, I have to squint to see through the bright glare. It reflects off the shining metal-topped benches, which are scattered with scientific instruments, high stools arranged along them at regular intervals. No one is sitting on any of these, but I get the impression that they have been recently vacated.

At the far end, there is a shiny metallic pod with a curved glass front, behind which is a small control panel and a swivel chair. On the wall there is the expected plan of the underground Research complex. The red letter R is positioned to show we are in a section dedicated to "Consolidated

Research".

'Nice place you have here,' I say as my hands are grabbed and roughly cuffed to the legs of the nearest bench. The cuffs are fancy tech. Nano locked. Authority issue. There's no slipping out of these.

The same happens to Mouse. The Black Knights leave. We have an audience with Evie White.

This is kind of what I wanted, but I could do with a little more of the power in this situation. I look at Mouse. She shrugs, or the closest equivalent possible, with her hands cuffed in front of her groin.

'So, you've got us just where you want us,' I say. 'I assume?'

Evie looks at us, stony faced. I can't even begin to guess what she wants.

'You've been getting into places you had no business to be, Oficier Lagrange. So yes, I would rather have you here.'

She turns away, picks up a beaker from the bench and inspects it like it's an alien artefact. This isn't her natural environment. What on earth has brought her here?

'I needed to take you away from temptation.' She turns back to face me. 'Lest you get the wrong impression.'

'As an Oficier of the city Authority, I have no interest in getting the wrong impression. What would be the right impression?'

Evie White throws the beaker at the wall, where it smashes and the pieces drop to the floor. The sudden, unexpected violence of the act makes both of us jump. I don't know about Mouse, but the cuffs dig into my wrist, pulling at my joints painfully.

'Now, now…' She wags her finger at me before turning and pacing away. 'Not so fast. I don't think you appreciate what you've stumbled into here. And if you understood it, you certainly wouldn't.'

'So,' I try again. 'What have I stumbled into here? Who is Lukas Deleon? What's he doing down there? What did he bring into Trinity?'

'So many questions. And not as coherent as you think they are. Lukas Deleon is working for me.'

'That much I figured. What did he bring into Trinity? Bombs...?'

'Oh no, I wouldn't risk that. There are plenty of ways to get explosives into Trinity. Mr Deleon brought something much more precious...'

'But the bag was empty...'

'...and much more impossible. But that shouldn't concern you. What he's doing now, on the other hand, could have much more explosive consequences for Trinity.'

'Bombs...?' I say, again.

Evie says nothing in response. She doesn't need to. Why would Evie White be getting someone to create bombs? That's going to be my next question, after this one, because I need to know who she's working with, and if that person is Eamer.

'How did he get free?'

Evie laughs. It is a cold sound; it jars my spine.

'You should ask your friend.'

A rush of adrenaline hits me. I glance at Mouse. She has her head bowed.

'Mouse?'

Mouse says nothing, continues to stare at the ground. I know that Evie's telling the truth. *Shit.* I didn't see that coming.

'Mouse?'

Louder. Insistent. We've known each other a long time. I've seen her grow up. I can't believe she'd betray me. This can't be what it feels like.

Mouse raises her eyes, but not her head. She stares at me

through her eyebrows. Her gaze is strong and *unusual*. I think she's trying to communicate something to me. I dearly wish I could interpret what it was.

'I couldn't tell you,' Mouse mutters. 'I didn't know much, but I did know that Deleon was free. And that Jack White wasn't.'

'But you couldn't tell me?' I couldn't believe what I was hearing. 'Those are two things I specifically remember having discussions with you about!'

'I was trying to protect you,' she protested. 'You can't be involved. What she's doing, it's... It's not your problem.'

I jerk my head down, towards my handcuffs.

'I think I'm pretty fucking involved now, don't you?' My voice cracks as I shout. 'It very much feels like it's become my problem. I don't remember you warning me not to come here?'

I can't believe how fucked up this entire situation has become. Everyone I thought I could trust, everyone I have surrounded myself with, one by one, they've wavered and fallen. James, and Parker, and Clar, none of them could help me, none of them saw what I was headed into, none of them could warn me, or save me.

Now Mouse, little Mouse, who it turns out *could* have done these things, *could* have stopped me getting to where I'm chained to a bench, at the mercy of...

At the mercy of who? Who is Evie White? Because she's not who I thought she was. I don't think this is what anyone thought she was. Her father is a cancer that has made this city sick, but she rejected him. She fell in love with the man who promised to rid us of our despot mayor. We trusted them to save us.

Now she's got him chained up, she's got me chained up. I look back to Mouse. Who is also chained up. Whatever she *could* have done, it wasn't enough to stop that. She's not working with Evie, she's not working for her.

'I thought I could keep you hidden.' There are tears in Mouse's eyes now. 'I thought I was protecting you.'

'You didn't say a word. You didn't give me a choice,' I snarl.

It came out harsher than it was meant to. I can see her shoulders go. I didn't mean to break her, but break her I have. She may be nearly thirty years old, but in many ways she's still the kid I watched grow up against the odds.

But that's my point. If she'd told me what she knew, I could have done something differently. I could have figured it out. *Head, heart, gut.*

Evie's thin, piercing voice chimes out again.

'Oh, this is wonderful!' she shrieks. 'What did you think you were going to do, little Mouse?'

'You couldn't possibly hide from both of us…'

OK, that's weird. She says that second bit without moving her lips. Mouse's head snaps around and now she's staring at the doorway.

'Hello Mouse. I'm sorry that we had to involve you in this.'

I can tell now the voice is coming from behind me. It sounds is the same, maybe slightly higher, fresher in pitch. Younger. I turn my head. I know who I'm going to see.

'It wasn't my decision…'

Seeing them here, now, in the same room, together, it's obvious who is who. This new arrival seems less burdened, less jaded. It's not that her counterpart looks older, it's just obvious that she's seen more.

'Well, it was, but you know. It was *her* idea. She said it would be fitting. I still don't know what she meant by that. She said it should be a surprise.'

I also realise that I should have suspected something much earlier. It is the first time I'm meeting this younger version. It was her older self who I interviewed in Administration earlier today, who I chased through the streets of Trinity in a ridiculous attempt at intimidation.

'So, there are two of you.'

It's not a question, it's obvious that there are. Up to now, it's only been a theory. One that I had attributed no credibility to. Faced with the reality of the situation, I thought I'd be more surprised.

'Well spotted,' says Younger Evie. 'It's very nice to finally meet you, Oficier Lagrange. I've heard so much about you.'

She doesn't remember me. Not like I remember the brat she was.

'Really?'

'Oh yes,' she smiles the smile I recognise from her older self. 'It seems I'm quite the fan.'

She looks at her counterpart meaningfully.

'Why are they here? I didn't think this was how we were going to do it?'

Older Evie glares. There's no mistaking who's the more senior partner. If this wasn't the plan before, there's no question that it is now.

'They were getting in the way. I had to remove them from proceedings. I don't like these things being left to chance. Not until we're ready.'

'And are we ready?' asks Younger Evie. 'Did it arrive?'

'It did. But we need more time before we get to full power. Deleon needs to clear the loading bay of his fireworks first. We can't risk a discharge with that amount of explosive in the vicinity.'

Younger Evie nods. She seems to follow what's going on, even if it's nonsense to me.

'But we're ready? The machine is prepped?'

'I assume so. I've been too busy trying to keep prying eyes

out of our business.'

I glance at Mouse. She's following intently, but she gives no impression that she understands a word of it either.

'You want me to follow up?' asks the younger woman.

'No,' Older Evie shakes her head, and walks to the door, pressing a gun that I didn't realise she was carrying into her younger self's hand as she passes. 'You keep an eye on these two. I'll check the machine.'

She doesn't leave space for a reply, and before she can give herself one, she disappears through the door and down the corridor beyond.

'What has she got you into? Why is Jack tied up down here?'

It's the first time Mouse has said anything for a while, and it's directly to the younger Evie White. The only Evie White still in the room. That Evie White shakes her head.

'I'm just doing what has to be done,' she says. 'For the city. For Trinity. When he found out the whole truth, suddenly Jack wasn't on board. She said...'

It's a defiant shake, but there's something in her demeanour that suggests she's not as certain as she wants to be that she's doing the right thing. It is reassuring, at least, that one half of Trinity's golden couple thought that blowing up the city was a bad idea.

'This future version of you,' I ask, 'the one who is calling the shots. Where is she from? *When* is she from?'

She turns to me, her expression clearly communicating that this is a stupid question.

'The future,' she scoffs. 'Not too far in the future, though. Just far enough that she can see where it all goes wrong. She's come back to fix things.'

'Just far enough that someone can invent time travel, too, I guess?' Mouse points out.

'You'd be surprised what they can do already down here,' Evie replies.

She pulls out a stool and sits down, glancing around the lab. I look around too, but I see nothing that I can interpret.

Does she mean here? Is this where it happens? Has it already happened? Is that what the computer pod thing is for?

If so, who? And where are they? Were they always in league with Evie White? Or was the technology co-opted, or stolen?

Evie White picks up a pen from the bench and fidgets with it. I get a strong sense that this version of her isn't sure of the answers to these questions, either.

'Isn't it risky, though?' I say instead. 'Messing with the timeline? Whatever you're doing, I would have thought you need to be careful. Or at least, she does. If she's trying to change her own future, especially working with you… doesn't that set up some kind of paradox? Isn't that potentially very dangerous?'

I don't know what I'm talking about, but I think I'm onto something. It might even be something that can get us free.

'Ha!' Evie puts the pen down, throws her head back. 'It would be. It definitely would be. But she's thought of that. I've thought of that, I guess. Will think of that. We've had to be careful up to now, but soon it won't matter. We'll be protected. And we can change the world.'

I don't know what she means. Fortunately, Mouse seems to be a step ahead.

'Is that where she's gone?' she asks. 'Is that what the machine is? Is it something to do with being able to change what happens without it causing problems for you?'

'It's…'

Evie looks around the room, like she's checking something, like she's making sure she can't be heard. I realise that, for however long her future self has been around, pulling the strings, she won't have been able to talk to anyone about any of this. Not her husband, or her sister. Certainly not her father. It looks like it's doing her good to talk. It seems like she wants to tell us.

A sly grin spreads across her face. She looks at me. I suddenly realise the implications of what she's about to say.

I'm not clear on what the stakes are here. Except for me, and for Mouse. Because if she's about to tell us anything of any use at all, then probably we don't have long left to live.

'Changing the past isn't a problem,' she says. 'That's been done before. But it's complicated. It's easy to mess things up. We've built a machine that will help.'

'Help to change things?' Mouse asks.

'The future she comes from,' Evie explains. 'It's not how things were meant to be, how things were written. Someone else got there first, made a mess of it.'

'She's come back to fix it?' I ask.

I can see Mouse's face. She's closed her eyes and is struggling to control her breathing.

'Fuck,' she exhales.

'You OK, Mouse?' I ask.

'I'm such an idiot,' she says. 'I didn't spot it. She's come back to fix it. But who does this? Time travel? Rewriting history?'

'The winners,' says Evie White.

'The winners,' repeats Mouse. 'Interesting you put it that way. Not the good guys?'

'It's not a question of good or evil,' scoffs Evie. 'Those are relative concepts. Winning is what matters.'

This is madness. She is mad. Or she will be mad. This version doesn't seem completely committed, despite what she's saying. The waver in her voice, the repeated glances downwards. They don't shout confidence at me.

'I presume she only needs a machine to keep reality from unravelling because she's about to do something that is going to royally fuck it up?' I say, trying to tighten the screws, to get her to squirm.

She is looking decidedly uncomfortable.

'Is she?' asks Mouse. 'Is this a good idea?'

'It doesn't matter,' snaps Evie.

'Even if she's only in it for herself?'

'She is me. If she's only doing it for herself, then she's still dong it for me.'

'Depends on whether you like what she's become,' I point out.

Evie says nothing. I look back to Mouse.

'It's OK, Mouse,' I say. 'You did what you thought you had to do. I don't blame you for that. We all have to make our choices the best we can.'

'I've made my peace with making bad choices,' says Mouse. 'I like to clean up my messes, though. How are we going to stop her?'

'Oi,' shouts Evie, cutting her off. 'No one is going to stop her. You're not really in a position to do very much.'

I look down at my cuffs. She's right, I'm not in a position to walk two paces, let alone stop a time traveller from corrupting the timeline. I look at Evie, who is pacing. Back and forth, back and forth, back and forth…

And then I see a face appear on the monitor that sits above the closed door. It leans in, filling the screen, then places a finger over its mouth. I can almost hear the "shhhhhh". Fortunately, Evie can't.

But I know that face. It's so-called Bjorn fucking Barlow. I shake my head. I don't know what he's doing here, and I don't know if he can see me, but he doesn't realise what he's about to walk into. I feel strongly that I need to warn him.

Which is weird, given how I've been feeling about him for the last few days. I don't have time to examine that.

Evie glances at me, and I stop mid-shake. She pulls a face. She knows something's up but, at just that moment, her Com beeps. She holds it up to her mouth, without taking her eyes off me, and answers.

Holo off. I'd hoped it would distract her, but she continues to stare right at me.

'Yes.'

'Evie, are you watching the security feed?' A similar voice, tinny and small from transmission, but unmistakeably the other Evie White, rings out.

'No, I'm watching the prisoners.'

There's tension there, some tetchiness in her tone.

'I need you here. We have a situation.'

'A situation?' This Evie seems confused. 'I have the prisoners here. What kind of situation do you have?'

'An old friend has put in a surprise appearance,' says the voice on the other end.

'Old friend of mine?'

'Old friend of mine. Someone I think you should meet. Before I have to kill him.'

'I'll be there.' Evie cuts the call.

She walks across to Mouse and checks her cuffs, then back to me to do the same. Satisfied that we're still unable to make a run for it, she activates the door and disappears into the corridor.

Before they slide shut, a wisp of a shadow slips through the other way. I think I hear it shout "follow her".

'Oficier Lagrange.' The shadow bows deeply, the light shining off his freshly shaven head.

'Bjorn Barlow,' I snarl. 'If I'd known that all I had to do was wait for you to turn up to rescue me, then I wouldn't have tried so hard to track you down.'

'I apologise,' says Barlow. 'But this was necessary.'

'Why the fuck are you calling him Barlow?' asks Mouse. 'Lek, what's going on here?'

The man I know as Bjorn Barlow, who Mouse just called Lek, turns to her with a smile.

'It's a pleasure to see you again, Mouse. Oficier Lagrange, here, first met me in difficult circumstances. I was necessary for me to practice a little innocent deception. Subterfuge. I was in search of information and I couldn't afford for my true identity to be known.'

'Making about as much sense as you ever do,' says Mouse. 'You can explain later. Or not. The key question I have is: can get us out of these cuffs?'

Barlow, or Lek, grins again.

'That,' he says. 'I can do.'

CHAPTER 23

Out of cuffs, it's not that I'm ungrateful, but I need some answers. I'm the senior authority in this room, but even Mouse knows more than I do.

That's not fair. Mouse often knows more than me. Maybe I'm just nursing a bruised ego. I'm not used to being the one in cuffs. I rub at my wrists.

Barlow is staring at me. He has his hands folded in front of him and an irritating, serene look on his face.

'Who the fuck are you, then?' I growl.

I had meant to approach this less aggressively. There's no need for confrontation, but I appear to be more irritable than I realised. Then I remember Sergey James and there's every need for confrontation.

'My name is Lek,' says the smug Monk, without reacting to the fact that I am obviously pissed off.

'Not Bjorn Barlow?' I ask. 'Who the fuck is Bjorn Barlow?'

'Not Bjorn Barlow,' says the man I should start to think of as Lek. 'You made him up, remember? He is the Grey Knight. I like that. It was clever.'

'So why did you pretend you were him?'

I think this is a fair question. It appears that he knows exactly what the name would mean to me.

'I had to get your attention.'

I don't know if he's doing it on purpose, but each answer frustrates and annoys me more than the last. It's in the delivery, I think. He's unflappable, but not in a good way.

'To what end?' I ask, exasperated. 'I haven't seen you since.'

'To *the* end. We are all headed, inexorably, in one direction. I had to make sure you were on board. Anyway, you had me followed.'

'And you made him jump off a building!'

There it is. That's where I snap. I lose my cool, surrender the upper hand, although I'm uncertain that's what I had.

'No,' he says.

It's one word, delivered definitively. *Head, heart, gut.* I don't need to wonder if he's sincere, if he's telling the truth. The universe hasn't left room for a shred of doubt in the wavelengths of the sound of his voice.

'That wasn't me,' he says. 'That was her. But he did it for a reason. It was good that he did it.'

I can't believe the words that I'm hearing. I explode.

'He's dead!' I shout. 'He's dead and you just stand there spouting...'

'No,' he says, again.

I stop. I don't understand.

'What do you mean, "no"?'

'He's not dead. That's what I explained to him. He's gone somewhere else. He's made the right choice.'

'Fucking religious nuts and their fucking delusional...'

'No,' he says once more. 'He's not dead. He's not gone to a better place. He's definitely not gone to a *better* place, but he's no longer here, not now. You'll see him again, though. Or...'

Entrapment

He trails off, drops into thought for a moment. He looks like he's trying to solve some really quite complicated mathematics in his head.

'He'll see you again, at least. You should trust him.'

I can't quite explain what happens in that moment, but I do trust him. I trust James and I trust Barlow, or Lek, or whoever he is. I take a deep breath and let James go. Everything shifts at that moment. I am no longer angry. I am intrigued.

'So are you really Brotherhood?'

Lek laughs. Wrinkles sparkle around his eyes. He doesn't appear to be that much older than me, but I get the impression of something ancient and timeless.

'No,' he smiles. 'I'm not Brotherhood. The Brotherhood died a long time ago, long before you were born…'

That can't be right. I remember the Brotherhood. They stood up to Chaguartay. Chaguartay had them dissolved.

'…figuratively, at least,' he says. 'I am Devoted. No more, no less.'

I stare at Lek. He's inscrutable. But I also know he's right. Not about the Brotherhood, although he probably is right about them. A religious order doesn't just blink out of existence like that, the rot would have set in long before.

But he's right, he *knows* things, things that Evie White doesn't know. *Can't know?* He's right in all the ways that she's wrong, all the ways that her focus on winning means she can never understand.

I understand. Suddenly, in that moment, I understand. I have to follow him. It's my only hope. Our only hope. *The* only hope.

There's a silence that seems to stretch time. I think it lasts forever.

'What now?' asks Mouse.

The silence is broken; the moment is lost. I forgot that Mouse is still here, but she asks a pertinent question.

'Yes, let's get out of here,' I suggest.

I mean out of this room, but I also mean out of Research, out of Evie's reach. I don't say it, but Lek seems, instinctively, to know. He shakes his head.

'No. I'm afraid that would be a terrible mistake. We can't let this play out the way she wants it to.'

I want to go to Eamer's. I need a drink. I want to get out of here. I hear the words in my head, hear the potential whine in my tone. I keep my mouth shut.

'We're never going to find her,' says Mouse. 'Not down here. It's a labyrinth.'

I think of the viewing room we stumbled across, think about how Evie White has been running rings around me all day.

'And not if she knows we're coming,' I say. 'She has eyes everywhere.'

'I know where she is, though,' says Lek. 'Both of her.'

'That's where we're going, then?' checks Mouse.

'It is,' says Lek. 'And we'd better hurry. I had someone follow her, but it's someone I really need to look after. The fabric of reality depends on it, somewhat.'

I recall the message that Evie had received from her future self. There is someone else roaming the complex, someone she hadn't seemed particularly pleased to have seen. They have to be with Lek.

I don't understand it yet, but I'm so close.

'And old friend?' I ask.

'Older than you could imagine.'

I move towards the doorway. I can feel my jaw tighten, my fists clench, almost involuntarily. I'm fighting it, and I don't know why. I trust Lek. It's sudden, complete, unquestioning; I *know* he's telling me the truth, and I know I don't have a choice.

But something within me resists. I think I'm afraid. What am I afraid of?

'Come on then,' I dig deep, feel the fear, let it go. As I have done so many times before. 'I guess we can't let her get away. Either of her…'

My heart is not fully in it. I turn to Mouse.

'You in?'

Mouse shrugs. That's about as much commitment as anyone has any right to expect from Mouse.

I force myself to walk out of the lab, one foot in front of the other, squashing down the sudden sense of foreboding.

Head, heart, gut.

I ignore them at my peril.

I don't have a choice.

However old he might be, the Monk is physically fit. We're walking, rather than running, but his pace is brisk and he stays well ahead of Mouse and me. He seems to know where he's going.

'You trust this guy?' I ask Mouse.

'With my life. Don't you? People tend to warm to him pretty quickly.'

'Yeah, I…'

I don't know how to say it to Mouse. The man I've met now is a whole different persona to the one pretending to be Bjorn Barlow. Once I realised this, the smugness melted away and left me with… what? Calm, serenity, peace. All things I don't think I need, but I can't help but grab onto.

And yet, there's the unavoidable sense that he's about to lead us into mortal danger. I can't reconcile the two. They're both powerful sensations and I can't pick a direction. It's astounding that I'm still moving forward because, in my mind,

I'm stuck.

Mouse doesn't seem to notice this. She carries on talking.

'I've known him all my life. If he says something, you listen. If he leads somewhere, you follow.'

I felt that. I was doing that, against my better judgement. At least against my sense of self preservation. Is this what made James throw himself from the roof?

'It's as simple as that?'

'Oh, it's never simple,' laughs Mouse, slightly breathless, as we trot to keep up with the pace. 'He's made it his life's mission to... well, to save time.'

I misunderstand for a moment, but I look at Mouse's face and I realise what she means.

'Wait. You're not serious? You don't mean he's really efficient, do you? You mean...'

'I mean, he's here to save time,' she repeats.

'To *save* time?' I ask. 'Like, time is in danger? What does that mean?'

'There's not a lot left if we run out of time,' says Mouse. 'Two Evie Whites can't be good for the integrity of reality. No one's really supposed to hop back and forth. You heard what Lek said. "We're all headed, inexorably, in one direction". Evie White would take issue with that. Well, at least one of her would.'

'Hold on,' I'm not getting this. Unless I am, in which case it's blowing my mind. 'It's a belief? The linear progression of time is an article of *faith*?'

'Don't be silly. It's a theory. A fairly scientific one, but a theory nonetheless. One that reality has usually disproved. But nature abhors a paradox so it tends to fix itself and the jury's out on how things are actually *meant* to be...'

'Right, so what's changed?'

'I don't know. There used to be safeguards, added

protections. Ways that the Devoted, or rather the Brotherhood, had to keep things on track.'

'And they're gone now?'

'Well, yes. But you heard what Lek said. They all went a long time ago.'

'And so far, so good? So what's different now? What's happened?'

'I think the answer to that is "Evie White"…'

Mouse is slowing down, and I think it's because Lek has stopped ahead of us. He seems to hesitate in front of an open doorway. I look back at Mouse. She's moving in slow motion, but she's not falling behind. I realise that I'm moving in slow motion as well.

'Do your limbs feel heavy?' asks Mouse, in a voice that sounds deeper than usual.

I see what she means. Ahead of us, Lek motions that we should gather behind him, against the wall. We seem to drift towards him, floating into place.

I can hear voices through the doorway beyond. They, too, are slowed down and slurred, but at least one of them sounds like her. Lek is listening intently.

'What are we waiting for?' I ask, but it feels like it takes an age for me to get the words out.

'I don't think we are.' Mouse's words stretch out to forever. 'I think this is just how long it takes.'

'Time distortion,' says Lek. 'Speak quick. Short words.'

I can hear a male voice, too. He's stuttering, stammering, seems to take forever to be lost for words. I assume that's who we're here for, who Evie was concerned about.

'Are we going?' I ask, with mammoth effort. 'Why is he…?'

Lek is off again. He pushes through what seems to be an invisible membrane and suddenly he's striding forward, heading through the doorway.

'You're asking the wrong questions,' he says. 'You need to ask her what the elephant is for.'

That question again.

And no, I still don't know what he's talking about.

Through the membrane, everything seems to move normally again, distortion free. Mouse and I follow Lek inside.

The room is vast, like the loading bay we saw before, except this one has a domed ceiling. Both Evie Whites are present and correct, one standing, shoulders slumped, looking lost, staring at a gun that has dropped to the floor. The other is standing behind a bank of computers.

The hesitant man is to our right, waving a gun around without seeming entirely sure what he's aiming at. He also now seems completely struck dumb.

At first, I think it's Lek he's surprised to see, but I don't think that's right. He seems to be gaping at Mouse. Mouse, to her credit, is doing an excellent job of ignoring him.

None of this, however, is what *I'm* staring at. There isn't a lot in this room: long wooden topped benches, the computer banks, some kind of generator, protective screens, a couple of forklifts parked next to a stack of crates, enough space for them to drive side by side around the perimeter. Then there's the cage.

In the middle of the room, there is a giant cage. Attached to the bars of the cage are thick, snaking cables, feeding electricity from the generator that arcs across the top, making the air thick with the tinny crackle of unconstrained power.

And in the middle of the cage there is an elephant. Now I want to know what the elephant is for as well.

This elephant is an elephant gone wrong, though. It's big, and wrinkled, and disappointingly grey, but its tail just ends, rather that forking out three ways into the traditional trident. It also does not have a halo, fiery or otherwise, but it's got a silver hat on. Its head looks too round. But those aren't the most remarkable thing about this elephant.

This elephant is real. It's alive. It's breathing, and swaying, and hooked up to the generator with wires. Its trunk is wrapped in gold foil. It looks like it's been drugged.

I look again. In the middle of the cage there is a full-grown elephant. A full-grown, fully alive elephant. Which isn't possible. Because they don't exist.

Elephants are a heraldic symbol, much beloved of many nations, notably Trinity's neighbour, Ashuana. They are not a real animal. Living, breathing elephants are not found in the wilds of… anywhere. And yet here is one, right in front of me.

I'm staring at it while the conversation continues around me. Neither Mouse nor Lek has moved and, apart from the staring from the man with the gun, nobody is paying much attention to us. The air is tight with tension and us bursting into the room has done little to dissipate it.

'This?' asks the older Evie White of the gunman, looking at the cage. 'This is nothing. Well, no, it's everything. This is Continuity. I don't have to worry about fracturing reality because I have Continuity to hold it together.'

I see a moment of confusion cross his face, before he swings the gun around to point at the cage, then back towards the older Evie White. If he's confused, the rest of us have no chance.

'So I can kill you both?' he says, in a voice that is vague, detached.

I don't know where it comes from, but suddenly I have a moment of clarity. *Head, heart, gut*, all aligned. I have no actual basis for any of what I suddenly believe, but it all makes such perfect sense I know I'm right.

This man is another time traveller. He's come back to stop Evie White from doing whatever she's doing. I glance at Lek, who is watching, impassive. I hoped to see a flicker of recognition that would give me the confirmation that they're working together but, whatever.

The elephant, which I still don't believe in, is some kind of machine… *In* some kind of machine? What's the point of it if it's not *part* of the machine? But this all has something to do with time. The way it slowed down outside the room, the way it's slowing down again now…

I see it this time, a pulse of energy bursting from the elephant, radiating out, like a wave, or a gust of wind. But I can see it, I can see the fuzziness spread, the faint shimmer as everything is engulfed, and everything stutters to a different pace.

Evie White, the one who isn't staring at the gun on the floor, pulls a gun from behind her computer bank refuge. Slowly, she raises an eyebrow as she brings it up to point at her adversary.

'Doesn't really matter,' drawls the man with the gun, a slow grin spreading. 'I can kill you, anyway. But thanks for the machine…'

He raises his gun too. He doesn't have as far to go, so he's aiming first. He's going to kill her. I know that look in his eye. I've seen it before.

With an instinct I can't control, I leap forward. I can't let this happen. I can't let her die, not with so many unanswered questions. Questions that I have a sense her younger self doesn't know the answers to. Not yet.

Evie White, either Evie White, isn't an imminent threat, at least not to me. I can't speak for the gunman, but I can't let her die. So, with an immense effort to overcome the inertia that is holding me down, I throw myself forward. I think I can tackle him to the ground before he gets a shot off.

At the same time, Lek also moves. I see him from the corner of my eye, turn my head towards the motion, take my eyes off my target. He's diving the other way, trying to put himself in between Evie and her would-be assassin.

I want to shout out, to stop him. He's a civilian, I've got this. He shouldn't be putting himself in harm's way. He doesn't have to worry. No one is going to get hurt.

That's the last thing.

No one is going to get hurt.

I misjudge my dive.

No one is going to get hurt.

With my attention on the actions of the Monk, the shot rips through my shoulder, turning me.

No one is going to get hurt.

My hand goes to the wound, my mouth opens to shout in pain.

No one is going to get hurt.

That last thing. It's a lie.

The second shot rips through my chest.

CHAPTER 24

ESTREL

Lek jumped back from the window, pushing me flat against the wall. He didn't say anything, and I hadn't been able to see who was in there, but I understood instantly that it wouldn't be a good idea for them to see me.

We heard footsteps, then the door slid open and a very recognisable figure emerged. Fortunately for me and Lek, in our inadequate hiding place, she turned the other way and hurried down the corridor.

'Hold on.' I couldn't quite believe my eyes. 'That was... Was that...?'

'Shhh,' Lek scolded.

I shut my mouth. We waited a moment for Evie White to disappear around the corner. This wasn't part of the plan. I was supposed to be avoiding her, at all costs. When Lek hauled me out of bed and dragged me down to Research, via The Catacombs, I did not imagine it was to find that she'd taken up residence in our lab.

Venn's lab. I'd barely had chance to establish my presence

before I'd gone to see Lek and everything had started to unravel.

'Yes, that was her.' He kept his voice low, hushed.

'Well, what's she doing down here?' I hissed. 'Evie White didn't have Research connections. Not back then, anyway. Not now, I mean. And that's Venn's lab! Is she OK?'

I'd not been here, in this time, for very long. A matter of days. It was still taking some getting used to the order of events.

Everything felt weirdly familiar. I guess not that weird. It felt familiar because it was familiar. I'd been here before. Not yet, but give it a few weeks.

Trinity didn't look like it had the last time I'd seen it, in my personal recent past, because that was years in the future. It looked like it used to, in distant memories. But those hadn't happened yet.

It was disorientating. But it was also intensely emotional. I'd hated this place when I'd first arrived. But I'd met people I loved. I'd met Mouse.

The entire period was a thrilling, passionate ride. I'd felt nothing like it before. I'd feel nothing like it again. That nostalgia was pulling at my heart. It hurt.

But I felt it again. I was back in Trinity. She was here.

Yet I couldn't see her. She wouldn't know who I was, anyway.

It was good I was getting in some practice, avoiding people. I had a timeline to preserve, a reality to protect. A future to fix.

'Venn's fine,' replied Lek. 'She's gone away for a bit. A holiday.'

This didn't seem like the time.

'A holiday?'

She was supposed to be refining her theories of time,

preparing to put a younger version of me into temporal purgatory. She didn't have time for a holiday. She hadn't been confident about the deadline I'd given her.

'I gave her some time off.' They way he said it left me in no doubt about who was in charge here. 'I thought it might be dangerous for her to stick around. And nothing impedes scientific progress like mortal danger.'

'Where are you going?'

Lek was on the move again, and he looked like he was about to disappear through the doorway. He turned to face me.

'There are some people I need to see.' He ducked his head to dart through the narrowing gap. 'But you should follow her!'

At least I assumed he said "see". It sounded an awful lot like "free". But with that, he vanished, and the doors closed behind him.

He hadn't left me much alternative. He held the security token. I couldn't follow him if I wanted to. I might as well follow Evie White. As long as she didn't see me, I could learn something useful, something that might help me, something that I could use. I knew I couldn't directly help myself once I'd arrived, once the loop had started. But maybe I could nudge, maybe I could steer things. All of this was about that woman, about stopping her ascent to power.

I set off in the direction that Evie had gone and, after a few paces, broke into a gentle jog. Once I reached the corner myself, I stopped and peered around. I'd caught up some ground on her, so from there I concentrated on trying to make as little noise as possible, adopting some kind of tiptoed shuffle.

It was probably fine. She seemed intent on where she was headed. I would be unlucky if she turned around now.

She went around another corner, this time to the right, and

suddenly I couldn't see her anymore. I wasn't going to panic. I knew what the tunnels were like in Research, and the probability was that I'd reach the corner, look around and see her halfway down the next, long, featureless corridor.

Still, I didn't enjoy taking the risk that I might lose her and, besides, this was my chance to make up some ground. I hurried to the corner and, again, peered around.

There was no one there. Of course. I had lost her.

The corridor did, indeed, disappear off into the distance, as expected. But the more I stared at it, the more I realised that there hadn't been enough time for her to have reached the end and turned another corner, not even if she'd broken into a run the moment I lost sight of her.

That had to mean that she had disappeared into a lab. I glanced up at the wall. The ever reliable plan told me I was in Zoological Research. I knew this zone. Those labs were big, built to hold all kinds of species, large and small, with huge cages in the middle, surrounded by benches, and computer terminals, and protective screens to shield the observers of the experiments that went on. Some of which could get very messy. I scuttled down the corridor to the first door.

It was open, giving me a clear view of what was inside. There was, as expected, an enormous cage, in which was what appeared to be an elephant. It had a silver metal dish strapped to its head, from which came a variety of antennae and cables. More wires were attached to its flank, its belly and back, and all four of its feet. Its trunk was wrapped in a gold material, with the most complex wiring spiralling off that. It looked sad and sedated. I couldn't imagine why it was there.

It couldn't be an elephant, though. It had to be some kind of experiment gone wrong. It was an ugly thing.

I took a couple of steps inside. Beyond the not-elephant, at a bank of screens, hunched a familiar figure. Evie Chaguartay.

Entrapment

I should have been expecting her, but there was still something wrong. This was Evie Chaguartay, after she'd offloaded her husband and reclaimed her name. My Evie Chaguartay, the one I knew and loathed.

That's not who I followed up the corridor, not who I saw come into this room. That was Evie White. Younger, seemingly more innocent, less tainted, although only because no one knew what she was planning.

Evie Chaguartay looked up and smiled at me or… Not at me. She was smiling at someone to the left of me.

I followed her gaze. There was Evie White, stood behind me. Between us was a gun that she was holding and pointing at my head.

'Is this him?' asked Evie White.

'It's him,' replied Evie Chaguartay. 'Hello, Estrel.'

'It seems that you've been expecting me?' I said.

I could see the tremor in Evie White's gun hand amplifying down the barrel in my face. I was pretty confident that she would not fire it. Not this version of her, anyway, not yet.

'I could see you coming,' said Evie Chaguartay, tapping the screen in front of her. 'A mile off. Evie here knew you were behind her. She brought you here for a reason.'

'So much for the element of surprise…'

This wasn't good, though. Not only was I expected, they'd drawn me here. I wondered where Lek was, if he'd find me. This was the problem with him only sharing part of his plan. When he wasn't around, I had to make my part up as I went along.

'I assume you're surprised, though.' She stepped back from the consoles and spread her arms wide.

'I was only expecting there to be one of you. That is correct.'

Evie White's gun was dropping now, enough for me to feel comfortable taking my eyes off her, not enough for me to go for my own gun. Yet.

'I can't place you.'

It was true. This version of Evie Chaguartay was definitely older, definitely from the future, just like me. But there was something about her I didn't recognise.

A different edge, a new sprinkling of ruthlessness. She'd lost something more. She'd been through something I didn't know about. Did that mean she was from my future, too? I did some quick calculations. She was from my future; we were both in the past. There was a paradox risk somewhere, but I couldn't wrap my head around it quickly enough.

Regardless, if she was here, then something was wrong. If she was from any time later than a couple of weeks away, certainly if she was from later than I was, then something had gone wrong. I was here to fix things, make it so that my former self would prevent her living to look like this.

If she was here, did that mean that I'd already failed?

'No, Estrel,' she said with a pained smile. 'I know you, but you don't know me, not like this. I came after you. Set off later, arrived earlier. I'm here to stop you.'

'Not me, though. Obviously.'

I relaxed a little more. Evie White had dropped all pretence of being about to shoot me, and if Evie Chaguartay was from my future, then that afforded me a certain amount of protection. I'd done my sums now. She carried the risk.

'You're here to stop original Estrel,' I asserted. 'You're early.'

She shook her head and laughed. I wondered why. If she was from my future, then I was protected from her. But she wasn't protected from me.

She actually did seem to be amused by something, but I

couldn't imagine what it was. She was vulnerable. Maybe it was just a smokescreen. I didn't think it mattered. I pulled my gun from the back of my waistband.

'No, Estrel, I'm here to stop you,' she said.

I took three strides back and brought my gun forward. I flicked back and forth between the two Evies. I had them both covered. It didn't matter what she said. I had the upper hand.

'You should probably drop that,' I said to Evie White.

Her gun fell to the floor with a clatter. She backed away from it, nervously. I didn't remember her being as meek as this. I first met her on the day she started her rise to power, but it was hard to imagine someone who couldn't hold a gun with conviction masterminding a bombing campaign that incited an uprising.

I looked at her older self. Had this version of Evie cowed her earlier self so much, and if she had, what was that doing to the timeline? Had her mere presence here changed things already?

I wasn't supposed to make direct contact with myself when I arrived. Both Lek and Venn had been very clear about that. I was developing a bad feeling about this whole situation, and I already had one of those. I thought I knew why Lek hauled me out of bed.

'You're not carrying anything?' I checked.

'I'm not,' said Evie Chaguartay, almost regretfully. 'But that's not what's important now.'

'Not important?' It was my turn to laugh. 'I can't kill her, not without corrupting the timeline, which I've been firmly warned not to do. But you? You come after me. There's no paradox in my killing you.'

'And yet you're not pulling the trigger. You have questions.'

Damn her. I did have questions. I wanted to ask Venn. I

wanted to ask Lek. I wanted to ask someone I trusted. But they weren't here.

'If you're here...' I began.

I stopped. Dozens of questions hung in the air, floating between us.

'That's the one,' Evie grinned.

I hated her more in this moment than I'd ever hated her before, and I'd hated her plenty. I gritted my teeth and squeezed the gun in my two hands, my finger itching towards the trigger. I knew she was trying to seed doubts in my mind. I knew she was stalling for time. I knew I was going to let her.

'You're not dead,' I snarled. 'I came back here to make sure I killed you. It doesn't work, does it? The loop. I trap myself for nothing?'

'No, you didn't kill me.' Evie's voice was gentle, mocking me. 'Give yourself some credit, Estrel. It's easier said than done.'

Everything is easier said than done. Mouse said that to me, once. *"Everything is easier said than done, except love"*...

'You want to try me?' I moved my finger to the trigger.

'I don't think you understand. You could kill me, of course you could. You even killed her, once or twice, I'm sure of it...'

She motioned towards her younger self. I glanced over. She looked baffled by the entire conversation. I wondered how much she knew, if that would help to keep things on track, continuity-wise, if she didn't know why she was involved, what the grand plan was.

'...but he couldn't go through with it.'

Evie Chaguartay finished talking.

'Who?' I asked the question, but I knew the answer.

'Him, Estrel Mark One. He couldn't do it. Millions of iterations. He fell in love, he fell down vertical shafts, he blew himself up with Resistance munitions. He did everything you asked of him. He ignored every word you said. But never, not once, could he bring himself to kill me.'

That didn't make any sense. That was knowledge that she shouldn't have. It was knowledge that no one would ever have, not even me. Once I satisfied the conditions of the loop, that was it. That would become the main timeline. I'd blink out of existence. Everything else would collapse and no one would know what we'd done.

Venn didn't even that she, herself, would know if it had worked. Once she'd created the conditions for it to happen, the plan was that she would step back and leave me to initiate the loop alone. That removed the paradox risk. That's what she thought.

It made sense as far as I understood it, but could Venn have been wrong? Everything was unravelling in front of me and the only answers I was going to get were from the woman in front of me.

I had to know.

'How do you know all this? Those timelines, they don't exist anymore. There's no way you could know about any of this.'

'I know I'm still alive,' she said. 'And besides, it's not as simple as that, Estrel. You really don't understand what you're messing with here, do you? Nothing is ever completely erased. It leaves a mark. I can see what you tried to do. Your tracks are still there, in the sands of time.'

'The sands of time?'

This all sounded very mystical and unlikely. And yet she knew. I didn't manage to kill her, but the loop must have worked. It must have had some effect. One she didn't like. She'd come back to fix something, to change something. Something I did.

'It's a fucking metaphor. Good grief, you're hard work. It

worked, OK? Your plan worked. I never rose to power. You stopped me. I rotted in jail for trying to blow up the city.'

Relief flooded through my body. It took all of my concentration to keep the gun pointing at her. Tears filled my eyes. It worked. I did it. I didn't kill her, but I stopped her. That was better, wasn't it? I never wanted a murder on my conscience.

But I didn't kill her. Now here she was.

I hadn't stopped her.

I had to stop her now.

Except...

'You seem awfully keen to tell me all of this?' I said.

I could feel myself getting twitchy. There was something else going on. *Does it matter? Should I just kill her now?* I glanced back to Evie White, swung my gun back in her direction.

'You don't need to worry about her,' sighed Evie Chaguartay. 'She's not going to shoot you. Any more than your younger self was willing to kill her. Honestly, you're like children!'

I swung my gun back to Evie Chaguartay.

'But you're not her. And I'm not him. And I don't believe you'd let anything, even something as cataclysmic as corrupting the timeline, get in the way of you getting what you want.'

'I don't think you want to do *that*, though.' Evie threw a switch on the console in front of her. 'I don't think you want to kill me.'

Damn her. She saw me now.

Electricity surged through the bars of the cage in the middle of the room. In a moment, all I could hear was a hum that caused all the hairs up the back of my neck to quiver to attention. Lightning flashes arced between terminals, over the back of the beast, who seemed agitated but remained silent.

Entrapment

A pulse of energy radiated out from the cage. The air fizzled and sparked, and everything slowed down, just for a moment. Something significant was happening. I opened my mouth to speak. It took an age.

'Oh, but I do,' I said, eventually.

I didn't know what was happening, but I knew I couldn't let it continue. I still didn't want to kill her. I knew I had to.

The air in the lab settled, and the normal flow of time reasserted itself.

'No, you don't,' Evie said, firmly. 'Think about it. If you kill me now, then this is when I die.'

'Seems obvious to me. And perfectly acceptable.'

'But if you do that, then it becomes what happens. It's written before you - the original you - even arrives here. Nothing you, or he, does can change that anymore. Continuity will prevail. He can't succeed, he can't kill me. Because you already did.'

I wasn't having that.

'I don't believe you,' I said. 'That's not how it works.'

'It's not?' Evie cackled. 'You're sure about that? You understand what's going on here?'

She took a step forward, arms spread wide, her chest thrust forward. She was, I noted, still mostly protected by the bank of equipment in front of her, but a shot to the head was all it would take.

'Go ahead, take your shot. If you're prepared to risk being wrong…'

'Doesn't matter,' I said. 'He didn't kill you, but we still got out of the loop. Whatever he did, it worked.'

'Probably,' shrugged Evie. 'You won't know, not for a while. And just imagine if you screwed things up before they even got going. You could have doomed him to fail. But if you want to take that risk…'

I stared at her. I didn't believe this. She was just trying to confuse me, to stop me from killing her here and now. If I did it, she'd be dead, my mission accomplished. But it wasn't supposed to be my mission. Not this version of me. I went to pull the trigger, hesitated.

'I...'

I couldn't do it. I couldn't take the risk. I needed to know what he'd done, what I'd done, to escape the loop if it wasn't to kill Evie White. I had so many questions. I couldn't trust her enough to ask her. But if not her, then who?

'You're asking the wrong questions,' said a voice behind me.

It was if he had read my thoughts. He probably had. I turned around.

'You need to ask her what the elephant is for,' said Lek.

Both versions of Evie laughed this time. It echoed around the lab, the reflected sound harder, crueller, than that which came out of their mouths.

I looked at Lek. Lek looked at me. Was that a look of incomprehension, or just one of regret? He was an inscrutable as ever. Damn him.

'It's Continuity,' said Evie Chaguartay. 'The elephant is part of the machine, and the machine gives me Continuity. *My* Continuity.'

'That's not an elephant,' I said. 'Why is everybody calling that thing an elephant? There is no such thing as an elephant.'

I struggled to compute what she was saying to me. She kept repeating that word. *Continuity*. I didn't understand. So I asked about the elephant.

'Spoken like a good Ashuanan boy,' she cackled. 'But I'm sorry, this is an elephant. We're making the impossible possible today. I thought it was fitting. Now, all we need is a paradox to fire it up...'

With a smug look on her face, she thought she'd won. I was sure of that. It gripped me tight around the guts, and I reacted with white-hot rage. It surged from inside me, my mind on fire, my nerves ablaze.

I swung my weapon. I needed to act. I knew I couldn't let her win. Except I didn't know what I was doing. I didn't know what I was trying to do.

I looked to Lek. His eyes were desperate. He seemed at a loss himself. I wasn't used to that. It seemed Evie had, indeed, taken him by surprise as well. I didn't even know how that was possible.

There was the suggestion of a sound, almost a pop, like we were trapped in a bubble of reality and someone had broken through from the outside. Two more people appeared in the lab.

I only saw one of them.

Mouse. I wanted to go to her, to wrap my arms around her, to feel her against me again. I wanted to kiss her in a dramatic, romantic gesture I knew she'd hate and so I'd never attempt.

She looked straight through me. She didn't know who I was.

It struck me through the heart, but this wasn't the time for that. This pain would die, it would disappear the moment we fixed the timeline and everything reverted to the way it should always have been. I would never remember how much this hurt.

I could use this emotion. I should use it, honour what it meant. It was why I was here, to make sure I never felt it again. It meant everything.

It was the machine. The machine was the problem. We could deal with Evie Chaguartay after we'd dealt with the machine. After *I'd* dealt with the machine. I pointed my gun, took my stance, prepared to fire.

What if I was being rash?

It wasn't working yet.

"...a paradox to fire it up..."

What if this was an advantage that I could exploit as well? Instead? I didn't understand what I'd been told. I hadn't been told anything, really. But if this machine could do what I thought it could...

Evie Chaguartay was still talking. I wasn't listening anymore.

There was no longer anything to prevent me from killing Evie White myself. I could start their machine with a perfect paradox. Me killing Evie White. Then the machine would protect... the *continuity*. No need to wait for my younger self, no more time loop, no more waiting for random chance, infinite monkeys or infinite Estrels to come good.

This was a better plan, surely? It was poetic that she would be the architect of her own destruction.

'So I can kill you both?' I think I said.

I felt myself rise out of my body and I could see everyone laid out like on a map. Me, both Evies, Lek, and this guy who I was pretty sure was Authority. And Mouse.

Mouse. She hadn't even recognised me. There's no reason that she would have. We hadn't met yet. But it hurt.

I'd dreamed of seeing her again. I literally dreamed, every night and then, once it had been proposed that I could go back, I had imagined this moment. I thought I'd prepared myself.

Turns out that it's not something you can prepare for. I felt like my heart had been ripped out, stolen from me. Yet she didn't want it. Not yet. I swallowed those feelings.

Evie Chaguartay pulled a gun. *Of course she did, I knew she'd have one somewhere.* That concentrated the mind somewhat. Lek's face, his apparent doubts about the Continuity machine, the machine that could save us all, all of that could wait.

'Doesn't really matter,' I said.

Which was true, it didn't. Because this Evie Chaguartay was from my future and there was nothing the prevent me from stopping her in her tracks. Now.

'I can kill you anyway…'

I allowed myself a grin.

I knew what I had to do now.

'But thanks for the machine…'

I pulled the trigger, and then I pulled it again. The sound of the shots echoed around the hangar, and with the act done, my mind snapped back to attention.

Neither Lek nor the man from Authority were where they had been a moment ago. Evie Chaguartay was still standing.

I glanced down at the dead body on the floor. I didn't recognise him, but I suddenly knew who he was. It was Simeon Lagrange. I hadn't met him before, the first time I'd come to Trinity.

And that made sense. Because I'd just killed him.

Electricity fizzed across the roof of the cage. The elephant cried out in pain.

All I could hear was the elephant's scream.

Another pulse of energy spread out across the lab. This one caught me like a wave, sent me spinning, balance gone, disappearing into the blackness.

Everything slowed. I didn't know how I could tell. I couldn't see anything.

Everything stopped. The blackness, the dark, was the space between the moments and it trapped me there. I hadn't gone anywhere, and yet I was nowhere.

That thought, the realisation, triggered a rush. Time flew at me all at once and I was knocked off my feet again, pushed backwards by the surging tide.

I was somewhere else. This place wasn't dark, but I still couldn't see. Shrouded in a thin mist, the visibility was about ten metres and beyond that, there was nothing.

I looked around in confusion. Lagrange's body had vanished, as well as both Evies, and Mouse... again, the shot through the heart, the pain of losing her. It was right there, everywhere I turned.

Lek moved into my eyeline. His head was bowed. He looked older, suddenly.

Relief. Wherever I was, I wasn't alone.

'Where are we?' I asked. 'What happened?'

Lek raised his head. His eyes were sunken, his face pallid and drawn.

'We're out of time,' he sighed. 'I brought us here. I need to think.'

He looked tired. He shook his head. I looked around me. This place really was nothing. I looked down at my feet. I'm not sure why. They looked pretty solid, which was reassuring in its unsurprising normality. I don't know why I expected to see through them.

I had a sense that I was somewhere I'd been before, but that it was different this time.

'When you say we're *out of time*...' I felt around for the words I needed. 'You mean we're *outside* of time, don't you?'

I didn't know that was my question, but now I'd asked it, I already knew the answer.

'I had to,' said Lek. 'I didn't know what would happen next. You shouldn't have shot him.'

'It was an accident.'

'I know. That's not what I meant. He's from your past. From *the* past, from your perspective, I mean. You shouldn't be able to kill him. Not without bad things happening.'

'Corrupting the timeline? But the machine...'

The machine was going to protect the timeline, to protect us, wasn't it? *"...all we need is a paradox..."*. Well, I gave it one, didn't I? I didn't mean to give it that one, but it shouldn't matter. The machine should be running, should be protecting all of it.

The change in Lek was instant.

'That machine should not exist,' he snarled. 'It isn't natural. I never saw it...'

The Cleric slumped to his knees and rubbed his eyes; the mist swirled up around him, over his head. He looked up at me. For a moment, it looked like he had a long, wispy beard before it drifted away.

'It can't be,' he said. 'That machine cannot be. She used me. I should have seen what was coming. I always know what is coming. But she managed to trick me.'

I sat down opposite him. I had questions.

'I know this place. How do I know this place?'

'You've been here before,' shrugged Lek, 'In a way. A version of you has. Or will do. Time is not linear, and nothing is ever erased.'

'Footprints in the sand...'

I understood. I wonder what happened, why I, the other version of I, found himself in this place.

'But you brought us here,' I said. 'We didn't break anything?'

'We didn't. But we should have done. We should have broken it all. But she...'

'She was a step ahead of us.'

That was a recurrent theme. I'd experienced this before. Not in a vaguely remembered, deleted reality, but in my life, in my recent past. Every. Single. Time.

'But how?' fretted Lek. 'How did she do it? That's not

technology that can exist.'

'And yet she built it?'

I was worrying about the old Cleric. I'd never seen him look this defeated. Could it be that the strain of his life's mission was finally getting to him?

'Not on her own.'

His face was set. I didn't ask what he meant.

'So what do we do now?' I asked. 'Can we go back?'

'I don't think we should. I don't think it's safe. We gave her a paradox, just like she always knew we would.'

'Not safe? Not safe for us, or…?'

'Not safe for anyone. I don't think she knows what she's unleashed.'

'What has she unleashed?'

I was going to have to work hard for answers it seemed.

Lek leaned back, took a deep breath, and fixed me with a stare. I knew what that meant. *Parable incoming.*

'When I was a boy, I used to run in the forest,' he began. 'I ran and ran all day, never stopping, never resting. One day, I reached the edge of the forest and I met a man planting saplings. I asked him what he was doing. He told me he was helping the forest to grow. I spent the day with him and then I ran home.'

It was peaceful here. The world was raging somewhere else, but this was a sanctuary. It was tempting. Could we stay here? Would we be safe?

'It was many years before I returned to the edge of the forest and, of course, it was no longer the edge. I came to the place where I had met that man. There was a clearing in the trees. Do you know why?'

It didn't matter what my answer was. It was bound to be wrong, and Lek was about to tell me what the lesson was. I shook my head.

'Small boys do not watch where they put their feet,' said Lek solemnly. 'Cause and effect, Estrel. It matters.'

'Right. But now there would be trees? After what she did?'

'There would be a clearing, and there would be trees,' said Lek. 'Both would exist at the same time.'

'That feels... confusing.'

'Reality, the timeline, has broken before, of course it has.' He winked at me. 'You will do it yourself on more than one occasion. We reset and we go again. One thing remains constant. Me. There was a time when I worried the world was going to disappear in a puff of smoke. You cause that...'

This was news to me. I was going to object, but he ploughed on.

'And then you fix it. This is different. This time, the world is going to burn. She can do what she likes and that machine... will let her. Nothing will make sense, chaos will reign. And I don't think she'll lift a finger to stop it. I think it's what she wants.'

'The world is going to burn?' I asked. 'How?'

'She's made everything possible all at once. All futures will survive, endure. Even those that were never meant to be. That's not how it's meant to work. There's no balance there. Too much energy flowing in, not enough reality to contain it. The pressure will build, and build, and build until...'

'Until?'

Lek held his hand, palm up, fingers gathered together. Then, making a small noise, "poof", under his breath, he spread his fingers wide.

'It explodes?' I checked. 'What, like, reality?'

'All of it. Every possible world, heating up until they can't take it anymore, then they're gone. All at once. Poof.'

'When?'

'That's not a very meaningful question,' Lek smiled.

'Eventually, once upon a time... Now? It all means the same thing in this context.'

'But we'll be safe here.' I searched in his impassive face for reassurance.

'No.' Lek shook his head. 'We're outside of time. Once there's no time, there's nothing to be outside of.'

'So what do we do? How do we fix this?'

Lek took a deep breath.

'We wait. We can't do this without help. We need to wait for reinforcements.'

'Rein...?'

I looked around at the vague nothing we were in. Where were reinforcements going to come from? *Who could even get here?* I sighed.

'Take me back.'

Lek shook his head.

'That's not a good idea. You don't want that.'

Lek's mouth hadn't moved. That wasn't Lek's voice. I turned around again. A figure emerged, a shadow indistinct from the mist. But I knew who he was. He was old. He walked with a stick. But he was me.

'Reinforcements?'

I turned back to Lek. He grinned.

'Just a few,' he said, as another figure appeared behind him.

This one was younger and dressed in a business suit. Another, in a white canvas jumpsuit. Still another, his face smeared with camouflage.

I looked around again. Everywhere my eyes went, more people emerged from the cloud, faded into existence. All of them were me.

'I asked the wrong question, didn't I? We're not going to fix this, are we?'

Entrapment

I took one last look around. There were tens, maybe even a hundred of me now.

'No,' agreed Lek. 'We're not going to fix this.'

'I am,' I said.

It looks like you've finished reading ENTRAPMENT…

Thank you!

I really hope you enjoyed it, and if you did it would be great if you could leave a review somewhere… Amazon, Goodreads, Social Media, just tell a friend - any of those would be fantastic and make all the difference for me, struggling little indie author that I am.

Next, if you'd like to stay up to date with what I'm writing and when you can read it, pop along to https://philoddy.com where you can find links to my own socials, and you can sign up for my monthly newsletter.

Finally, there are other books I've written and contributed to, so if you're not sure what to read next, check out:

ENTANGLEMENT SERIES
    Echoes
    Eclipse (coming early 2025)
    Enlightenment (coming late 2025)
    Exodus (coming 2026)
FOR CHILDREN
    The Man In The Moon
AS CONTRIBUTOR
    Royston and District Writers' Circle 40th Anniversary Anthology
    There Are Many Ways Of Getting Lost: The Royston Writers' Circle Lockdown Anthology

About the Author

Phil Oddy lives in North Hertfordshire and writes stories about how to cope in a confusing world, cleverly disguised as sci-fi/fantasy adventures. Find his website at https://philoddy.com - everything he's currently up to should be on there.

He is happily married with two sons, and has promised everyone lavish gifts if he ever writes a bestseller, so if you've bought one of his books then they all thank you.

Despite a long and successful career as an IT analyst in both the public and private sectors, writing is something he seems to be unable to prevent himself doing which means that by encouraging him you're either feeding an addiction or providing therapy. You can pick which.

When his fingers are too tired to carry on typing, Phil likes to relax by reading something by David Mitchell (either one is fine) or binge-watching Drag Race.

Printed in Great Britain
by Amazon